BANNED BOOKS, CROP TOPS, AND OTHER BAD INFLUENCES

ALSO BY BRIGIT YOUNG

Bright
The Prettiest
Worth a Thousand Words

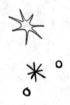

BANNED BOOKS, CROP TOPS, AND OTHER BAD INFLUENCES

Brigit Young

ROARING BROOK PRESS
NEW YORK

Published by Roaring Brook Press
Roaring Brook Press is a division of Holtzbrinck Publishing
Holdings Limited Partnership
120 Broadway, New York, NY 10271 • mackids.com

Our books may be purchased in bulk for promotional, educational, or business
use. Please contact your local bookseller or the Macmillan Corporate and
Premium Sales Department at (800) 221-7945 ext. 5442 or by email at
MacmillanSpecialMarkets@macmillan.com.

Library of Congress Cataloging-in-Publication Data

Names: Young, Brigit, author.
Title: Banned books, crop tops, and other bad influences / written
    by Brigit Young.
Description: First edition. | New York : Roaring Brook Press, 2024. |
    Audience: Ages 8–12. | Audience: Grades 4–6. | Summary: Sheltered
    small-town teen, Rose, forms an underground book club for banned books
    with Talia, an outspoken new kid from New York City.
Identifiers: LCCN 2023046325 | ISBN 9781250901514 (hardcover)
Subjects: CYAC: Prohibited books—Fiction. | Book clubs (Discussion
    groups)—Fiction. | Middle schools—Fiction. | Schools—Fiction. | City
    and town life—Fiction. | Friendship—Fiction. | Jews—United States—
    Fiction.
Classification: LCC PZ7.1.Y7424 Bad 2024 | DDC [Fic]—dc23
LC record available at https://lccn.loc.gov/2023046325

First edition, 2024
Book design by Trisha Previte
Printed in the United States of America by Berryville Graphics, Martinsburg,
West Virginia

ISBN 978-1-250-90151-4
10 9 8 7 6 5 4 3 2 1

For my precious friends, Alex Whatley and Laura Mulcahy,
who came roaring into my young life and, through
times light and dark, remained steadfast

School is a battlefield for your heart. So when Rayanne Graff told me my hair was holding me back, I had to listen. 'Cause she wasn't just talking about my hair. She was talking about my life.

ANGELA, MY SO-CALLED LIFE, PILOT EPISODE

But you don't have to take my word for it.

LEVAR BURTON, READING RAINBOW

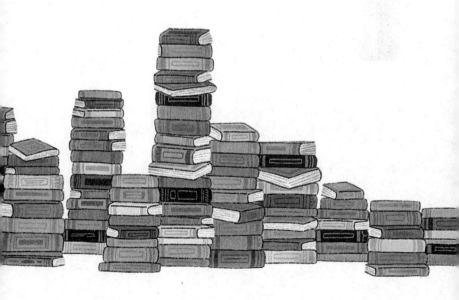

Rose Stern fastened the top button on the shirt her mother had placed out on the bed for her that day, and it pinched her skin.

"Mom!" Rose yelled out. "It doesn't fit anymore!"

Rose hadn't thought she'd grown much over the summer, but when she undid the top button beneath the collar, she felt able to breathe again. She faced the full-length mirror that hung over her door, its pink and white swirls of paint chipping off the sides. She'd had the mirror—and pretty much everything else in her room—forever.

Rose let her fingers drift to the center of her clavicle. Without the buttons there, that crevice made the perfect home for a necklace. She opened just one more and reached for the heart-shaped silver jewelry box that her aunt Laura had given her for her Bat Mitzvah the year before. She pulled out a golden chain that held a little bird. Pretty. She clasped it behind her neck and tilted her chin side to side to take in the effect.

Well, nothing she could do would distract from the

newest crop of pimples moving in right below her hairline. But it was a start.

She undid one more button, creating a V-neck style, so the necklace would stand out.

Lots of girls at school wore multiple necklaces at a time. The glamorous girls like Gabbi, Aaliyah, and Piper. They sashayed into school like it was a photo shoot. How did they do that? Did their moms know how to create those styles for them? It was a mystery.

Should she double up with another necklace?

No, that wouldn't suit her. And Charlotte would say she was trying too hard.

Ugh. Why was she thinking so much about clothes? If anyone knew how shallow she could be, they'd judge her.

As Rose pulled her fine auburn hair up into a ponytail, her mom opened the door, where the mirror hung, and Rose stumbled back a step.

"Oops! Sorry, sweets." Her mom was a stay-at-home parent, but she dressed in nice skirts like she was going to an office.

After a yank on the ends of her hair to secure it, Rose grabbed her schoolwork folders—stuffed to the brim with extra papers from the days she'd just missed over Rosh Hashanah—and turned around to see her mom pulling a different top out of the closet.

"Try this." Her mom handed her a sandy-beige turtleneck

and then hurried about the room to swipe up any clutter—a pencil that had fallen off the desk, a few stray sheets of choir music . . .

"No, it's okay. I think I made it work." Rose placed a hand beneath where she'd unfastened three buttons and added the golden dove.

"No, honey, the buttons could pop." Her mom nodded to the other shirt that lay on her bed. "That one works." She paused midcleaning and said, "Oh—you're wearing that necklace? It's not too fancy, you think?"

"I don't think so?" Did it matter if you wore a fancy necklace to school?

But her mom was right about the buttons. If too many popped, it would be a nightmare. She changed her shirt and took off the necklace. It didn't show under a turtleneck, anyway.

"Come on, love, we should get going." Her mom held out Rose's jacket as they left the bedroom and headed downstairs.

"It might be hot later," Rose said.

It was that time of year in Michigan when the morning started out frigid and yet by afternoon Rose could get a sunburn on her cheeks as she walked the dogs at the rescue with Charlotte.

"But it's cold *now*." Her mom gave the coat a little shake in Rose's direction.

Rose wanted to argue. Almost. It was a pain to shove it into her tiny locker. But one look at her mom and she changed her mind, taking it.

She threw on her backpack and grabbed a protein bar from a ceramic bowl by the front entrance as she left.

On the drive to school, they passed by pretty much all of Cove Lake: the narrow homes sitting close together with small concrete steps for a porch, like her own; the town's single apartment building; the busy roadway that shot off toward the grocery store and shopping outlets; the two restaurants, tailor shop, clothing store, and three banks that made up Center Street; and, closest to their destination, the fancy houses with multiple stories and enormous yards, one of which even had a pond.

Her mom pulled up to the school. Its tennis court and enormous field stood empty as the students milled about the flagpole and the wide pavement entryway. The crowd grew quickly at this hour.

After two full days off, the taste of honey and McIntosh apples still lingering on her tongue from the holiday, Rose wondered what she'd missed.

But through the window she saw the person who would fill her in. Rose tapped on the glass and waved as Charlotte spotted her and bounced up and down.

"I love you!" her mom cooed in the one second the door opened before Rose scurried out.

"You too!" Rose hollered back as she hurried toward

Charlotte, who waited for Rose every morning by the left pillar.

"Missed you!" Her best friend enveloped her in a hug that felt extra warm in the chilly morning air. Charlotte's loose, cedar-brown curls smelled cinnamony, just like her house, Rose's second home, where something was always baking.

"How many Jewish holidays are there, anyway?" Charlotte linked her arm around Rose's. "You guys really love to party."

Rose laughed. That was true. "Too many," she answered.

As the sidewalk and concrete entryway filled to the brim like they did every morning, the school entrance finally opened. Throngs of students stormed right in, texting and chatting.

There was comfort in being back.

Charlotte and Rose followed behind the first wave of students into the hallway and upstairs, jostled about between the bigger boys in their class, while Charlotte whispered into her ear, "What do you think she'll look like?"

"Who?" Rose dodged a girl's waving arm as it tried to catch attention from somebody up ahead.

"The new kid!" Charlotte burst out, her round hazel eyes lighting up.

"What?" Rose glanced around like maybe she could spot them. There was a new kid? *Nothing* new happened in Cove Lake. Let alone a whole person.

"You didn't know?" Charlotte asked.

As they entered the school and swerved left toward their

lockers, Rose answered, "How would I? I only hear things from *you*!"

"I forgot to text you." Charlotte shrugged. "Found out yesterday afternoon. Today's her first day. Mr. Morrison had us do a whole how-to-welcome-people activity." Charlotte rolled her eyes. "It was hilarious. And guess what?"

"What?" Charlotte had Rose's full attention. Muscle memory led her to her locker.

"She's from *New York frickin' City*." Charlotte emphasized each word and raised an eyebrow. "So you know what *that* means."

But Rose didn't know what that meant.

What would someone from New York City be doing in Cove Lake, Michigan?

Rose shoved her backpack and coat into her locker.

She'd known everyone in school her whole life. The last time they'd had a new kid was maybe in sixth grade? And that girl was from Kalamazoo, an hour away. Rose had either gone to daycare or started kindergarten with all the other students. She could summon memories about everyone.

Rose headed to class.

Sneakers squeaked on the speckled-tile floor. Zion and Scarlett, their year's on-again, off-again couple, walked down the hall holding pinkies. Principal Thomas greeted various groups as he made his way through the eighth-grade hall. A pack of theater kids burst into a cappella song, the high notes bouncing off the walls as a couple of people shouted at them, *"Would you stop?"*

Where was the new kid?

In English, Charlotte asked Paige Retford if she'd seen the new girl or knew her name yet. Charlotte and Rose were in Girl Scouts with Paige, so she always chatted with them even though she was in a whole other world outside of Scouts meetings. Paige lived on the periphery of the popular girl group, always around them but never quite in the inner circle.

Paige was one of those girls with perfect necklace/shirt combos. And she was *so* blond.

"I think I heard Mr. Thomas say her name's Delilah?" Paige twisted a lock of flaxen hair. "I didn't see her. But somebody said she got kicked out of her old school." Paige lifted her shoulders and let them drop. "I guess we'll see?"

Then she went back to listening to Piper and Aaliyah's conversation.

Over the next two hours, Rose heard more about the new girl.

"Scarlett saw her in the office. She said she wears all black," Rose overheard Bree Ryder's crowd of friends joking in the hall on the way to math. "That's, like, a New York thing."

"Ha. What do you know about New York?" Bree cackled. "Have you ever left the Mitten?"

"I go on plenty of spring break trips to Nana in Cincinnati, thank you very much," Bree's friend replied as their belly laughter faded behind Rose in the hallway.

Without Charlotte in her math class, Rose sat on the outside of all conversation, but she heard some low murmurs of "So has anyone seen this new kid? What's up with her?"

Rose sat facing forward in her usual front-row spot, textbook, pencil, and paper out, ready. Yet she yearned to turn around to hear more.

"Let's give her a spot with us at lunch," Rose managed to catch one kid saying above the muttering.

"You don't even know her, what if she's sus?" another chided them.

Rose hadn't thought of that yet. Who would the girl sit with?

As Mrs. Williams, in her perky and smiley way, jumped into approximating irrational numbers like she was a host on a TV show, Rose tried to picture showing up to a new school building—walking up to the unfamiliar doors, finding the right room, searching for an ally . . . She could never handle school without Charlotte by her side. Their moms liked to tell a story that in kindergarten Charlotte came up to Rose's mom at the end of the first day and said, "We're best friends now. You have to plan a playdate." And they'd been together ever since. You *needed* someone by your side.

Maybe they could reach out to the new kid and help her.

On the way to history class, Charlotte sidled up to Rose. "Any sightings?"

Rose shook her head. "But I heard she wears all black."

"Emo!" Charlotte joked.

Maps decked the walls around them. A banner above the dry-erase board up front read *History is a form of time travel.* An American flag hung in the side corner a few feet from the teacher's desk, and a thin mural depicting the first lines of the Declaration of Independence wrapped around the top of the room. Mrs. Paterson sat under the overhead lights that were so bright they'd keep you awake no matter how late you stayed up doing homework, and she gave each kid a small nod as they came in.

Mrs. Paterson reminded Rose of a flamingo in human form—dresses always bright, fluffy hair in an updo, pink lipstick, and heels that Rose could not imagine balancing on all day. She was probably about thirty. Maybe forty. She was one of those people where it was impossible to tell.

"Nice to have you back." Mrs. Paterson held out a hand for Rose's papers.

Rose fumbled in her folder and pulled out the work. Charlotte had emailed her everything.

"I sent you the others on Google Classroom," Rose reported.

"I'd expect nothing less." Mrs. Paterson gave her a closed-mouth smile of approval.

And Rose felt her shoulders relax an inch. It might've been stupid, but she always worried teachers would be annoyed that she had to miss so many school days in the fall. Luckily, Mrs. Paterson didn't seem to mind.

The bell rang, and right on time, Mrs. Paterson popped up.

Charlotte eyed the door, searching for the girl named Delilah.

Rose heard her sigh and give up.

"Monday, we finished review. Tuesday, we set up the landscape. Now we really get going," Mrs. Paterson began. "We're going to watch a film today..."

Whispers of "Yes!" rippled across the room.

"I know, I know." Mrs. Paterson smiled. "But really take it in. It's essential. And there *will* be a quiz after!" she added to an "Aw, man!" from Zion as he dramatically threw his head back and let his gangly legs stretch out straight and go limp in front of him.

"To frame the importance of this," Mrs. Paterson went on, ignoring him, "I want to remind you how much background we need to truly understand this semester's unit..."

And then the door creaked open.

A black combat boot pushed it ajar, and a head of nearly black hair with blue streaks in it peeked inside. A hand with nude-pink nail polish swung the door out so forcefully it smacked the wall.

And, standing in the doorframe, was a girl.

She stepped inside, holding a backpack strap.

She wore a shirt so short that a couple of her ribs showed, not merely a slice of torso like the other girls at school. That was obviously against the dress code.

"Hey?" the girl said to the teacher, but really to all of them.

It was her. The new girl from New York.

And while Rose still didn't know and couldn't describe what Charlotte had meant by "New York frickin' City," she could *see* it. And it was standing right in front of her—another world in a black crop top.

Her top *was* way too short. Right? Rose almost wanted to turn around and ask everyone if they'd seen it, too. Instead, she checked in with Charlotte. And, from Charlotte's side-eye, Rose could tell she'd noticed the same thing.

The newcomer's hair fell in front of her eyes. When Mrs. Paterson introduced her, the girl blew it away and looked directly out into the crowd of faces, scanning them as if she were looking for something interesting and was disappointed she couldn't find it.

Rose tried with all her might not to stare. But she couldn't help it.

Had this new kid really been kicked out of her last school?

"Welcome." Mrs. Paterson put a hand on the girl's back. "Folks, this is Talia Anderson." Checking the clock and noting her new student's tardiness, Mrs. Paterson leaned in toward her and said, "It's hard to find your way around here at first. It's a labyrinth."

This struck Rose as an obvious white lie. The school's structure was pretty straightforward—three hallways with eighth graders on top, grades stacked on one another like logs, and one mobile classroom outside for the art and science room.

But it made sense for a teacher to be nice to the new kid. Rose tried to imagine it: thirty strangers gawking, taking you in, deciding you were this or that thing. Rose would crumble in that kind of situation. Although maybe in a city you were used to thirty strangers gawking at you, because Talia Anderson didn't look like she was crumbling at all.

"Ugh, no, it's not that," Talia groaned, inching her face closer to Mrs. Paterson's, like they were talking one-on-one. "I was tied up by paperwork. Took hours just to make sure I was in the system or something. Schedules, IT errors, the works. It never ends, right?"

Rose had no idea what she was talking about. But it was weird that she spoke to the teacher like they were both adults. It felt a little . . . disrespectful. Like . . . that was her teacher. Not her friend.

Talia Anderson sighed a small sigh and strolled toward the open seats in the back.

Rose refocused on Mrs. Paterson. She'd seen the New York City girl. It was over with.

But she couldn't help it. She wanted to know more.

Would people want to talk to Talia Anderson, or would they think she was too weird-looking?

She definitely looked weird to Rose. But was it a bad weird? Rose wasn't sure. Maybe it was cool. That kind of cool where someone isn't trying. There was no way Rose could even *think* of that outfit, let alone pull it off. Rose and Charlotte were not kids who ever got to see the spotlight. And that suited the both of them just fine.

"Where were we..." Mrs. Paterson regrouped. She poofed up the sleeves of her dress and continued the lesson.

"So! We'll spend a large chunk of our time on America's role in World War II. You'll learn all about the background leading up to the conflict, why the US entered the war after the attack on Pearl Harbor, and how America ended it by saving the lives of potentially millions of soldiers and citizens with the bombings of Nagasaki and Hiroshima." Mrs. Paterson pivoted to the SMART Board and pulled up the syllabus. "Like I've said, there's quite a lot to cover!" She hesitated, noticing something in the back of the classroom.

"Yes?" She pointed. "Talia?"

A rustle could be heard from the mass movement of thirty torsos turning toward the new girl.

"I'm confused." Talia leaned forward on her desk and held on to the ends of it.

"Yes?" Mrs. Paterson repeated.

"You just said America saved a ton of lives with the bombings of Nagasaki and Hiroshima?" Talia bit the eraser tip of her pencil.

Mrs. Paterson waited a beat, then reiterated, "Yes, I did."

"I mean..." Talia glanced around at everyone as if something crazy was going on. "I've read that the atomic bombs killed *way* more people than the number of people they would've saved. Like..." She looked to the other students once again, as if someone there would obviously join in and back her up. "They're *atomic bombs.* Have any of you guys read *Sadako and the Thousand Paper Cranes?*"

Utter silence replaced the rustling. All that could be heard were the far-off voices of hall monitors chatting, way out beyond the door.

Rose held her breath. Was this girl serious? She had just walked into their classroom, and immediately she was small talking with the teacher and then *questioning* her? Mrs. Paterson had an actual *master's* degree in history. She'd told them. She should probably have been teaching at a *college.* And just because Talia Anderson was from New York City, she thought she knew better than a teacher? After less than ten seconds?

Talia's fingers strummed on the desk. Rose noticed a smattering of symbols and sketches drawn with pen decorating the skin. A crescent moon with a dangling star. A little cartoon boat. A flame.

"I think you'll find there's much to learn on the topic," Mrs. Paterson responded gently. She returned to the SMART Board and took a breath in to speak.

"But—" Talia interrupted again.

Someone coughed into their hand as they said, "Shut up," and a few people giggled, including Charlotte.

Rose twisted her neck again to study Talia. She must have

been embarrassed. Rose could feel her own stomach flutter and ache at the thought of that humiliation.

But Talia appeared . . . unbothered.

Mrs. Paterson jumped in and shut down the room's growing electric energy: "Talia, we're skipping ahead here. Let's have a chat after class. Mmmkay?"

Rose watched Talia shrug and shake her head. She whispered something under her breath. Rose wasn't sure, but she thought maybe Talia said, "I'm just saying . . ."

And then Talia noticed Rose's rubbernecking.

Heat rushed to Rose's face. She knew she should turn away like the other kids already had. She'd been caught.

Everyone wanted to know about the new kid—that wasn't odd of her—but she still felt like a complete weirdo.

But instead of glaring at her or something, Talia simply nodded, lifted a hand, and mouthed, "Hi."

Rose snapped back to the front.

As Mrs. Paterson set up a documentary about life in Germany after World War I, Rose heard wisps of laughter in the back of the room. Were they *about* Talia, or was she joining in, too?

And was that true what she'd said about the atomic bombs? Rose didn't know anything about them except that they'd been dropped on Japan in the war. That was it. How would this new girl even know all that stuff?

Rose's dad would hate the way Talia was talking about America. Like they'd done something evil.

Rose swallowed hard and tried to concentrate on the film.

Watching the black-and-white footage, she diligently took notes. Bullet point after bullet point. Attention darting between screen and page.

What would it be like to just waltz into a room and act so . . . What was it?

Unafraid.

And *rude.*

Clearly, the new girl wouldn't need Rose and Charlotte to help her feel comfortable. It was like she was already more confident in five seconds than Rose had been . . . well, ever.

Rose scribbled:

• *Dependent on other nations*

• *Job crisis*

• *Lack of opportunity*

But with her left hand, she ran her fingers through the ends of her straight, copper-colored hair.

How would it look, she wondered, painted a loud, vibrant blue?

Then she shook off the thought, focused on the task at hand, and let her palm fall on the familiar wooden desk before her.

o ✳ o

Rose watched as Talia Anderson strode into the school cafeteria, a crocheted bag hanging on her shoulder and a book tucked just below her armpit. She didn't look from table to table, unsure and alone, like Rose had imagined that morning. She simply made her way toward the hot lunch line as kid after kid came up to her and glued themselves to her sides, talking to her about who knew what. Aaliyah and Gabbi didn't even get school lunches, they brought them from home, and yet they waited in line with her.

Rose and Charlotte sat in their usual nook toward the back corner and observed the welcoming ritual taking place.

"Someone needs to tell that girl it's fall," Charlotte declared, whipping her eyes away and focusing on her food. She pushed aside her Tupperware full of veggies and dug into her mom's famous grilled cheese. Charlotte's mom worked full-time as a nurse and still managed to send all four kids to school with homemade lunches. She was involved in the PTA and showed up to school board meetings and fostered dogs from the rescue. On top of that, she was their Girl Scout troop leader and never missed a meeting.

Rose's mom always said, "I don't know how she does it. Jennifer the Supermom!"

Rose's mom had fibromyalgia and other unexplainable health problems, so she was in too much pain to complete her to-do lists a lot of the time.

Sometimes Rose wondered what it would be like to have a mom like Jennifer. It seemed fun.

Not wanting to get caught staring again, Rose copied Charlotte and shifted her focus back to her lunch.

"Her shirt's just not very appropriate." Rose opened her years-old lunch box decorated with cartoon pugs.

Two boys started pushing each other in the corner. A teacher hollered at them before a real fight could begin. The bigger boy walked away mumbling.

"They should just be allowed to battle," Charlotte deadpanned. The tips of her mouth rose in her ever-mischievous grin. "Like in a cage match. Just let them get it over with, and they'll be best friends again by tomorrow. It's a boy thing." Charlotte sighed. "They're just like the dogs."

Rose chuckled. "That's true."

Rose couldn't wait to get back to the rescue center. The troop had decided to go above and beyond that year and work toward the Silver Award outside of regular badges. Their proposal involved two walking sessions a week, plus a fundraiser to help the rescue gain enough money to rent the empty floor above them. The rescue needed more space, and that way they could maybe even bring in new dogs.

And if Rose kept up her volunteering and never let her grades drop below a B+, her parents would finally give in to her decade-long campaign for a pet dog. This year she had to prove she "understood responsibility" so she knew what it meant to have an animal. They were probably right. A dog took a lot of care. She saw that at Cove Lake Rescue.

Girl Scouts had always been Charlotte's favorite thing more than Rose's, but this year, with the dogs, Rose could try to make it hers, too.

"How was George on Thursday?" Rose asked about her favorite one, the perpetually unadopted senior shih tzu/Min Pin mix who had a few medical conditions and only two legs. He was the one she wanted to adopt.

"He missed you like I did," Charlotte reported. "He doesn't get all excited for anybody like he does for you. Even Paige and Addie, and they were there the most at the end of summer."

Rose wished that didn't make her feel so special, because it shouldn't matter which dog loved which person . . . But it did. She couldn't hide a smile. "He's a sweetie," she said.

A spasm of laughter ricocheted through the room, and Rose instinctively turned to look. It was the group surrounding Talia Anderson. She'd settled at Bree Ryder's table. Well, that would make Charlotte like her even less. Charlotte was in youth group with Bree at church and said she'd always been snobby. But besides Charlotte, *everyone* wanted to be around Bree. She was super pretty, with perfectly zit-free brown skin, great taste in outfits, and a megawatt smile. But although she was friends with the popular girls, she had her *own* group, and that made her even cooler. Not to mention that a few of her videos racked up thousands and thousands of views online. She did dances on them or something like that.

Rose wasn't allowed on social media, and she'd never seen them.

It made sense that Talia would want to hang out with someone widely adored like Bree.

"It's just, like ... you don't talk to Mrs. Paterson like that," Charlotte said, alerting Rose that she was once again taking stock of Talia, too. Charlotte shook her hair—which she styled in a manner she liked to describe as "Kate Middletonesque"—off her shoulders and glowered at Bree's table. "I *will* fight for her and defend her honor."

Rose knew Charlotte was joking, but she had seen Charlotte smack a boy upside the head once for calling Rose an "ugly ginger" back in fifth grade, so she knew her best friend wasn't all talk. Charlotte wore either cutesy, girly stuff with frills and sequins or fangirl shirts from her favorite shows like *Stranger Things*, and she had the face structure of a Kewpie doll. But she also held herself like she was a much older kid—sometimes high school boys tried to talk to her, which creeped her out big-time. And since she'd presumably reached her full height and shape already at about five feet seven inches, she was taller and stronger than plenty of the smaller boys at school.

It would be a huge mistake to mess with her.

Rose snickered into her almond butter and jelly sandwich.

"What?" Charlotte asked with a full mouth.

"You're just funny, that's all," Rose answered. "You really love Mrs. Paterson that much?"

"She knows how to make history not boring, so yeah!" Charlotte smacked a hand on the table in joke passion.

Peeking over at Bree's table, Rose noticed it had gotten so full that a couple of boys were forced to hover at the ends of the table.

How did this newcomer, who looked so different, already have it so easy? It was sort of unfair.

"Why do you think everyone cares so much?" Rose asked Charlotte before chomping on a baby carrot. "About the new girl?" She knew she was a hypocrite. She'd been thinking about Talia all morning.

"Because we're bored out of our gourds. She's the belle of the ball now, I guess." Charlotte surveyed the crowd around Talia and gave a tsk-tsk. "It's so annoying. Just ignore her."

And Rose really tried to ignore Talia Anderson.

Over the next week, she ignored Talia as she moved from group to group, conversing with everybody. Well, except for kids like her and Charlotte, who were never the center of anyone's attention.

She tried to ignore Talia's continued pestering of Mrs. Paterson in history and also Mr. Alexie in English, where Talia publicly declared that *The Call of the Wild* by Jack London was "wholly irrelevant for kids today," whatever that meant.

And Rose ignored how hard Charlotte gritted her teeth at all of Talia's raised hands and loud opinions.

And Rose tried even harder to ignore the boys gossiping

in between classes about how "gorgeous" Talia was, because she didn't want to care what boys in her grade thought about any of that stuff, or she'd have to start wondering what they thought about *her*, and that stressed her out.

"They're just saying she's cute because she's new," Charlotte would explain whenever Talia came up, which was often over the next week. "Ignore it."

So Rose ignored. Ignored, ignored, ignored.

But eight days after Talia Anderson swept into Cove Lake Middle School, there came a day Rose could *not* ignore her. She couldn't even try.

From Rose's spot in the twelfth row of the synagogue's sanctuary, as she listened to the haftorah and marveled once again at how if Jonah had just followed directions, he wouldn't have been swallowed by a huge fish, she glimpsed, up toward the front, a head of dark hair with bright blue streaks.

Yom Kippur ended the week of High Holy Days that began on Rosh Hashanah, and that year it took place on another set of school days. It was the most sacred of holidays, on which congregants fasted all day long and feasted after sunset. And there was a *lot* of praying involved.

Yom Kippur was the kind of holiday that people came to temple for even if they never attended otherwise. Unfamiliar faces filled the sanctuary, which was part of why security was so tight that year. The temple had had a bomb threat the year before, so even regular members of the congregation had to show their High Holiday tickets at the door alongside those who only came once a year.

So maybe the blue-streaked girl in a white dress was just someone Rose didn't know. Or maybe someone from Hebrew school had changed their hair. What were the chances the new kid was Jewish and would go to her temple? Almost zero. There were five Jewish kids at Cove Lake Middle School, none of them at her temple, so it *couldn't* be her.

But it had to be. Rose peeked between heads and shoulders and inspected her.

The girl wore combat boots that kicked back and forth, her heels lightly tapping the bottom of her seat. She sat next to an old woman with gray hair and a lacy white kippah. And when she put a hand on the old woman's back, guiding her toward the correct page in the siddur, Rose could barely make out what looked like pen markings below the girl's knuckles.

And then, just like that first day in history class, as if by some sixth sense she knew Rose was staring, Talia Anderson turned back and looked directly at her.

Grinning, Talia motioned with a tilt of her head toward the exit. She spoke into the old woman's ear and made her way out of the aisle.

Did Talia want *her*—Rose—to meet outside?

No. Absolutely not. Rose couldn't. Talia disrupted class. She dressed like she wanted to get stared at. It was almost like she didn't even speak the same language as Rose or Charlotte. Leaving services for her couldn't lead to anything good. And why would she be interested in Rose, anyway? It made no sense.

Talia stood at the exit in the back, right before the huge wooden doors. Her hand was on the doorknob, and she motioned, *Come!*

Talia's bracelets jangled, and Rose almost wanted to shush her.

And was she wearing red lipstick? *On Yom Kippur?*

Still . . . Rose couldn't believe Talia was Jewish, too. Rose's dad had grown up in town as the *only* Jewish family in school with his brothers, and he thought five kids—even though they spanned three grades—was like having your own personal gang. Like the T-Birds in *Grease* or something. But it so wasn't.

Because of that, he would probably like it if she talked to Talia.

Rose checked out her parents. Her dad appeared bored, as usual, but her mom sat somber and near tears, like she got sometimes during prayer. She had a massage ball behind her back to help with her pain, and she moved against it in tiny circles to rub her muscles.

If Rose talked with Talia, she could tell Charlotte everything about it—report things that Charlotte might be curious about, even if Charlotte had been pretending that she didn't care.

Right? Charlotte had said, *Ignore her*, but Rose knew, without a doubt, that if she passed up an opportunity to learn more about the new girl, Charlotte would be annoyed.

Rose murmured to her parents that she had to use the bathroom and whispered, "So sorry . . . So sorry," to every pair of knees she slid by.

And she followed Talia through the exit and out the door.

o ✳ o

"So I'm not alone," Talia said after striding several feet in front of Rose before pushing open the doors to the courtyard.

Temple B'nai Tikvah was built like a square, with a memorial courtyard in its center and the educational rooms on the lower floor in the basement. As kids learned how to chant Torah, the light snuck in from soil-level windows.

In the enclosure, names of lost loved ones were engraved on each stone that made up the ground, and in the center stood a large Holocaust memorial boulder surrounded by a moat of pebbles and a few potted chrysanthemums. Two miniature gardens for the older kids and some raised herb beds for the little ones decorated every corner.

Rose whispered, knowing voices tended to echo a bit between the brick walls. "I can't believe you're Jewish!" She regretted the words immediately, mostly because they sounded too enthusiastic.

She felt butterflies in her stomach. But they weren't butterflies. Why did people say that? They were spiders. Spiders skittering about her insides.

"Ha!" Talia plopped on the edge of a small stone wall that made up one side of a closed-in rain garden the kids tended to each year. Behind her, a row of coneflowers had turned brown but still shot straight up toward the sun. "How *would* you know?"

"Yeah, well, of course," Rose agreed, sitting down on the wall and trying not to overthink how far away she had placed herself from Talia.

"This town is, like, shockingly homogenous." Talia stuck her calves out into the sunlight. She wasn't wearing tights. "I told some girl I'd be gone for Yom Kippur, and she said, 'What's that?'"

"Oh, *none* of them know. None of them know anything." Rose surprised herself by laughing and felt a few of the spiders leave her.

"It's gonna take some getting used to," Talia said. She ran her fingers through her shoulder-length hair. "You ever been to New York?"

"No. But I've always wanted to see the Statue of Liberty." The wall leading up Rose's home's staircase held a framed photo of her mom standing at some kind of fence, grinning, the statue a speck behind her in the water.

Talia let out a small laugh. "It's super touristy."

"Oh," Rose said. She had no idea what to contribute to this conversation.

"Oooh, but the statue has that amazing poem, yeah?" Talia lit up. "*Give me your tired, your poor, your huddled masses yearning to breathe free . . .*" She intoned the words like an actress might, full of feeling. "Something like that." She dropped the performance and ran a finger back and forth beneath one of the gold chains hanging around her neck.

"You have it memorized?" All Rose had memorized was the daily recitation of the Pledge of Allegiance.

"I like words." Talia's smile was so broad and stretched so wide you could see her gums.

Rose noted that inked words decorated not just Talia's hands but her arms. Rose wanted to try and read the penned phrases, but instead she faced front.

"I wish it could be warm forever, right?" Talia arched her back a bit, like she wanted all of her skin to touch the sun. The V-neck on her white dress cut sharply into her chest.

Rose's thick cardigan felt hot in late September's surprising heat.

Rose tried to imagine wearing Talia's dress. Her pale complexion would probably look blotchy next to the snowy white. And she'd want to put her arms over her own small chest and cover up.

But Talia elongated herself, not at all self-conscious, letting her head fall back to bask.

"So who forced *you* to come?" Talia broke the quiet, lifting her legs up and down like she was doing a quads exercise.

"Me? Oh, no one forced me." Rose straightened her legs, too, and they went far out past Talia's. Her feet touched the ground while Talia's hung above it. "We're here a lot."

"Oh. Huh." Talia brought her chin down and locked eyes with Rose. "Bummer. My grams made me. My parents don't really care about this stuff."

The eye-to-eye contact made her feel like she couldn't

even blink. In the bright light, Talia's irises held shades of amber.

"My dad's kind of Buddhist-y, actually," Talia said, and the amber twinkled.

"*Really?*" Rose had never met a Buddhist. Or if she had, she didn't know.

"Oh yeah. He's really into it. He told me that one time, after a week of silence at a meditation retreat, he looked down at his cereal and—out of nowhere—he *understood the meaning of life*. It just hit him!" Talia acted out a mind being blown at a bowl of cereal. Her impression was so good that Rose couldn't help herself and let out a giggle. Talia raised her thick eyebrows up and down. "Cool, right?"

"So what *was* the meaning?" Rose hated how interested she sounded. She could feel herself moving closer to Talia on the wall without trying to.

"He forgot." Talia clapped her hands together and cackled. "By the end of the cereal bowl, the thought was gone."

"That's so funny," Rose said, even though she wasn't sure if it was. It was . . . *something*, though. A cool story. In her head, she could hear her grandpa call Talia's dad a "hippie," but she pushed Grandpa Jacob away.

"*I* think we each have our *own* meaning of life." Talia hopped up and circled the memorial stone, lightly kicking little pebbles with the heels of her boots. "Like, everyone has a reason they're here, and it's just theirs and just for them."

Rose could not believe she had just met this girl—and

still not even officially—and they were talking about the purpose of being alive. Charlotte would definitely say it was awkward.

"What do *you* think?" Talia asked, whipping her head toward Rose, even as she kicked a few more stones.

"Um . . ." Rose searched herself. Talia Anderson wanted to know what *she* thought about the meaning of life. Why did she feel like she needed to give a good answer? She had nothing to offer a kid from New York who knew how to use words like *homogenous.*

But Rose sat up straight. No matter how it might sound, Rose knew what she thought.

"I think it's to be a good person. To do good deeds."

Through the glass door exit, Rose spotted a couple of kids she knew from Hebrew school walking the hall with their families. People tended to show up at different times on Yom Kippur, since the praying went all day. Cara Morales and Ariella Weiss strolled together with their parents behind them. Cara had always been a friend to Rose, but Ariella . . . Well, a couple of times she'd said Rose wasn't really Jewish because her mom had converted. Rose's mom had been raised Catholic by two grandparents Rose had never even met. But Rose knew she was just as Jewish as anybody else.

Were Cara and Ariella squinting at her because of the sunlight coming through the window or were they judging her for hanging out with a girl who dressed like Talia did on the High Holy Days?

"I like that." Talia punted a pebble, and it flew all the way to the dirt beneath some bushes by the wall.

Rose had to get back. She should say something and leave.

A flock of birds flew out of the nearby oak tree, and the falling leaves cascaded downward in droves. Rose watched the red and brown fall on the cobblestone.

"Can you believe we have to turn in homework from these two days?" Talia's arms fell and smacked down by her sides, and she walked back to Rose, who was still by the stone wall.

Avoiding Talia's intense gaze, Rose fixated on the journey of the reddest leaf of all, so red it looked like it had been painted that way. "It's no big deal, right?" she said.

The leaf hit the ground.

Talia let her jaw fall. "Are you serious?"

Rose had no idea what Talia meant. Had she said something wrong?

"Where I'm from? *Everybody* gets the holidays off. Like, the whole school." Talia's complexion reddened. "We shouldn't have to do the homework, at the very least. It's our *holiday*!"

"Well—" Rose started.

Rose saw Ariella and Cara, this time without their parents, returning to peek through the glass.

She had to head back to the sanctuary . . .

"Where I'm from, you don't just get our holidays off, but

Eid, Chinese New Year, Juneteenth, and everything people celebrate! Tomorrow we'll have tons to catch up on just because of our *identity*. Who we *are*. A *religious minority*. It's unfair! Don't you think?" Talia inched closer to Rose with each question.

"Yeah, I guess." Rose tried to avert her attention from Cara and Ariella's spying. "But, like, there's only a few of us. So . . . it would make it tricky for everybody else to change the calendar, right?"

"Oh, come on." Talia put a hand on Rose's arm and searched her eyes again. "Is that what you *really* think?"

And Rose froze.

Was it unfair? It did really stress her out that she wasn't allowed to do homework during those days, so then she had to cram at night, and she missed so many days in September and October that Halloween time usually felt like a constant game of catch-up. But that wasn't the worst part. The worst part was that no one else at school could really understand.

Even Charlotte had joked earlier that Rose's people "really love to party." But it wasn't like she just got the day off to hang out and relax! Rose had laughed at that comment at the time . . . But *was* it funny? Was she being overly sensitive to think it wasn't?

"I guess it's not fair that all the big breaks are just around Christmas and Easter." Rose recognized the truth she felt in her words as she spoke them. She let herself meet Talia's stare.

"Exactly!" Talia lowered her voice to a quiet, sneaky rasp: "Have you ever said anything? We should say something."

"Oh no." Rose could feel herself blushing. "It's just . . . the way things are."

Some birds flew to a useless, dead-leaf-filled stone bird-bath. Small brown ones, who would soon disappear in the oncoming winter.

"But things don't *have* to just be the way things *are*," Talia insisted with the same tone she'd used to grill Mrs. Paterson. She returned to her previous seat on the wall. She touched the dead coneflower and pulled off a dried-up petal, then blew it onto the ground. "Do you know what I mean?"

Rose opened her mouth to say, *I better get back*, but Talia interrupted her.

"I'm gonna show up to school on Christmas." Talia grinned. She swung her calves back and forth against the stone and beckoned for Rose to sit closer.

Rose did. Out of the corner of her eye she saw that her friends from Hebrew school had left. Good.

"I'm gonna break into school and make it a school day. And we can learn stuff ourselves. Like how Mrs. Paterson's class is *absurd*, for example!" Talia clenched her fists and let out a little yell. "I hate it! Oh, and we'll create some incredible project that no one else gets to do because they're missing school for midnight Mass or whatever!" Talia giggled.

Rose couldn't help but giggle, too. "And if Hanukkah

overlaps, we can put the menorah in the school window!"
She covered her laughter with a palm.

"Ha!" Talia shot up from her seat. "I'm in! Christmas School Day protest! We are evil geniuses!" She held out a hand. "I'm Talia, by the way."

They probably both knew that Rose knew that already. But it was still nice.

"Rose." Rose shook her hand.

She hadn't ever thought Talia would be so friendly with her. Rose wasn't Bree or Piper or . . . anybody.

"I better go back in," Rose finally said. Although she now sort of wished she didn't have to.

What would happen if she stayed?

"One more second," Talia said, like she could read Rose's mind. She squatted and rummaged through a crocheted bag she'd put on the ground. And she pulled out a book. "Check this out. I just finished it."

Talia held the book out to Rose.

"I think you'll, like, *get* it." Talia pointed at her and then let her hand drop. "They don't want to tell us *this* about our precious history, that's for sure."

"Oh, okay. Thanks." Rose took the book. The cover displayed a picture of a girl's face fading away over the image of an old-timey boat. The words above the illustration read *Fateful Passage: The Story of a Young Girl Aboard the MS* St. Louis.

"Let's go." Talia started back, striding toward the door and leaving Rose scrambling a foot behind.

"When should I give the book back?" Rose asked in as soft a voice as possible as they returned to the overly air-conditioned building. "I have lots of school reading, so—"

"Give it back whenever! I always have more to read," Talia answered, her volume much louder than Rose's. "How about by the time we're eighty, so I can pass it down to my grandkids? Ha!"

They slid back into the prayer service and went their separate ways.

What had just happened?

Talia was ... *nice*. If a little bit weird, too.

"Rose!" Behind the rows of seats, Cara Morales caught her by the arm and whispered, "Who was that?"

"Oh, she's from school," Rose explained.

"She's sorta ..." Cara scrunched up her face, searching for a word.

"Yeah, I know," Rose said, almost like she was apologizing. "She's new."

"If you come with us and our little brothers, then you can join the kids' service instead of having to sit here," Cara told her. Cara's braces and retainer had given her a slight lisp, but she was still the most glamorous of all of the Hebrew school kids. Her cream-colored, puffy dress made her look like a bride.

"I have to ask my parents first," Rose whispered back, and went off to see if she could make her escape like the others.

Rose liked the kids' service best. She loved the guitar, and the way the kids laughed and played.

Back inside, tiptoeing by the far end of the aisle so she'd draw less attention to herself, Rose returned to her parents, *I'm-sorry*ing over many knees for a second time.

"Mom," she murmured. "Can I go to the family service? My friends are going with their little siblings."

Her mom pressed her lips together. They were bare, without their usual mauve-shaded lipstick, because on Yom Kippur women technically weren't supposed to wear makeup. Even though almost *every* woman around them wore some, she liked to follow the rules. Predictably, her mom shook her head no, and Rose knew to go back to her seat next to her father.

When she squeezed in beside him, he patted her knee. One of his legs bounced a little, so she knew the fasting was getting to him.

Rose could feel the light weight of the book in her hands. She slid it onto the thigh opposite where her father sat.

Its pages were worn and dog-eared, its cover slightly shredded in one corner. Rose turned it over to read the back's description:

In 1939, Raizel flees Hamburg, Germany, on a ship bound for safety in Cuba. But when the boat arrives at port, it is denied entry. As the ship circles off the coast of Florida, hoping for mercy, the fate of its passengers lies in the hands of North America. From the perspective of the fictional Raizel, this book tells the true story of the MS St. Louis, a boat of refugees fleeing certain death in Eastern Europe in World War II.

"Hey—absolutely not in here," her dad muttered when he spotted her reading. He took the book without checking its contents, put it under his seat with their things, and handed her a siddur.

Rose faced straight ahead. The white of the robes on the rabbi and cantor and the decorated wood of the ark struck her as beautiful. It always had.

It was so bizarre and funny that Talia went to the same temple . . . Maybe it was okay to be friendly with her. Being welcoming to strangers was a good deed, one of the best deeds of all. And Charlotte was always talking about doing good deeds, especially as a Girl Scout. So she'd understand that.

Through a sliver of space between several congregants' heads, Talia turned back once again to Rose and smiled her bright, gummy smile.

Rose nodded at her, thinking of Christmas School Day, and smiled right back.

4

She held on to the wet railing of the ship. They could see the shore. And if they were turned away again, she knew what could happen. She had to get to the land.

What if she jumped? What if she dove into the choppy waters of the sea and swam toward the glistening sand of Miami? The white buildings, full of people with homes and schools to go to and families that could own businesses and walk the streets freely?

Mothers on the ship had started to cry.

Rose wanted her own mother with every cell of her being. She wanted her arms, thick and dependable and smelling of lilac cream, wrapped around her.

And then a group of men came toward her. How could that be? How did they get there? She screamed. She couldn't stop screaming.

"Rosie! Rosie, what's wrong?" Her mom was there. The faint scent of lilacs overtook Rose. She fell into her mother's chest.

"Did I make noise?" Rose asked. Her room was still dark. The digital clock on her bedstand read 3:45.

She'd never had a dream like that before, where she woke up yelling out.

She'd finished the book earlier that night, in a mad rush, waiting for—just stupidly expecting—some sort of a happy ending. For a hero to come.

The story of the MS *St. Louis* was crushing. The novel followed Raizel, a teen passenger on the ship. Port after port, country after country, refused entry to her and the 936 other Jewish refugees from Germany. And America refused them, too. America—her country, her home—had sent a boat of refugees back to Europe while Hitler was in power. In the story, after Raizel landed in France and was eventually captured, nearly all of Raizel's family ended up in the camps. The book's final scene depicted Raizel and her only surviving cousin reuniting in New York, staring out at the coastline, hand in hand.

The note in the back of the book said that in the 1930s America maintained a strict quota for how many Jewish refugees were allowed in its borders. A lot of America, the note said, didn't want *any* of the European Jews coming there. How could that be true?

Her dad's great-great-grandpa was murdered by the Nazis in some small town in Ukraine, along with his great-aunts, great-uncles, and their kids. *Everyone.* Her grandpa Jacob used to talk about it all the time! Whenever he did, her dad would always joke, "Don't worry, Dad, I know. I've got a set of bags packed, ready to go, just like you taught me."

But *was* it a joke?

Did her *dad* know about the MS *St. Louis*?

She wished she had never read about it.

Instinctively, Rose took the book, which lay next to her pillow, and moved it farther away from herself. It fell to the carpet.

Her mom reached down and picked it up.

"What are you reading?" She flipped through the pages.

Rose didn't say anything.

"Of *course* you're having bad dreams." Her mom put the book on the bedstand, cover down. She flipped Rose's sweaty pillow and fluffed it. Then she pulled the covers up to Rose's chin and rubbed her back through the comforter. "Don't read this stuff."

Rose fell back asleep to the sound of "Everything's okay, sweetheart. You're so safe," repeated again and again.

Every day, Rose brought the book back to school to return to Talia. But she never found the right moment. At first, she thought maybe she'd see Talia at synagogue for the holiday of Sukkot a few days after Yom Kippur, but she wasn't there. A week went by. Talia continued to seep into the school's various cliques with ease. Rose couldn't go up to her. She wasn't in those groups, and what would they think of her?

And then another week passed. October was flying by, and Rose *still* hadn't tried to talk to Talia about the book.

What did they even have in common besides B'nai Tikvah?

But every time Talia saw Rose, she nodded, and Rose nodded back. Sometimes they even exchanged a tiny wave, or—once—a fist bump as they passed in the halls. It felt like there was some secret between them, but if someone had asked her what it was, Rose wouldn't even have known.

Maybe that was why she didn't tell Charlotte about their talk in the courtyard, even though she told Charlotte everything. And even though the whole point of talking to Talia in the first place was to share information with Charlotte . . . That just didn't feel right anymore.

Rose thought Charlotte hadn't noticed the nods and waves.

But one Wednesday, as the third week in October officially brought in the cold, and a bundled-up Rose arrived at the rescue, Charlotte was notably quiet.

Both their moms dropped them off on Lincoln Avenue at the same time.

Cove Lake Rescue stood in a two-floor building a block off the Center Street downtown strip. On the top floor hung a FOR LEASE sign where there used to be a gym, its front still plastered with pictures of veiny, tan men lifting weights. Hopefully their fundraiser could help secure the rental of that space.

The rescue's sign stood proudly above its entrance, with a bumblebee-adorned BEE KIND garden flag and a rock painted

JESUS SAVES on the soil on either side of its doors. Adoption and fostering information decorated the windows.

As Charlotte and Rose hopped out of their cars, Charlotte's mom yelled out, "How are you, Rosie Posey?" Charlotte's mom always looked a little tired but never stopped smiling. Her features were pert and animated, just like Charlotte's. That day, she wore her chestnut hair back in a messy ponytail, and a bright magenta lipstick lit up her face.

"Hi, Jennifer! Good!" Rose waved.

"Coming by this weekend?" she asked.

"Yup!" Rose chirped, because that was what she always did.

If you were lucky enough to be one of the Holmes kids' best friends, your sleepovers involved "home spa" time making sugar scrubs and face masks, morning pancakes morphed into any shape you requested, and a general feeling that you were a part of one big family party. It was the exact opposite of Rose's quiet house. "My bonus kiddo," Jennifer sometimes called her. And Rose ate it up. Who didn't want bonus family?

"Sleepover Saturday? Have her stay through the troop meeting Sunday?" Jennifer called out to Rose's mom. Rose's mom hopped out of her car to go discuss it.

And Charlotte and Rose headed into the rescue.

"Paige was supposed to come today." Charlotte spoke toward the floor.

"What happened?" Rose asked.

Charlotte shrugged. "She bailed."

Indoors, the two rooms on either side of the front area held kennels. The backyard served as a play space for the dogs to run around. Dog toys littered the grass, including the remains of some that had been shredded by a few of the larger pups.

In the front, volunteers came to collect the dog they'd walk for the day. The girls were only allowed the ones deemed "nonaggressive," although Charlotte always said she "wanted the toughies." So far, Mariah had just laughed her off.

Mariah wasn't the official owner, but she practically ran the place. She wore her usual tie-dyed bandana over her braided, beaded ponytail, and an oversized T-shirt with sweats. Mariah made her way over to them in slow strides, her hands pressing into her lower back. Rose wondered if she had pain problems, like her mom did.

She greeted them with a "hi, ladies," and then headed back to the kennels to get George for Rose and two others for Charlotte.

Charlotte signed them in and twisted the pencil between her fingers.

George was so pumped to see Rose, it was tricky getting his leash on. His little tail wagged at maximum speed.

"Good boy, good boy, oh, I love you," she baby-talked him.

Rose and Charlotte headed off around the neighborhood.

Rose's mom sat in her car, reading, while Charlotte's had gone.

They rounded their first corner, and Charlotte's dogs both stopped. One of them relieved herself on the dying grass by the curb. Rose squatted down to scratch behind George's ears.

"So what's up with you and Talia Anderson?" Charlotte followed the lead of her duo as they made their way forward, past the small houses with sheltered front porches. A few American flags dotted the landscape, along with a host of bridal wreath spirea bushes, their branches bare.

"What do you mean?" Rose remained a step or two behind Charlotte, because George used a doggy wheelchair and moved more slowly than the others.

"You guys obviously know each other. I was just curious." Charlotte strode along, taking little hops over places where the cement of the sidewalk lay in unattended piles of rubble.

Charlotte didn't miss a thing.

Rose couldn't see Charlotte's face to read how she was feeling. She picked up George and raced a little faster to catch up.

"She goes to B'nai Tikvah, actually," Rose said.

"Huh?"

"Synagogue."

Rose knew it was strange she hadn't told Charlotte. She still didn't quite understand why she hadn't.

"What?" Charlotte stopped, and her terrier took the

opportunity to mark his territory on a lawn. "No, no, the curb." Charlotte attempted to move him, but it was too late. They kept walking. "And you were going to tell me this when?"

"Sorry. It just wasn't a big deal. I saw her there, and that's that," Rose said, wishing Charlotte would slow down.

Charlotte's terrier barked at another dog across the street, and they led the pack away.

"Marlon—treat! Marlon—treat!" Charlotte threw one down, and he gobbled it up, forgetting the excitement of the stranger dog.

"I just didn't think about it," Rose said as they passed a couple more dilapidated houses with FOR SALE signs in front. This neighborhood shifted block to block, with one home clearly well cared for followed by another that appeared tattered, dotted with a couple of houses that looked haunted.

"That makes sense now." Charlotte lowered her speed and walked side by side with Rose along the grass by the street while Rose and George took the sidewalk. "I noticed she wasn't there the same days as you, and then you guys were all 'Hey, girl!' 'Hey, girl!' with each other, so . . . now I get it. I thought she was skipping, since she got kicked out of her old school." Charlotte giggled as one of the dogs wrapped itself up in the other's leash. She knelt down to help them out. "Goofballs."

"I don't know if it's true she got kicked out . . . ," Rose said softly, watching Charlotte untangle and love up the pups.

"So did you talk to her?" Charlotte straightened, and they turned their second-to-last corner. Another nice block.

"A little." A breeze struck Rose, and she shivered.

"Are you, like, friends now?" Charlotte asked.

A few chimes filled the gusty air with music.

"No," Rose answered, knowing that was true. "But she's pretty nice." Rose saw a pinecone trailing along with George's wheels, and she reached down to fix it, getting a lick on her cheek as a thank-you.

"So she wasn't a nightmare like at school? Wow." Charlotte lifted her hands as if she'd lost a round of cards, giving up.

"She's not *that* bad at school." Rose noticed a tall purple flower in front of a house with bird feeders hanging from its small front yard's lone tree. How was that plant still in bloom?

"Now she's got problems with Mrs. Paterson because we're not learning enough about women during World War II?" Charlotte gave her signature raised eyebrow and her pursed-mouth look of *that's weird*. "I almost fell out of my chair. I'm sorry, but were the women *soldiers in the war*? They *weren't*. I guess that makes me a terrible person. Giddyup, cuties!" Charlotte commanded the dogs as they turned the final corner that would bring them back to the rescue. "Everybody likes her, so I guess that's . . ." She trailed off.

Rose didn't have anything to say. They really didn't need to make it a thing.

"I'm just saying," Charlotte went on, seemingly unable to stop herself, "Talia thinks she's better than us because she's from New York City. I want to be, like . . . girl, I don't need to go to some murder capital of the world, thankyouverymuch. I'll take Cove Lake any day."

"She's not so bad," Rose repeated.

Charlotte paused. Her hair, which had been tucked into the back of her coat, fell out strand by strand the farther they walked. She tugged on the leashes to move the dogs away from some candy wrappers they'd found. "Why not throw trash in a trash can? This world is not your dumpster, people!" Charlotte complained to the concrete.

Rose thought of Talia handing her the book and saying, *I think you'll, like, get it.* Rose hated how much she loved that Talia thought that.

Something stopped her from telling Charlotte about that part.

"Anyway, listen to this: Yesterday I came into my room to find my headphones stolen *again*! But Ava is saying she didn't steal my stuff. I'm going to put hot glue on them next time and catch her in the act." Charlotte's grin slid up the side of her face.

"You are hilarious." Rose loved every bit of Charlotte's little-sister-revenge fantasy.

"Siblings. You're so lucky you don't have any," Charlotte

added, and she went on with other stories about the dramatics in the Holmes household.

Now that Charlotte knew Rose talking to Talia wasn't a big deal, she returned to her normal self.

They ambled their way back to the shelter where Rose's mom's car sat parked. Rose hated to think badly of her mom, but why did she have to wait in there the whole time they walked the dogs? Maybe she could run an errand or something.

Her mom waved, and Rose motioned, *One sec*.

Rose and Charlotte handed the dogs back to Mariah. As always, Charlotte had a hard time letting go. She kissed and hugged each dog like she'd never see them again, even though they went every Wednesday. Then Mariah returned the dogs to their crates and shuffled off to the door, where she opened it and thanked them over and over for the troop making the time to help. Sometimes it felt like too many thank-yous for what they were doing. The fundraiser would make the real difference. They had to get to work on that, and soon.

Before they split for the night, Charlotte threw an arm around Rose and said, "Us against the world, bestie." And she hugged her. "Night! Text me!"

As Rose's mom drove them home, she asked, "How was it?"

"Fine," Rose reported as she looked out the window at the sunset's soft orange light. Night came earlier and earlier every couple of days now.

At home, she went right to her desk and completed the homework she'd started earlier. She reviewed the sheet music for school choir. She helped her mother set the table and sat through her parents' dinnertime discussion of scheduling on the weekends. At nightfall, she read the end of *The Call of the Wild* and crawled into bed.

Fateful Passage lay in her backpack, tucked away on a hook in her closet. She kept it there like if it stayed hidden, then maybe it could ward off any more nightmares. She hoped only the simplicity of dogs and music and the present-day world she lived in would make their way into her dreams.

5

Charlotte missed school the next day. She had woken up with some kind of flu. Rose's mom, knowing Rose might catch it, forced her to drink some disgusting water with vitamin C powder in it and checked her temperature three times.

Days without Charlotte were quieter. No chatter. Just heading straight down the hall, sitting at her desk waiting for class, and, at lunch, finding one of the girls in the troop to sit with. At least, one of the girls who wasn't at a "no-go" table. Certain groups were no-gos. They were closed off—members only. That day, Rose looked for Paige, but she was at the far end of Piper, Gabbi, and Aaliyah's table. A no-go. Rose searched for the other Scouts: Two were with the theater kids, and a couple of them usually studied in the library and weren't there. Then Rose spotted Addie Herning, one of the girls in their troop. She sat with a random assortment of kids. Perfect.

Rose slid in beside her, and automatically flipped some

hair in front of her face to hide the pimples that attacked the areas near her jawline.

"Oh, hey!" Addie moved her tray over so Rose could fit in. Addie's parents had magically let her get multiple piercings on each ear, and she wore what must've been two dozen bracelets, so she sounded like a musical instrument when she walked. Besides the troop, she'd also been in Rose's class a hundred times over the years. It was a bit of a mystery why they hadn't ever become better friends.

Rose opened her Tupperware container full of pasta primavera and let herself fall into the rhythms of their conversation. Addie was in the middle of insisting that it was harder to find plus-size clothing for teens than for adults and that wasn't fair, and that society hated fat people. Another girl jumped in to say that you could get all clothes online, so why did it matter if they were in a store, anyway?

Addie grumbled, "You're basically a Barbie. You don't get it."

And then a kid named Connor Roadson—his fully freckled face gleaming with mischief—stumped them all by saying, "Yeah, but what if I *love* going into the girls' section and freaking out all the old retail ladies in person with my outfit choices?" To which they all squealed with laughter.

He stood up, wearing a turquoise skirt over a T-shirt and jeans, and said, "Let me tell you the story of *this* one."

Rose knew he wore girls' clothes sometimes. Everybody

knew it. But she'd never heard him talk about it before. And he had her in such stitches with his story of the shocked ladies at the Nordstrom his grandmother took him to that she had to take a break from drinking, or she would've spit her water out.

As Rose left the cafeteria, she spotted Talia standing with Bree Ryder by the stairwell, their heads thrown back, giggling as hard as Rose's table had earlier.

Bree kept saying, "I know, right?" and Talia shook her head again and again, and said, "You have to stop, dude."

Rose stood by the lockers nearest to the cafeteria door, watching. Why couldn't she move away?

She wanted to know what they were talking about. The meaning of life? New York City? Something from the secret manual that cooler girls had?

Her bag instantly felt heavier with the reminder of the book inside it. This was her chance to give it back. No Charlotte around thinking it was "weird." No explanation needed.

Before she could make a decision one way or the other, Bree called her out: "Hey, Stern."

"Hey." Rose tried to sound self-assured and strong, to use the voice her mom coached her on when they practiced school presentations. Ugh. How embarrassing she thought that way. But the thing was, she'd never really talked to Bree. Not since the great Pokémon recess games of second grade. There was a difference between being in school with someone for years and actually *speaking* to them.

"Rose!" Talia motioned for her to join, and then she swung an arm around Rose's shoulders. Rose couldn't believe how excited Talia was to see her.

"Where's your sidekick?" Talia asked.

Bree covered her mouth like she had to hide how funny that was to her.

Would Bree be shocked that Talia knew Rose? She didn't look it.

"Sick," Rose reported. She lifted a finger to say *one sec* and fumbled to open her backpack. Then she held out *Fateful Passage*.

"What's that?" Bree asked, taking a step closer toward it. Her short haircut made her silver earrings stand out. They sparkled in the hallway light.

"Did you read it?" Talia grabbed both of Rose's arms.

The book nearly fell out of Rose's hands.

"Y-yeah. Yes," Rose stuttered. "It was actually probably the saddest thing I've ever read." She caught the lump in her throat and swallowed it away.

Her dream came back to her in a rush. Safe land, visible but unreachable.

"Yeah, I know." Talia might've been swallowing a lump, too, from the looks of it. The whites of her saucer eyes grew a touch pink. "I knew you'd get it."

Talia reached for Rose's hand and squeezed it. "Doesn't it make you *furious*?" As she said "furious," her entire body instantaneously simmered in rage—ring-covered fingers clenching and unclenching, her nostrils slightly flared, her wide, bright smile a world away. "And you think Mrs. Paterson is about to tell us about it? You know what she said to me after class my first day? She said, 'We teach the standard. And we teach what students are ready for.' What does that *mean*?"

"What's up?" Bree asked, lightly smacking Talia's shoulder so she'd tell her. "What's the book? Is this that banned books list stuff?"

"What?" Rose snapped her head in Bree's direction. What did she mean? What list?

But before anyone could clarify, Mrs. Caputo, the office administrator, appeared.

It was like she'd come out of nowhere in a puff of smoke to join their little circle.

Kids heading toward the stairwell or their lockers peered over in curiosity.

"Excuse me, girls, is that a book from our library?" Mrs. Caputo asked in a sugary voice. But something lurked beneath it, Rose could sense it.

"No." Talia's tone went cold. "It's my dad's."

"May I see it?" Mrs. Caputo held out a palm.

Without thinking, Rose handed it over right away. She heard Talia let out a tiny, nearly imperceptible groan. Rose had messed up, but she didn't know how.

"Is this for a project?" Mrs. Caputo asked, brow wrinkled, scanning the back of *Fateful Passage*.

"Why?" Talia asked, her hand on a hip. "No extracurricular reading allowed?"

Mrs. Caputo lifted her head up from the book. She peered up and down at Talia and pasted on a toothy smile. "Here at Cove Lake Middle School, we have a set of rules we follow. We care what our kids are up to."

"My dad gave that to me. I mean, for God's sake—" Talia challenged her.

"Language," Mrs. Caputo warned.

"Are you serious—" Talia started, but Rose instinctively put a hand on Talia's arm to stop her.

Mrs. Caputo paused. She spoke through her teeth, smile still on. "I will take this for the remainder of the day. I'll check and see if it's an approved school grounds text. We'll bring it back for you as soon as we've got that cleared up, Miss Stern, Miss Ryder, and Miss . . . Anderson, yes?"

Then she tucked the face of Raizel right under her arm along with folders and textbooks she'd already been carrying and sped off.

"Wait, what?" Talia yelled after her.

Mrs. Caputo stalked down the hall, stopped at the office doorway, and glared Talia down.

"Don't worry," Bree muttered into Talia's ear. "Mrs. Caputo's just an ice queen. She lives to torture children." Bree paused and added wistfully, speaking into the distance, "Her cousin saw BTS live, though. I heard her tell somebody."

Rose wondered if Talia and Mrs. Caputo would stop

staring at each other if one of them blinked. Mrs. Caputo broke first and disappeared into the office.

Talia cursed. "This stupid, stupid school."

"Bell's about to ring." Bree swung a fuchsia bag over her shoulder and skipped off toward class. "Don't worry about it, Talia. It's not a big deal."

"Come on." Rose inched toward science.

Talia followed, head down, talking to herself.

"What is this about a list?" Rose swung the door open and hustled toward the warmth of the insulated mobile classroom.

"Are you kidding? I thought you knew. You haven't heard about this? Some parents banned over forty books from the school grounds. It's the first thing that came up on my Google search when I officially knew I was going to move here." Talia spoke like Rose was incredibly ignorant. "Are you seriously saying you don't know about it?"

"Wait, it's really on a *list*?" Rose asked right as they reached science, her mouth bone-dry. "You gave me something I *could get in trouble for*?" Rose whispered, but it felt like a scream.

"How did you not know about it?" Talia lashed out at her, the warm, open Talia of the synagogue courtyard transforming into a tense, harsh, entirely different person.

Maybe Charlotte was right to be suspicious of her.

Standing next to Rose's seat at the science table, gripping its side, Talia snarled, "This banned books list is hateful. The whole school is. You should be proud that just by reading, you fought back."

Talia walked away and slumped down at a different table, legs splayed out before her.

Rose sat, knees together, face forward, back straight.

She could feel a couple of her face muscles twitching as she tried to stay calm and focused for class.

What would Mrs. Caputo do? Why had Talia spoken to her that way? What would happen to them?

6

"So . . ." Her dad fiddled with his glasses and cleared his throat. Her father was lanky, like Rose, with a crop of messy, graying brown hair that he had to cut constantly to look as "sharp" as he liked. At dinner, he kept on his button-down work shirt, and that night he spoke to her like she was in one of his work meetings. "I'd been under the impression that school was off to a good start this fall?"

He poured Rose some ice water from their white ceramic jug, and she thanked him.

In their dining room, a cabinet filled with silverware and serving plates passed down from her dad's grandma stood in regal stacks behind the glass. They only used them on Shabbat. On the other wall hung a dozen framed photographs, mostly of Rose at different stages of her life: trying ice cream for the first time with Grandma Adele, running in sprinklers with her cousins, and performing at the fifth-grade talent show with Charlotte. The only new ones that had been put up in years were her humiliating school photographs. Why did she always look like she'd just eaten a slug right as some-one told her to smile?

The most recent picture captured one of her worst breakouts.

"You've got that great project going on with the dogs and the Girl Scouts, and you're doing your homework—I think?" He checked with her mom, who nodded enthusiastically.

Rose got along fine with her dad, but it wasn't like he knew that much about her life. He was so busy with his job doing "cybersecurity consultations," whatever that meant, that he didn't exactly keep up on the details of Rose's days.

"But reading this book," he went on, putting down his fork and shaking his head before setting his elbows on the table and looking at her. "I just don't get it. Didn't you know you were breaking the rules?"

"You never told me about it!" she said much louder than she'd meant to. But it was true. Was this one of those things everybody in Cove Lake knew except her? Like when her parents shut off the news as she came in the room and then she went to school the next day and she heard kids talking about some horrible incident in the world she knew nothing about?

"I think what Dad is trying to say"—Rose's mom jumped in, doing what she tended to do and saving them from ever really getting heated—"is that we were surprised to get the call. You're not in trouble, honey." Her mom turned to her dad. "Even *I* didn't know that was one of the books on the list, Seth, and I saw it in her room the other night." She took a sip of her wine and spoke into the glass to say, "It's a long list."

"No, no." Her dad jumped in, in his own attempt to reassure Rose. "Not if you didn't know about it. Like you said. It's tough, kiddo, because even if you don't know a rule, if you break it, the consequences can be the same." He spoke to her like she was six. "If I don't know the speed limit, but I go way over it, I still get a ticket."

Rose described how Talia had given her the book, how she'd read it and it was really good but also upsetting, and then Mrs. Caputo took it away and told them it was on a list of inappropriate materials.

Her mom explained that over the summer a few parents had complained about the content in some books in the school library. The school board was in a review process and would eventually decide which books to remove (or not), but until then, none of them were allowed at the middle school.

"But why was *Fateful Passage* on the list?" Rose asked her parents. She'd gone over and over that question since Mrs. Caputo took it away and couldn't figure it out. "We're learning about World War II anyway."

"Who knows why?" Her dad opened up a spritzer and took a swig. "Everybody has an agenda these days."

"But, Dad . . ." She had the sense she should speak carefully and deliberately. "You know the book they took from me is about a boat of Jews that President Roosevelt sent back to Europe? And hundreds of them died in the camps?" Rose had to admit that she didn't think "everybody has an agenda" covered the topic enough, considering the subject matter of the specific book she'd read.

"Rosie." Her dad paused midsip.

She could feel a lecture coming.

"Yes, I looked up the book," he said. "First of all, do you understand that in 1939—and we're not talking '43, '44, if you know what that would mean here . . . The president had no idea what would happen to those refugees." He used his fork like chalk on a chalkboard, gesturing it around to point to imaginary countries and marking the boat's travel as he said, "They were sent to England and Belgium and what have you, *not Germany.*" He waved the fork in front of his face like he was shooing her nonsense away. "Some of your information is *off*. Like, my dear, Roosevelt is someone we should be *thankful* to for going to war and *helping* us, and hey—maybe that's why some parents don't like the book? They don't want you learning the wrong story?" He lifted his shoulders as if to say *I don't know*, and Rose understood that was his way of trying to stay light, of trying to not seem angry with her.

But she couldn't believe that was all he thought about it. Really? He just didn't mind a Holocaust book getting taken off the shelves? Why didn't he care more?

Before she could even work up the bravery to challenge

him, which she knew could start some squabbling between them, her dad muttered, "You sound like Aunt Laura."

Aunt Laura was Rose's aunt-in-law and had been her mom's roommate in college. She'd been dating Rose's dad's brother, and she introduced Rose's mom and dad to each other. The rest was history.

Aunt Laura was "a radical," her dad always teased.

He resumed eating, and Rose could tell the conversation was over.

But that didn't feel fair.

"I'm sorry, but that just seems like . . ." Rose wanted to say, *an excuse*. She wanted to say, *one side of a story* or *just your argument*, but a lifelong feeling crept in. Her dad knew more than her. Her mom knew more. They always had. Rose knew new ways to do math problems, she knew how to work apps on their phones that her mom couldn't figure out, but they knew the world.

Yet it simply couldn't be true that they knew *all* of it. Could it?

"Fine, Dad," she said instead. "Fine. I'm sorry . . . This won't mean I can't get a dog at the end of the school year, right?" She heard her voice crack slightly. Maybe they didn't notice.

"No, angel, of course not," her mom reassured her.

"No!" Her dad softened. "We just want you to have good standing at school, okay? That's it. You're good! We're good! Yeah?" He looked toward her mom again, like he always did, to see if he was saying the right thing.

"That's right," her mom confirmed.

Rose left dinner as fast as she could.

That night, after she dutifully completed her homework, her phone lit up with texts other than just Charlotte's.

> Hey it's Talia, Paige gave me your number

> Im really sry. I can be kind of a jerk sometimes when I get all worked up

> You actually read it and that's awesome. I didn't know if you would. I give books to people all the time and they like never open them lol

> You're a good person

> > It's ok

She could not believe Talia Anderson was texting her. A streak of bravery found its way to Rose's fingertips as she wrote, I'm glad we're not getting in real trouble or anything. It's all so stupid. Then she added, I didn't even know about this list thing. Sorry.

Why was she apologizing? Sometimes life felt like one apology after another.

Actually, she should've been upset with Talia. She'd been so tough on Rose. And why hadn't she explained to Rose about the list? Did she really just assume Rose knew?

Tiny dots appeared where Talia was typing. The dots stayed there for a long time. Maybe a minute or more. Lying in her bed, Rose just watched them. Then the words rushed in:

> It's more than just stupid tho. They're telling us we can't read books about the frickin holocaust? Did you know they say it's because the characters SWEAR? I just . . . so if they hear me swear will I get banned from school too lol then I'm in serious trouble. Also there are "descriptions of puberty" in it? Like, I can't even read about what's happening to my own dang body? Trust me, I've noticed what's occurred lol.

Haha

> The thing is I don't feel like that's the real reason they don't like it. Or maybe not the whole one.

Maybe

Talia's texts were getting . . . a little intense. Rose knew she couldn't match that in return. Plus, maybe it really *was* just about the couple of swear words the passengers used.

And then a link appeared. Rose clicked it, and a video popped up of a person at a microphone yelling at a group of exhausted-looking adults who sat behind a large table. The title read COVE LAKE SCHOOL BOARD MEETING ERUPTS.

Check this out, Talia wrote.

But before Rose could respond, her mom came in. She was dressed in her usual purple robe with her hair twisted up in its nighttime braid. Rose dropped the phone onto the bed beside her.

Her mom reminded her it was getting late. She plugged in the warm, planet-shaped night-lights that surrounded her room. Rose had loved space as a kid, all the way up until sixth grade. She had a Mae Jemison poster, and her lampshade was decorated with the moon in all its phases. Plastic stars adorned her ceiling.

Rose's mom scooted about and picked up some clutter. Rose wished she'd done that herself beforehand, so her mom didn't feel the need to. Sometimes that made her mom's chronic pain worse.

Then her mom came to sit next to her on the bed. She stroked Rose's hair, making Rose sleepy.

Rose had to respond to Talia to let her know why she'd stopped texting back. As her mom watched, Rose messaged, gtg parents.

"So the girl who gave you the book goes to B'nai Tikvah, huh?" Her mom eyed the turned-down phone.

Rose pulled the covers up to her chest, and her mom smoothed them out.

"Yup," Rose said.

"I think I heard about her. Talia? Evie's granddaughter?" Her mom twisted an earring in circles.

"Yeah, her name's Talia Anderson. She's new this year."

Her mom nodded slowly. "It's really kind of you to be friendly to the new kid."

Rose let the room fall into silence. Then a car drove by outside, breaking the neighborhood's evening stillness.

"You know, I used to get in trouble at school a lot." Her mom's voice was as lilting as all those years ago when she'd read Rose *Goodnight Moon.*

"Yeah, right," Rose snorted.

Her mom's head slanted toward the window. "No, it's true. I did." She sighed with an exhale so tired and long it could've made the curtains flutter.

Rose tried to picture her mom as a kid, lying in bed and having the same talking-to with her own mother. Rose wished she could know what her mom's mom would say about that. But her estranged maternal grandparents were an off-limits topic.

"It doesn't really matter what the school board says, right?" Her mom took Rose's hands in her own, and they felt wonderfully familiar. "What matters," she went on, "is *your* school year..." Her mom had a pretty, forgiving smile that gave her face the comforting glow of a bedside lamp. "You just watch out for your *own* life, sweetheart. No need to rock the boat, right?"

"Right," Rose said. One of the planets, in the corner of the ceiling by the door, hardly lit up anymore. A dying Neptune.

Why did she still have this space stuff when what she

actually liked was working for animal rights and singing along to her '90s music and hanging out with Charlotte?

"Can we take down the planet lights?" she asked.

Her mom glanced up, as if she'd forgotten they were even there, although she plugged them in every night. "Sure, angel," she said.

She let go of Rose's hands and kissed her forehead before leaving the room.

Rose popped up to check her phone and see if Talia had written anything back. And she had:

She'd sent link after link after link . . . And Rose figured, fighting tired eyes, that if she wanted Talia's approval, she needed to click on each and every one of them. Like homework.

But why did she want that approval so badly? What would it even mean to be in Talia's good graces? She wasn't sure. After all, just hours earlier she'd been wondering if Charlotte was right about Talia.

But still—she dove in.

What the Uptick in School Board Book Bans Means for American Education

The Surprising Story of America's First Banned Book

Rose went back to the first link, the Cove Lake school board meeting. She pulled her cover over her head like she used to when she stayed up late reading books. Light filled the little blanket cave. Rose tried to listen to what they were saying, but some of it made no sense to her. The people at the microphone were so, so angry. One of them had brought a poster with pages from a graphic novel taped onto it. The scene the woman read aloud from was about two people being what Rose's mom would call "intimate," and Rose turned the volume down despite the fact that she was wearing headphones. She peeked over the covers just to make doubly sure she was alone. Then she listened in again.

She saw the video was an hour and a half long. Impossible. She could already feel her eyelids falling. She couldn't keep going, so maybe she'd text Talia that she'd finish in the morning but she'd looked at a lot of it?

But before Rose clicked out of the video, a scene in the school board meeting woke her right up. It jolted her awake so forcefully that she may as well have had a swig of her dad's daily morning coffee.

In the tiny screen in her hands, standing at the microphone, reading aloud a list of books, stood Charlotte's mom, Jennifer, emotional, her dependable smile absent, her voice hoarse, imploring the school board to remove every single one of forty titles from the school grounds.

7

In between classes, Rose dodged Talia.

With Charlotte almost always by her side, how would it work if Talia rushed up to her talking about banned books, books that *Charlotte's mom wanted taken out of school*?

During English class, as they split up in groups to find examples of symbolism in *Call of the Wild*, Rose could hardly focus.

Jennifer. Her second mom.

Why did she think *Fateful Passage* was bad?

Jennifer texted Rose's mom "chag sameach" on holidays because she'd learned the proper Hebrew phrases at her work at the hospital. And she was so understanding that one time when Rose accidentally threw a ball through one of the Holmeses' windows during an ill-fated game of catch, Jennifer had said to a humiliated Rose, "We all make mistakes. It's okay." In fact, she said that all the time, about any tough moment any of them had.

Had Jennifer actually read *Fateful Passage*? Maybe she just didn't understand that it was an important story.

It didn't make sense!

She couldn't let Charlotte hear Talia talk about this whole thing. No way. Charlotte already thought Talia was a "nightmare." Charlotte did not like her. It was palpable.

Why did this girl come to school and mix her all up?

She needed a pillow to scream into.

But instead of screaming, she pointed out to her classmates that the dog's journey in the book took him from civilization to the wild, so maybe that meant something important.

Meanwhile, texts from Talia poured in:

> We should talk. Are you free at lunch?

> Hey I hope I didn't freak you out with all those links

> Btw are you ok with your parents? Did they get mad?
> Sorry I'll stop writing you a novel here haha

It *was* a lot. Too much.

Rose could hear Charlotte's mom's voice in her head. Jennifer hadn't been yelling, like the person in the meeting who had spoken before her. She'd sounded sad. Pleading.

"I am a working mother—a pediatric nurse. I have four children. One boy, three girls." Jennifer had paused and taken a breath, dabbing under her eyes with a tissue from a to-go tissue pack. "I always knew I had to keep my eye on my kids' phones," she'd gone on. "On what they could find online. But I *never* suspected I'd have to fight *even harder* to watch out for what's available to them at *school*. In the *school library*. It's a betrayal of a parent's right to protect their children."

Half of the room had clapped.

Rose wondered what would've happened if Charlotte's mom had spotted *Fateful Passage* in Rose's hands before Mrs. Caputo had. Would she have taken it, too? Would she still want to teach Rose her fondant techniques on weekends with Charlotte and her sister if she knew Rose was reading a book on the list? Would she think Rose was a bad kid? Would this be the first time she couldn't find it in herself to say, "We all make mistakes"?

Rose avoided Talia all day. She made sure to get to class right when the bell rang and run out immediately so Talia couldn't catch her to talk. She hid in the bathrooms between English and history so Talia wouldn't spot her.

But at lunchtime, escape would become unavoidable.

Maybe Rose needed to try and expand their cafeteria group, so it wasn't just her and Charlotte. That way, if Talia came over, it would seem more natural. Other people could talk to her, too.

As they walked in, Rose said, "Hey, want to sit with Addie and those guys today?"

"Naw." Charlotte headed for their spot by the nook, where they could lean against the wall and stretch their legs out on the bench. Plus, it was right next to a huge window, so some cold air crept in and cooled them down after enduring the school's heat going up to full blast. "Let's just be together."

Maybe Rose could grab Talia first, before she found the two of them and started in on the topic of the list, and let Charlotte know Rose had read a book that Jennifer wanted off school grounds.

They opened their lunch boxes and spread out their choices. Charlotte held up a molasses cookie her mom had made. "Jackpot."

Or maybe Rose could get the first word in. Perhaps Charlotte would be on the same page as Talia, after all.

Charlotte was her best friend. She could tell her anything.

"Hey, what's the deal with this banned books list, do you know?" Rose tried to sound casual. She focused on removing the cherry tomatoes in her pasta with a fork. Her mom knew she hated them, but she never stopped trying to convince Rose they were delicious. "I heard somebody talking about it," Rose added.

Charlotte shook her head. "Pssh. My parents say you can't even trust half the stuff people write."

"So you knew about a list?" Rose asked. What did Charlotte know? What did she *think*?

"I heard some books here and at Emma and Noah's school were super inappropriate," Charlotte said matter-of-factly, referring to her high-school-aged siblings.

"Whoa," Rose said. "I didn't know about it until yesterday."

"It was a thing over the summer. Some people got all

worked up. One of the other parents showed my mom and dad some stuff in a couple of crazy books in the high school library, and my mom freaked. Found some here, too, I guess." Charlotte started in on her cookie and leaned her body against the wall. "But I was at camp, so ... no skin off my back! Hey—check out Scarlett and Zion."

Rose looked up to see them getting *really* close to one another at the opposite table. They looked literally in love.

"I'm so glad I don't have a boyfriend," Charlotte went on. "It must be so much trouble. Emma says so. And, like, until you can drive, it's kind of embarrassing, honestly. That's what Emma says. You're going to have your *mom* drop you off on a *date*?" She grimaced. "Blech."

"So how were the books inappropriate?" Rose tried to scope out the cafeteria for Talia as subtly as possible.

"Hey—would you rather have a rat terrier or a Jack Russell terrier if you *had* to choose?" Charlotte moved on.

"Rat," Rose answered into her food as she mentally shut out the crowd gathering around a fistfight a few yards away. Another day, another round of punches.

She'd gotten as much as she would out of Charlotte about the books for the time being, and the signs didn't point to Charlotte's view differing from her mom's.

Rose saw Talia leave the lunch line, set down her tray, and spot Rose in the corner. So Rose took action.

"Hey, I gotta go to the bathroom." Rose hopped up and bolted toward Talia.

On the side of Talia's tray sat another book—*Of Mice and Men*. Rose had heard of it.

As she passed Talia, Rose nodded toward the vending machines that stood right outside the cafeteria's doorway, a few feet away from the entrance to the school. She could sense Talia following closely behind.

The teacher on cafeteria-door duty let them go ahead when Rose pointed to their destination. Rose leaned against the large red Coke sign and took a breath. Hopefully Charlotte hadn't seen. She'd wonder what they were talking about. She'd feel left out.

Talia played with the gem on her choker necklace. "I've been trying to catch you between classes all day, but you're MIA." Talia rested her back right next to Rose. "Did you read through the list?"

Rose had. She didn't know most of the titles.

Talia spoke so close to Rose's face that Rose could smell her strawberry gum. She listed all the middle school books and the reasons she thought they had been challenged by parents.

"The whole Girls Club series isn't allowed because, like, *periods*, I guess," Talia was saying, shaking her head in disbelief. "*The Kid Who Jumped over the Moon* has a boy with gay parents. Like, wooow. Shocker. How will I grow up in a world where I read a book about a kid with gay parents, right? Will that make *me* grow up to ..."

She paused, and Rose waited for her to say *be gay too*, but instead Talia said, "... have gay parents?"

Rose snorted and covered her mouth.

Her laughter seemed to spur Talia on. Talia's gruff voice rose in volume, and her gestures expanded so much as she railed against the list that Rose took a tiny step away.

"Can you believe a biography of Ruby Bridges is banned? Ruby. Bridges." She cursed under her breath.

Rose didn't know who that was, but she nodded, pretending she did.

The roar of a hundred kids talking at once poured out toward them from the cafeteria's open doors, but it was white noise.

"It's messed up." Rose needed to get back to Charlotte soon. But she also wanted to know what Talia had to say ...

"Kids all over the country have started banned books clubs," Talia reported, her whole face brightening. "They've started showing up to school board meetings. And fighting it."

Talia pulled on Rose's arm to move her away as someone came over to use the machines. It was Connor Roadson.

"Hey, guys!" Connor greeted them.

Rose lifted a hand to say hi as Talia told him good luck on his upcoming basketball game.

Connor thanked her and put a dollar in the machine next

to them, but it spat the dollar right back out. He tried to flatten it over and over against his knee.

Rose couldn't help but notice that he was wearing a skirt again. Or was it a tutu?

Linking arms with Rose, Talia strolled a few feet closer to the school's entrance, out of Connor's earshot.

Rose could feel a touch of the air outside seeping in through the doors' cracks.

"So." Talia locked her gaze on Rose again. There were no glints of amber there in the hallway light, her irises only coal. "Want to start one with me?"

"Wait . . ." Rose's pulse quickened. "Start what?"

"A group where we read the banned books. A book club!" Talia squeezed Rose's forearms, linking the two of them together.

Rose's heartbeat thudded in her ears. She pictured hiding books from her parents, then getting caught, losing George forever, the principal personally reprimanding her, her teachers hating her, Jennifer thinking she had changed irrevocably for the worse . . .

"But I don't want to get in trouble." Rose's body crumpled in apology. Then she explained, "I'm getting a dog at the end of the school year if I don't mess up. And my parents really don't want me, like, rocking the boat." She hated hearing her mom's words come out of her.

"Oh." Talia drooped, like a bloom that had gone days without water. "No, I understand."

She perked up slightly as a few boys walked out of a classroom and toward the cafeteria. She waved.

Rose wondered what it would be like to be friends with packs of guys in school. What did Talia talk about with them? Did she just joke around? Or did they all have crushes on her, and did Talia know it?

"We can talk more about this later, okay? See ya." Talia headed off to follow the boys.

Jealousy shot through Rose, though she couldn't quite tell if it was the attention Talia got or the loss of attention Talia had been giving to her.

"I'll think about it," Rose said, loud enough for Talia to hear. And then she raced after Talia and met her in the cafeteria's doorframe. "Wait," she said. "Do me a favor and don't talk about it in front of Charlotte. Okay?"

Talia grabbed her pinky and squeezed it with hers. Then she gave her a huge hug, tight, and Rose didn't know what to do with her own arms. She hugged Talia back with a pat.

Talia jetted off to the boys, who made their way across the room.

When Rose got back to her seat in front of Charlotte, Charlotte stayed on her phone.

After a couple minutes of silence, Charlotte said, not looking up, "So you and Talia are, like, buds now?"

Rose was so stupid. Charlotte must have seen them hug in the doorway. Why hadn't Rose just ended the conversation earlier? She'd messed up. She knew Charlotte would hate seeing her befriend a girl she didn't like.

"What was that all about?" Charlotte asked while still on her screen.

Rose did not want to lie. Lying made her feel gross. She remembered one time when she'd promised not to use her dad's work computer, but she did, and she thought she'd gotten away with it, but he told her he could see the search history. He must have known she'd been looking up the bio and photos of an actor she had a crush on. Knowing what her dad had seen, Rose had wanted to evaporate from the planet. He'd claimed he wasn't mad about what she'd looked at, but rather "the fact that she'd lied." The shame she'd felt had eaten away at her for weeks.

But then she *did* lie.

"She's going to volunteer one day at the synagogue with me. I was just explaining it all to her." The falsehood came so easily. Rose didn't even stutter. Or blush.

"Hmm." Charlotte put down her phone. "That was a *big* ol' hug." She spoke into her bread. "Do you remember when Talia said in history that she was happy we were going to Toronto for the school trip because Canada is 'better' than the US? Can you believe that?" Charlotte took a big bite and declared, lifting a finger into the air, "As my grandpa would say . . . 'She's a couple bricks short of a load!'"

In spite of herself, Rose cracked up at Charlotte's delivery of her grandpa's voice. "What does that even mean?"

Charlotte snorted and swallowed before throwing her head back and swigging down her pop. "Anyway, I cannot *wait* for the trip. I love how the school is like, 'Toronto was a huge center for war industries in World War II, so it'll be so important to look at it,' but really, it's just *close by*. Hilarious."

They chuckled together, but Charlotte broke it up when she asked, "So that's all you guys talked about?" She adjusted her fabric headband.

Before Rose could reply, Connor Roadson popped up behind her shoulder.

"Finally got it!" Connor held up a bag of Doritos, and Rose laughed politely.

"Good job!" She shot him a thumbs-up.

He took his seat down the table from them with Addie and a couple of friends.

"You'd think if you were going to be a weirdo and dress up in girl clothes, you would at least try to look *nice*," Charlotte muttered into her fork. "Real girls put in the effort, you know? Why does he get to slide by?" Charlotte let out a hollow laugh, like it was just any other joke.

But Rose halted. That was really mean.

Charlotte *could* be sort of mean sometimes.

Did Charlotte ever say anything about *her* behind *her* back?

"I like his outfit. It's great he's himself." Rose could hear her own clipped tone.

She had hardly eaten, but she cleaned up her space, anyway.

"Um . . . Okay? So you run off with Talia Anderson, but now I'm a jerk? So sorry." Charlotte pushed her lunch forward and leaned back again, crossing her arms. "I always thought, like, the best thing about a best friend is that you can say stuff and they still know you're a good person and they won't judge you? But fine."

Rose didn't want Charlotte to be angry at her. "Hey—" she started to say.

But Charlotte grabbed her wallet and through gritted teeth said, "I want more ginger ale," and stalked off.

This year was not going how it was supposed to go. Were she and Charlotte in some kind of fight? Just because Rose talked to someone else? Because she snapped a little? Wasn't she allowed to snap sometimes? Rose had easily forgiven Talia for snapping at *her*!

The whole day was too stressful, and it was just getting worse. She had lost her appetite.

Rose stood up and grabbed her stuff. She looked around at who else she would sit with if she left Charlotte's side.

From afar, Talia saw her and waved. Bree did, too. Addie and Connor and others with them were laughing about something. Everyone looked like they knew exactly where to be.

Rose gulped down some water and threw the rest of her food away before heading to the doors. She stood in their frame once again. This time alone.

Where did she even plan to go? From afar, Rose saw Charlotte head back to her seat and realize Rose wasn't there.

Rose didn't *want* to be there if Charlotte was going to be short with her for such ridiculous reasons.

Rose noticed Talia hopping up to chat with some people at a table nearby, then picking up her phone, thumbs out.

A text popped up.

Talia was writing to Rose.

Ask your mom if you can come over today?

Rose saw Talia put her phone down and keep talking.

Okay.

Anticipation fluttered through Rose.

But I have to be home in time for dinner.

Rose texted her mom right away to ask and prayed the answer would be yes.

She messaged Charlotte that she had an upset stomach.

And then she asked the teacher at the door if she could study in the library.

Once there, she ran her fingertips along the edges of titles, looking for something, though she wasn't sure what, until the bell rang.

8

Rose's mom insisted that she talk to Talia's mom before the two of them headed over there. Talia said it was no problem. So when they met outside the school, Talia shared her mom's information in a text to Rose's mom. She told Rose they'd be walking. Avoiding Charlotte, Rose hurried off with Talia as fast as she could.

Besides troop meetings and the occasional group project, Rose had never gone to someone else's house before. Except Charlotte's, of course.

"So where do you live?" Rose asked, entirely unsure what they were supposed to discuss besides the book list.

They rounded the side of the school that led to the fancy houses and headed onto Elmswood Avenue. The loud mayhem of the post–school day energy faded into the distance. They could still hear some whistles from coaches on the fields, but that was it.

"Cove Lake Towers. We live with Grams there. For now. Until my parents find some real work. It's just temporary." Talia shook her head to swish hair off her cheeks.

"Cool!" Rose wondered how big of an apartment it had to be if it housed Talia, her grandma, and her parents. It must've been pretty roomy.

"But that's not where we're goooiiing," Talia singsonged with a skip and a spin. She giggled and walked backward, her arms and fingers reaching out for Rose.

Rose shivered in the cold and scurried to catch up. "What do you mean?" She walked in long strides next to Talia's small skips.

Talia seemed uncaged out of school, like she could dance the whole way home.

"We're meeting Bree downtown," Talia said offhandedly. "I want her to join the club, too."

"But what about my mom?" Rose tried not to sound panicked. "Won't your mom call her back and tell her we're not at your place?"

This could end everything. No dog, no time with Charlotte, maybe even no school trip in the spring if she did something like this. Plus, Rose hadn't even agreed to do this club thing...

They passed a house with an elaborate garden and a small balcony on the top floor, and Talia muttered, "Looks like the Kennedys live there."

"But—" Rose tried again, the downhill slope of the avenue making their whole pace feel too fast. Like they could trip over their own feet.

"My parents are really cool," Talia explained, wrapping

a robin's-egg-colored scarf tighter around her neck, which made the blue in her hair stand out more, and tucking the front into her black jacket. "They don't care what I'm doing. They trust me. I mean, back in the city I took the subway to school by myself."

Rose's mind filled with every terrible option. What if her mom drove by and saw her? What if Charlotte and her parents did? What if she couldn't get home? How would she get home? When did she have to leave to make sure she got there in time? Would her mom call Talia's mom to check up on them? That was something Rose's mom would do.

And what if Talia got angry at her for something again? Rose hadn't really liked that side of her.

But Talia led her onward, and after about fifteen minutes, they arrived on the Center Street strip.

"Here it is," Talia said, her hands on both backpack straps, the tip of her nose and her cheeks all rosy from the chilly air. "So many banks."

A couple of twentysomething-looking guys flew by on skateboards, followed by the occasional pack of boys on bikes. Here and there, someone yanked open the heavy doors to a bank to use the ATMs. There had been more stores once, her dad had told her, but a lot of them had closed down. There were FOR LEASE signs up in a couple of the buildings. But new businesses were starting to crop up here and there on the main strip—like a children's clothing shop, a fabric and yarn spot that offered sewing classes, and the Silver Selkie, a clothing store filled with outfits Rose's mom deemed "inappropriate" for her age, as well as being "outrageously expensive." At the end of Center Street stood a large wooden gazebo that locals decorated every season. Families sat in it to eat takeout, and high schoolers often hung out inside to do whatever high schoolers did.

Rose liked Cove Lake. There was a reason her grandparents settled down there. It was safe and quiet, with a small park in every neighborhood. All summer long, if you went to Cove Lake beach, you'd find someone you knew to spend the day with. Her grandparents had liked it well enough to be close to the only Jewish family among the population of a couple thousand for decades until her dad was a teenager, so that sure said something. "Good schools," her grandpa Jacob always said. "All that matters are the schools." And, her grandma Adele would add, "It's nice and *quaint*," pronouncing every sound in the word like the concept of "quaint" was precious. Kind of funny, actually, that they said that even after all the bullying her dad claimed he'd gone through at school. But maybe they didn't know about it.

"At least it has the Silver Selkie!" Talia chirped.

And they strolled past the deli and headed toward the store.

"I've never been inside," Rose admitted.

Talia stopped in her tracks. "No way!"

Before Rose could explain that she only shopped at the outlets with her mom, Talia yelled out, "Breeeee!"

Bree hopped out of a car and rushed toward them.

Rose had almost forgotten that she was about to hang out with *the* Bree Ryder. How was it possible?

She should've been excited, but all she could think was that she was bound to say the wrong thing. A teeny flutter made an appearance under her belly button and worked its way up to her chest.

Talia placed herself in between Bree and Rose and linked arms with them. She led them toward the Silver Selkie. The sky was gray, and everything felt chillier in its gloom. And a little scarier.

"Bree." Rose attempted to push her voice above a mumble. "Your dad just dropped you off here by yourself? He doesn't mind?"

Bree looked at Talia. And Talia at Bree. And they both leaned over and clutched their bellies, hooting with laughter.

"Isn't she hilarious?" Talia said.

"Wait. No, no, seriously, what's the deal with your parents? Is this a jailbreak?" Bree put her hands on her hips and looked like a detective summing Rose up.

Rose didn't say anything because she didn't know if they were laughing *at* her or not. An alarm went off in her body, an immediate stiffening from head to toe, telling her to go home. She didn't know these girls.

"I'm joking." Bree gave her shoulder a light smack, and Rose, in her nervousness, almost jumped.

"My dad didn't even let me walk here alone!" Bree went

on. "My mom listens to a whole bunch of true crime podcasts, and my grandfather says it's rotted her brain and that kids used to do everything alone." She shrugged.

So Bree's parents could be protective, too. Wow.

Rose's muscles unwound a little, and she followed Bree and Talia into the store, a realm of clothing racks and dangling jewelry. The store was bigger than it looked outside. Huge phrases lit up every wall, like DARE TO DREAM and YOU ARE ENOUGH.

Two middle-aged women in body-length winter coats stood inside perusing items, and Rose could swear they were looking all three girls up and down with disapproval.

Talia and Bree grabbed hangers and held them in front of their figures, yes- or no-ing each one.

"These are for you." Talia dropped a small stack of items into Rose's arms.

And they made their way to the fitting rooms.

"I think those ladies were watching us," Rose said as quietly as humanly possible through the purple velvet curtains that separated them.

"Oh, don't worry," Talia comforted her at full volume. "They're just jealous of our youth."

Right when Rose was wondering why Talia had invited her to the store when she thought they were supposed to be talking about all the school board and banned books links she'd sent her, Rose heard Talia say, "So I was thinking—if you're both in—we could call our club the Banned Books Brigade."

Rose sat on the small stool in the dressing room, a dress, a skirt, and two shirts hanging behind her. She did not want to change. The curtains didn't shut one hundred percent. And how would she look in these things? They'd already laughed at her.

And what would happen if she joined? First of all, she didn't even really know what an outside-of-school book club did. Was it discussion questions like in class? And how secret could it possibly be? Because Charlotte could *never* know.

"Love it!" Bree's voice rang out from behind the curtain closest to the wall. "Alliteration—me likey. LOL, you guys, this looks terrible on me. One sec, I'm coming out."

So Bree was officially joining it with Talia?

Some tiny part of Rose, a part she didn't particularly like, couldn't stand the idea of not being included. Not when she'd come so far as to be out at a clothing store with two girls everyone wanted to be friends with. That made her *so* superficial, didn't it? For a second, she couldn't stand herself.

"It's just that everybody has a 'Banned Books Club,'" Talia gabbed from her spot. "Who wants to be the same as every-body else?"

"Wait, so how many places is this happening in?" Bree asked.

Talia went on to tell her all about schools taking away so many books that some class libraries in some states sat nearly empty and school librarians either took a stand or retired, and how, even at public libraries, some librarians were getting threatened or even losing all their funding.

After the mini speech, Rose heard Bree and Talia shriek at each other's outfits.

Rose stayed behind the curtain. The mirror out there would show a nervous, pimply, gangly girl.

"You look like a movie star!" Talia cooed to Bree. "Like Halle Bailey!"

"No way. I look like a . . ." And Bree used some harsh words Rose chose not to hear. Because that wasn't how Rose talked. And she wouldn't know how to fake it when it was her turn.

Rose pulled out her phone to see if her mom had texted. Nothing.

But she did have a text from Charlotte:

> Didn't see you after school. Paige is bailing again for next week, but Addie said she'd help us start planning the fundraiser. I think Paige has gone full popular girl vegetable.

So after that awkward lunch, was she in a fight with Charlotte or not? It seemed like not.

She didn't want to think about the fundraiser. Not right

then. She had to go out and show herself in something! Mortifying.

But why was she panicking? It was stupid. She could do this. It was just clothes.

Rose stood up and let herself feel the soft fabric of the green top Talia had handed her.

"Rose, let's see!"

Rose could see the tips of Talia's slightly muddy boots visible underneath the barrier between them.

"One sec," Rose peeped.

She changed into the emerald shirt. It clung to her skin and cut off way too high.

But she pulled open the curtain and forced herself to step out.

Bree gasped. "Stern!"

"You have *abs*?" Talia fake-pushed Rose, like she was mad Rose hadn't told her. But why would she have mentioned that?

Rose shook her head so hard she could've lost one of her fake pearl earrings. "Only because I have no *hips* or anything *else*," she insisted, taking in Bree's and Talia's figures in their outfits and noting that *major* difference between her and them. Especially with Talia, who had what Rose's grandma Adele would probably have called an "hourglass figure."

"Girl." Talia held on to Rose's arms, which remained tight by her sides, her hands covering up her tummy. "You have to own what you *do* have! You are *amazing*!"

"With the red hair and green, you're like some kind of . . . Scottish warrior queen!" Bree acted out a tough-girl, Viking-like stance.

Rose couldn't help it—a grin swept over her. "Scottish warrior queen?"

"Yeah!" Bree assured her. "You should be that for Halloween. Are you going to Piper's party?"

Rose shook her head, and Bree mouthed, "Oops," and blushed.

Bree didn't need to feel bad. It wasn't like Rose expected to get asked to that party, anyway.

Rose would be passing out candy with Charlotte.

But she did wonder . . . How did you get invited to a party like Piper's?

"Come here, come here," Talia said, and as all three stood in front of the mirror, she commanded, "Kiss face!"

They pouted their lips while she held up her phone and took a picture.

Rose ruined the photo by turning red at the last second and throwing her palms over her face. The lens caught her hands in midmotion and a light peach blur distorted the image. She'd taken a million selfies with Charlotte, and of course she'd photographed her own face a hundred times in private. But she always deleted them after.

"Stern, let's see those smackers!" Bree directed in such a goofy voice that the next photo captured the other two girls with puckered lips and Rose with her mouth wide open in a guffaw.

"I have to send this to Dillon. We look so cute." Talia fiddled with her phone, and Bree went back in the booth to change.

"Who's Dillon?" Rose grasped the ends of the shirt she was wearing. A shirt, she had to admit, she liked a lot. Not like she had anywhere to wear it. Were they going to buy them? Rose only had a little money.

As they all started to change and reveal one more outfit, Talia explained that Dillon was one of the people she messaged with online. She liked to talk to people who wrote to her, and sometimes it turned out they had a lot in common. Talia had started chatting with Dillon because he was also from NYC, and they posted a lot of the same political stuff.

"We message all day," Talia told them, like it was no big deal. "Not just Dillon, but a couple of other activists from the city."

How did she know who these people really were? What if they were fake profiles or something? Rose's mom had told her horror stories.

After they showed one another their second outfits, the salesperson from the front came back to check on them.

"Is there anything I can help you girls with?" The girl must've been around college age. She fit right in with the store—long, dreamy brown hair and loads of accessories. She held a hand on her hip, features expressionless.

"We're good!" Bree shouted out.

And as she walked away, Talia whispered, "She's annoyed with us. Let's go."

"We're not going to buy anything?" Rose immediately grasped for the back zipper on the too-tight dress she had just changed into.

"Heck no," Talia said. "You think I've got any money? Ha!"

Rose came out holding all the clothes on hangers, ready to put them back, but Talia and Bree were empty-handed. They told her to leave them there, and the salesperson would put them away.

And even though it didn't seem like they were in trouble, they hiked out of the store so fast that when they reached the outdoors, they panted between giggles.

"Where to next?" Bree's eyes widened in Talia's direction.

Rose stopped herself from saying she had to go home. She was in it now. Her cell phone gave her one more hour until her mom would expect her back, probably pulling up in Talia's mom's car.

"Wherever we want!" Talia spread out her arms and faced the melancholy sky like she was just daring it to bring her down, before leading them toward more adventure.

9

It turned out, walking in circles around the main street strip while no one knew where you were counted as an adventure all in itself. It didn't seem so bad, and definitely not dangerous... Was this what her parents were afraid of? Mostly, Talia and Rose just cracked up as Bree did goofy stuff.

When a few boys around their age biked by, Bree called out, "Hey, cuties!" and then they ran. Ran and ran until they were a couple of blocks away.

Talia laughed so hard she said she might pee her pants, and that made all of them crack up even harder.

"Do you think they'll come back this way?" Rose asked once she caught her breath, but Bree just went, "Psssh."

But Rose's nerves did kick in as time ticked on, and Bree and Talia wanted to mess with people more and more.

After the bicycle boys incident, Bree stood in front of a duplex on the edge of where Center Street turned residential and performed full-on choreography to a song she said was called "Heart Shaker" by Twice. Talia dared her to keep doing it until someone walked out of the front door.

Rose pictured someone yelling at them. Or calling the police.

"Stop it, people will get mad," Rose lamented, as Talia went, "Keep going, you're so good! I think I see someone in the window! Oh my God!"

Bree *was* really good. Were those the dances she posted online? No wonder she had so many views. It almost distracted Rose from her worries.

And finally, when a young dad and his baby stepped out of the front door and onto the porch, the dad said, "Excuse me, ladies," and Bree shrieked.

The three of them ran away once again.

The dad didn't seem mad at all—mostly amused. Rose felt light-headed. Fear floated away from her, replaced by some kind of unfamiliar thrill.

And then, out of sight from biking boys and those who caught them dancing, Bree eventually called her dad to pick her up, and Talia walked Rose home.

"That was actually . . . fun." Rose smiled as they turned onto the block that led them to her neighborhood.

But the thought of her mom wondering when she'd be home hit her hard, and her face fell. Rose checked her phone to make sure she had plenty of time before she had to set the table for Shabbat. They didn't really follow all the Shabbos rules or anything, but her mom made challah and they said the prayers every Friday night.

"You thought it wouldn't be?" Talia asked.

Before Rose could answer, Talia changed subjects. "So what's the deal with you and Charlotte?"

"We've been best friends forever," Rose told her. "You know how it is."

Talia shook her head. "Not really. We moved from neighborhood to neighborhood a lot. No one really..." Talia sucked in air and bit her lip before saying, "*Stuck.*"

"You seem like it's not hard for you to make friends," Rose said under her breath. Oops. Maybe it sounded like she'd been watching Talia too much.

"School friends are one thing, but *real* friends are another." Talia kicked a stick a few times, and it fell off the curb. "Why can't Charlotte know about the book club?"

Rose could feel Talia peering at her as she faced straight ahead. She spotted the house with a metal deer statue on its front yard, which meant they were close.

Rose wanted to be a real friend, not just a school one...

So she gave in. "Charlotte's mom was at the school board meeting. In the video."

"She's one of *them*?" Talia put her hands to her heart and froze in place.

"She's really nice." Rose should've known Talia would react that way.

"Her mom or her?"

"Both!" Rose insisted, losing herself for a moment and gripping the sleeve of Talia's black, loose jacket. She couldn't let Talia turn on Charlotte.

"Okay." Talia paused. "Well, I guess . . . we're not our parents, right?" She scrunched up her nose like she was thinking it out.

"Right!" Rose agreed, letting the coat go.

Talia skipped forward and wrapped her arms around herself with a "Brrr."

As early twilight rolled in, Rose was minutes away from officially being late to set the table. The lights inside the houses they passed grew brighter, like candle flames all around them.

They arrived at the house next to hers, and Rose stopped walking. "That's me over there."

Talia checked out Rose's home as she spoke. "I just think reading the banned books together would be, like . . . like you said about the meaning of life? Good deeds? It would be a good deed to change the town for the better, you know?" She paused and added, "At least for me, if I'm gonna have to live in it!" And then she burst out with her trumpetlike "Ha!" that Rose was getting used to.

Would a club make the town better? She didn't know how. Or what that meant.

But Talia had remembered what Rose had said about the meaning of life. She'd thought about it. That felt . . . nice.

Rose didn't want to walk right in front of her house with Talia, in case her mom was looking out the window, waiting.

Rose tilted her phone out of her coat pocket and checked the screen.

A text message from her mom read I called Talia's mom, but she didn't pick up. Are you ok? Rosie? What's up?

Oh no. Rose might have a heart attack if she didn't get inside that door soon.

But Talia wasn't moving, so Rose forced herself a few feet forward, toward the front of the small concrete path that led to her porch-lit door.

Through the window, Rose made out her mom's silhouette.

She turned to Talia to say goodbye.

Talia shuffled her feet.

"So . . . the *real* reason you wouldn't join the Banned Books Brigade is because you don't want to do something different from Charlotte?"

Was that the reason? Rose didn't know anymore.

Then Rose saw her mom peeking out from the curtain. Oh lord, it was like a horror movie. Her mom's pale skin, the way she stared through the glass. She must've been wondering why Talia's mom hadn't driven them home. Oh no.

She had to end this. Anything to shut it down before her mom decided to come outside and saw them. She'd know for sure that Rose had lied about being at Talia's, since Talia's mom wasn't there dropping her off.

"Yeah, let's do the club," Rose said, heading toward the door. "But I *have* to go."

"Yay! One book a month, okay?" Talia said, loudly enough that Rose could hear her on her way to the navy-blue welcome mat.

Rose waved goodbye, and Talia strode off.

What had Rose just agreed to?

"Hi, Mom!" Rose greeted her with as upbeat a disposition as she could muster.

"Talia's parents didn't pick up," Rose's mom said as Rose walked in. The creases on her mom's forehead deepened as a shred of anger bubbled up beneath her concerned voice. "Where's her car? Everything okay over there? Why on earth didn't you respond to my message?"

"I'm so sorry. We were having so much fun that I didn't look at my phone much," Rose said, knowing her mom always encouraged her to be on screens less. "Talia lives in an apartment with her grandma and parents for now until they can get a job. I think her mom was really busy while we were there. She dropped me off on the corner. She had errands to run the other way."

As she spoke, a strange spark of pleasure lit in Rose—her mom hadn't really known where she'd been.

And she didn't know Rose could look like a warrior queen, either.

But then it went out, the spark doused with cold water. Her mom didn't deserve to be lied to. Everything her mom did she did for Rose. What was she thinking? And what if she'd been caught?

"Oh—they're unemployed?" Her mom wiped her hands on her red apron and untied it, losing the earlier edge she'd spoken with. "That's so tough." She stretched to the side and groaned, rubbing the muscles between her ribs. Cooking dinner put stress on her mom's pain.

"Yeah," Rose said. It had to be tough . . . But Talia had made her family sound so glamorous. It made Rose wonder what Talia kept to herself.

Rose's phone lit up with a text from Charlotte:

. . . You there?

I know you weren't sick lol

I lowkey made you mad earlier

We're good, right?

Hey! Sorry!

Yeah, we're totally good. Sorry I got grumpy.

k. c u tomorrow

Rose wasn't sure if she *was* sorry for snapping at Charlotte. She was always the one who was sorry, whenever they got into a little spat here and there. One of them would get annoyed with the other, they'd stop talking for a few hours, and Rose would apologize. Why didn't Charlotte ever say she was sorry back?

But it didn't matter. Better to have things back to normal.

After Rose washed her hands and settled in, they opened up the cabinet for the nice china and set the table. And as her mom put a vase down and adjusted a couple of stems to give the bouquet the perfect shape, she spoke quietly to Rose: "Honey . . . just be careful with that girl. I know Talia's type. Please."

And then, acting as if nothing had been said, she hurried off to kiss Rose's dad as he came through the door.

10

On Halloween Charlotte and Rose passed out candy to the Elsas and Pikachus who came to Charlotte's door. Charlotte dressed up as Wednesday Addams, and Rose wore her Stitch onesie from the year before.

Down the hall past where Rose and Charlotte sat at the front door, Charlotte's parents threw a Halloween gathering for adults. Her teenage siblings were off doing who knew what, and her little sister was trick-or-treating in the neighborhood. Rose's parents were back at their place, giving out candy and delighting over the little kids in their costumes.

Charlotte made pretty much every kid who came to the door laugh or blush as she complimented their costumes, while Rose held out the cauldron-shaped candy bowl.

And it was fun! But Rose wondered what Talia and Bree were doing . . . What costumes did they wear? Were they in nonstop hysterics like they had been the day the three of them went downtown? A day she hadn't told Charlotte about?

"Did you know Piper's having a Halloween party?" Rose asked Charlotte as they sat in chairs behind the door, shivering slightly from the cold that kept flooding in and out, in and out each time a trick-or-treater left. Charlotte's knees bounced.

"*Trick or treat!*" a Moana and a cowgirl hollered at the screen door. The lucky pair took the last candy in the pot.

Charlotte and Rose shut the door and bounded up the stairs to Charlotte's room.

Were Talia and Bree having the time of their lives? Dancing? Which other kids got invited? Did Paige? Definitely Paige. Was she even in the troop anymore?

"I didn't know about Piper, but duh," Charlotte said, plopping into her faux fur lounger chair and picking at a zit on her cheek. "That's what girls like that do."

"Don't do that!" Rose smacked Charlotte's hand down.

Charlotte hardly ever got blemishes on her luminous skin, so when she did, she didn't know how to handle it.

"My mom says it can get infected that way, and you can get sick from it." Rose lay down and let her head settle on the edge of the fur.

"Your mom finds a cause of death for every situation," Charlotte teased.

Rose chuckled, popping a Milky Way in her mouth. "True."

"Girls like Piper want to be with the boys and act like they're somebody special or something," Charlotte grumbled. "It's way more fun to be with you. Now, let's go hide in Ava's room so when she gets home, she's terrified! We can go under the bed. Maybe I can start by scratching underneath it with something that makes a creepy noise! Bwahaha..."

Rose wasn't so sure about Charlotte's summation of girls like Piper. Rose had hung out with Bree and Talia, and they didn't seem like they were trying to act more special than anybody else. But instead of saying anything, she followed Charlotte to Ava's room.

Right before Ava arrived home, Rose checked her phone and saw a message from Talia:

> We'll start with the novel She Wore Red because it's been banned, like, everywhere, and they hate it so much. We need to get copies!

"Who's that?" Charlotte peeked over at the screen, which glowed even brighter in the darkened room underneath the bed frame.

"My mom," Rose lied, tucking the message away.

And they stayed there, waiting and giggling, as Rose fought off the part of her that wanted to check her phone again, the part that hoped for even more secret, hidden messages.

Rose continued to hide Talia's texts from Charlotte's hawk-eyed attention.

And there were a lot of them.

Before they could start the book club, Talia said they had to get the books for all three of the Brigade's members, and it wasn't as easy as it sounded. There were only two copies of *She Wore Red* at the public library, and both of them were out. Talia was on the wait list for whenever one came in, but who knew how long that would take. Maybe the book would never come back in. Maybe whoever had it would lose it. Maybe—Talia messaged her—the school board parents would come for the public library next.

They couldn't buy a copy online, or their parents would know, and the nearest bookstore was a twenty-minute drive away. Talia said her parents didn't care if Talia started the club, but they weren't about to spend the money on a bunch of books for her friends. And Bree couldn't tell her parents about the club, because they'd get worried that she'd get in trouble.

Just like when they'd gone downtown together, hearing about Bree's parents worrying gave Rose the feeling that maybe she wasn't as freakish as she sometimes felt.

Talia kept asking Rose for more ideas on how to get the books, but she avoided answering. In her heart of hearts, she hoped they never got them. That way, she could still become *real* friends with Talia Anderson and Bree Ryder, but she never had to risk her parents' dismay.

But a week and a half into November, Rose discovered she'd been added to a group text with Bree Ryder and Talia Anderson. Talia wrote:

> Ok guys ive been taken off the waitlist!!! She Wore Red is there waiting for us! Let's go to the library tomorrow and take it from there. Right? If we're

going to form a banned books club we have to stick together, yeah?

Rose couldn't. She had dog walking at the rescue. But something stopped her from telling them that.

Plus, she could still make it there if she went with Talia and Bree right after school and left on time.

So she wrote back, Ok! Let's do it.

At lunch, Rose watched Bree Ryder's table. Or what was becoming Bree Ryder and Talia Anderson's table.

What would happen if Rose just stood up, carried her lunch bag over, and sat right down between all of them?

She'd make Charlotte feel like she was nothing.

What if she brought Charlotte with her?

No. Charlotte liked things the way they were. That was the thing, wasn't it? She only liked things as they had always been.

And Charlotte was a good friend. A good student. A good daughter. Rose was those things, too.

But what *else* could she be?

That night, Rose tried on one of her button-ups. She undid the bottom four and tied the shirt up so that it landed right on her belly button. She unfastened the top two. The next morning, she decided, she would put on that top and a short black skirt with fleece leggings underneath her puffy, cold-weather coat. At school, in the bathroom, she'd take off the fleece and tie the shirt up, just low enough to slide by the dress code.

11

Rose told Bree and Talia that she only had a little over an hour before she had to leave the library, and she convinced her mom she had enough time to walk to the library with Bree Ryder for a school project before the rescue started. Rose's mom had known Bree's mom for years from PTA stuff, so she didn't question her choice of study mate. Perfect.

Her mom said to text her when she left and when she arrived, and that she'd pick her up to take her to the rescue.

But why? It was three blocks away! Rose tried to appreciate what she did get from her mom—a free pass to walk somewhere without her.

And that way she didn't have to go back into the bathroom before leaving school and put her fleece leggings back on, untie the knot she'd made, and tuck the shirt back into the skirt to look like she had when she'd left home that morning.

She could simply bound out into the world, her bare legs as cold as Talia's.

Rose had kept her eyes down all day long so that she

wouldn't see anyone's reaction to the new slip of skin between right below her belly button. She had hardly been able to look at Charlotte, who had murmured under her breath, "Wow. New look."

When they arrived at the library, skin chapped from the cold, Rose wondered why she hadn't gone inside much since she was little. The space was cozy after their trek through the freezing air. A small display read COVE LAKE ARTISTRY THROUGHOUT THE YEARS and presented wooden carvings of animals, paintings made by residents, and carefully knitted shawls. In the children's section, papier-mâché Elephant & Piggie characters smiled down upon tiny rocking chairs, and by the YA area, a poster read NATIVE AMERICAN HERITAGE MONTH with a map beneath it displaying where the Potawatomi, Ojibwe, and Odawa tribes used to reside hundreds of years before, and where many still did. A large table surrounded by folding chairs sat in the middle, probably for study time.

"This is so nice," Rose whispered to Talia and Bree.

"You're surprised?" Talia cocked her head to the side. "I'm here, like, every day, and I'm not even from here!"

Rose flushed from forehead to chin. It seemed absurd she was in a secret book club when she didn't even read that much.

And it hit Rose that basically . . . she was a boring kid. She knew about dogs. She could answer questions correctly for homework. And—she'd recently discovered on

Halloween—she wasn't bad at face painting. And that was it. Wow. Thrilling. Every yearbook signature she'd ever had just said "You're so sweet!" or "So nice being in your class! Have a great summer!" like she had brought nothing to the school year.

What was she doing there?

Talia led them toward the middle school section in the front of the children's area.

She tossed her jacket onto a chair, and Bree and Rose followed suit.

"Hey, Mariko!" Talia greeted a young woman sitting behind the main desk with pink tips on her bleached platinum hair. Mariko, typing away on a laptop with polka-dot reading glasses balancing on the tip of her nose, acknowledged them all with a welcoming, dimpled smile.

Talia bounded toward the last shelf, passing row after row, as she whispered to Bree and Rose about the library's ins and outs.

They arrived at the last shelf, attached to the wall and covered with packs of books held together by rubber bands. Slips of paper tucked underneath the bands contained printed names in alphabetical order.

"Okay, my books are right at the top there—ANDE6891." Talia pointed far above where she could easily reach.

Luckily, Rose could. She spotted the letters *ANDE* and stretched her long arm to the upper rows.

As she touched the book bundle with the tips of her fingers, she felt her tied-up shirt rise much higher. She pulled it down with her free hand.

"The lady running for governor said she wants to cut state funding," Talia said in a low voice beneath her. "I'm worried for Mariko. What if this library can't pay her anymore?"

"How do you know all this stuff?" Bree whispered back.

"I was wondering the same thing!" Rose jumped in, finally snagging the stack of three books and bringing them down for the other girls.

"Aha!" Bree rubbed her hands together in anticipation.

Talia took the pack of books and knelt down onto the gray-blue carpet. Bree and Rose joined her. Talia slowly pulled off the rubber band. The first books were a graphic novel called *March* by John Lewis and something titled *To Kill a Mockingbird*. As far as Rose knew, they weren't for the club, so Talia must've been reading them on her own. On the bottom was *She Wore Red*.

All three of them put their hands on the cover.

The title words popped out in scarlet above an illustration of the back of a girl's head, her hair long and a rich blackish-brown. She stared out at gray waves that led to a skyline Rose didn't recognize.

"I feel like we're doing a magic ritual." A grin crept across Bree's delighted face. "Like it's a little witchy." Whenever Bree giggled, as she was doing then, her eyebrows—thickened with black brow filler—rose up like each and every cause of laughter was a pleasant surprise.

Talia held the book to her chest. "Maybe there *is* a magic to it." Talia's features widened with a touch of wonder, and she looked from girl to girl. "Like we're a book coven."

"Well, hi!" a boy's voice said, and they all let out little screams.

"Sssssssh!" multiple unseen people chastised them.

Their laughter came out in silent wheezes.

"He saved us from the book's spell!" Bree held a hand over her mouth.

And for some reason—maybe the book's spell—Rose was having the time of her life. And all over finding a book.

Connor Roadson stood above them, a pack of books under his arm, his ever-friendly face pointed their way, the library's bright light making his strawberry-blond hair appear extra strawberry. "You all okay?"

They shot their hands up toward him, and he pulled the three to standing one by one.

"Where's Charlotte?" Connor asked Rose.

And he didn't intend it in a mean way. But Rose felt the magic slip away a little. And she checked the time. Forty-nine minutes until dog walking.

"And *what* were you doing on the floor?" Connor looked out of place in the library with his Cove Lake Ravens sports team clothes and dirty sneakers. "I'm here wandering around while my little brothers check out every Justice League comic known to man." He paused and surveyed Rose up and down with a teensy smirk. "Don't *you* look cute?"

"Right?" Talia tapped Rose's shoulder with hers and then ruffled the top of Rose's hair before leading them to another spot in the library.

Rose smoothed down the frizz Talia had created. It took all her inner power not to blush from hairline to toe. She managed to keep it to her cheeks. Her fingers shot to the undone button at the top of her shirt, and she twisted it back and forth in little half circles.

They hustled over to a table in the kids' section, which was covered with crayons and paper.

Talia immediately grabbed some and started to sketch. With orange, she outlined enormous flames, and with yellow, she added radiance around them.

As Talia drew, she told Connor about the school board's list—to which he responded, "Oh, I know. My parents might start a revolution because of it."

Bree revealed to him that they were going to start to read all the books together, as many as they could, and they needed to get copies.

"You know I'm joining you guys. Right?" Connor demanded rather than asked.

Talia hopped up and squeezed him tightly around the neck. "Happy to have you!" She sat back down, a smile behind her eyes as she doodled.

Didn't Talia and Bree worry that with more people joining, they'd increase their chances of getting caught? Could they trust people to keep it all secret, so no one got in trouble?

But if Connor reacted that swiftly and positively to the question of whether to join, maybe lots of other kids, not just Talia, thought reading these challenged books was the right thing to do.

"So do we just share the one copy?" Connor suggested. "Like, each person gets a week?"

Rose fiddled with the button so hard that it could fall off. No way could she finish all that extra reading in a week. She'd have to stay up way later, and then she'd be exhausted, and she'd do worse at school and all her activities, and the thought of it made her muscles clench up.

"No way," Bree said. "I have gymnastics, coding, and my Korean studies along with all our work, and—"

"You're learning Korean?" Rose interjected under her breath.

Bree did *so* much. And she was also saving Rose, who had a much easier schedule but still couldn't handle adding too much more.

"I get it." Connor ducked down, avoiding his little brothers, who walked by in a different section. "I had to quit half the activities I wanted to do because basketball is so intense."

Somewhere in Rose's brain, she had known that Connor was a minor sports hero in their school, but she never paid attention to sports, so it didn't mean much to her.

The group fell into a lost-in-thought quiet, with Connor squatted next to the table, tapping a foot, and Bree gazing around at all the posters on the walls as Talia drew.

And then Rose had an idea. But . . . could she say it, or would it sound stupid? She let herself speak, even while not knowing if she should:

"I used to help the choir teacher? She would give me sheet music, I'd go scan it, and then she'd email it to the students and parents," Rose offered, her nervous energy shifting from twisting the button to her gold stud earring, which led to its back popping off. She crouched down to find it.

"Wait, I know how we can do that!" Connor, from his spot hiding from his brothers, helped Rose look for the fake gold on the maroon carpet. "I saw my parents use a scanner on their Notes app. I'll do it!"

Connor explained that it would be a gargantuan task, but he could absolutely pull together the images into a file and send it to them. That way, they'd each have a copy and could take a full month to read it. In the meantime, they could put their names on all the holding lists for the other books.

"Yes!" Talia dropped the crayons and clasped her hands under her chin in little-kid delight. "Super-brilliant idea, Rose!"

Biting her lip as she smiled, Rose accepted Talia's high five.

Talia told them that would work great, except for when they got to *Ella & Elliott*, which Cove Lake Public Library didn't have. They needed to get an interlibrary loan, and that required an adult card—a kid's account wouldn't cut it. But they'd cross that bridge when they came to it, she said.

"Why do we have to start with *She Wore Red*, anyway?" Bree asked as she reached down and picked up the back to Rose's earring, which she'd apparently spotted.

Rose whispered a thanks and took a seat next to Talia.

"Because of this." Talia whipped out her phone and they crowded around its glow. "It'll just be noisy for one minute, Mariko!"

If Charlotte had been there, she would have pointed out that Talia acted like she was entitled to special treatment by feeling she could make noise in the library, and Rose wasn't sure that would be wrong.

"So the book is about a girl whose parents are from China, and they struggle to make it in America. Okay? Now listen to the complaint..."

On the lowest possible volume, they heard a voice. A broad-shouldered man, checking back at the audience with every sentence, addressed the crowd. Rose remembered him. She was pretty sure he was Piper's dad.

"It is a *parent's job* to teach their kids about prejudice, alright?" His pointer finger punched the air.

A small crowd off to the side cheered for the man speaking.

"Yes. Thank you!" he said back to them. "The author of this...'book'"—he used mock quotation marks even though it inarguably *was* a book—"moved here as an immigrant. She writes of being poor. This woman then graduated from *Harvard*! Ironic that she's putting down this country after all it gave her. I *refuse* to allow this *crap* to sit on my daughter's school shelves. She will *not* come home thinking there's something wrong with *her* or where she *lives*. No sir. And if this lady doesn't like it—she can leave."

More cheers.

"Because he's mean, and I want to make him *mad*." Talia grinned a sneaky grin. "I want to start with the ones that get hated on the most. You agree, Connor?"

"Obviously." He drummed his palms on his thighs. "Awesome!"

"But one thing," Talia told them. "Bree and Rose could get in trouble. And they're being super brave. So this *has* to be secret. Okay?"

Rose couldn't believe it. Talia was protecting them. *Her.*

"Thanks," Rose murmured.

And Talia gave her hand a quick squeeze. They were in this together.

Rose wanted to check her phone and see how much time she had left, but she didn't.

A trio of toddlers dashed by where they sat, knocking a few books off the wall, as women ran behind the little hooligans begging for quiet.

"Let's check out whatever books we can now?" Connor asked. "For scanning?"

"Yeah, let's see that list." Bree pulled out her phone.

Talia, still filling the library with the sound of a YouTube video, jumped around in the school board meeting recording to show them moments in which a parent complained about a particular book.

But Talia didn't show them footage of Jennifer Holmes.

And Jennifer was absolutely not a *mean* person, like Talia had described that guy in the *She Wore Red* rant. Or even an *angry* person. Not even in the school board meeting! She had just seemed . . . *really* upset.

Rose wanted to say something to the group about all of that. But she didn't know how. What if they thought badly of Charlotte and her mom forever?

Talia stopped the recording and led them to the books, and Rose silently followed the group through the shelves.

But as the three of them mocked the parents in the meeting, a ripple of nausea overtook Rose.

Was all of this just one big betrayal of her best friend?

"What if some of those people are just really worried about their kids?" Rose spat out in a voice just above a whisper as she stopped walking. They were standing in front of the biography section, and Rose looked away from the kids and toward books on Alexander and Eliza Hamilton. "Maybe their kid was, like, getting nightmares from one of them or something?" Rose went on. "And they, I dunno, meant well?"

Rose waited for blowback as she stood under a poster portrait of Simone Biles.

Connor stroked his chin like a beard was there, his magenta-painted nails chipping off. Talia shifted her weight from one hip to the other. Bree leaned back against the bookshelf.

Then Connor spoke. "I mean, I think if they don't want their kids to read it . . . they could just have *their* kid not read it. Not *everybody's* kid. Right?"

Rose shrunk. She'd done wrong.

"But that's still a good point," Connor went on. "They're not all, like, *evil* or something."

"Yeah! Good point, Rose." Talia wrapped an arm around Rose's neck and pulled her in.

Rose let out the breath she'd been holding and allowed herself to take in the kids around her. None of them appeared bothered in the least.

"Yeah. That's so real." Bree nodded thoughtfully as she let a finger slide across a row of book bindings.

And they moved on, searching for more titles.

They hadn't kicked her out. They had listened to her. Maybe she could belong with them after all.

Maybe she wasn't betraying anyone.

As the group roasted a cheesy old biography of Miley Cyrus, Rose joined in their laughter. It was easy, and these kids didn't mind her being there. Maybe they even liked it. She felt that warmth you get when it's snowing outside and you're wrapped up in a blanket.

But she was almost out of time with them. She hated even looking at the minutes disappearing on her phone . . .

Rose texted her mom.

> Hi! We're still working on the project, so I'll have to miss the rescue. Would you mind picking me up an hour later?

The dots appeared.

The dots disappeared.

She alternated pressing her thumbs hard against her middle and index fingers as she waited.

Talia and Bree and Connor had something to say about every book—what they thought looked good about it, what the parents probably objected to in it, and what they'd heard about it before.

Rose so wished she could jump in, but she hadn't heard of any of them.

Then the text her mom had finally crafted arrived. It read:
Okay, honey. Give me an exact time and I'll be there.

Rose's fingers released. And she let herself just listen.

But ten minutes later, the texts came in from Charlotte:

> Where are you?

> Mariah is asking where you are.

> Addie's here, too.

> Are you ok?

> Ok we're just going to start without you then.

Rose wrote as fast as she could, So sorry, not feeling good! I meant to tell you earlier! Talk to you later though!

And then Rose turned to the kids and asked a question she realized had been bubbling up inside her the whole time. "Did that guy in the video talk about *Fateful Passage*, too?"

"No, but apparently a bunch of antisemites flooded it with one-star reviews on Goodreads, so there's *that*," Talia groused.

After they grabbed a handful of titles, they checked out the books on Talia's card and sat on a bench outside, shivering. They huddled together under the rising November moon and watched school board clip after school board clip from other places—not just Cove Lake—until Connor's dad picked him up, Bree's mom got her, and Talia and Rose sat alone together.

Talia was deep into something on her phone.

"Sorry," she said after a minute. "Dillon again. He's low-key genius about literature."

"Nice." Rose rocked back and forth in the cold. Talia kept texting Dillon, and Rose wondered if she'd spend all their waiting time ignoring her. But eventually Talia put the screen away.

"So you missed walking dogs, huh?" Talia flipped her total focus to Rose.

"How'd you know about that?" Rose wondered for a second if Talia was psychic. If anyone was, it would probably be her.

"I've noticed," she said. "You and Charlotte talk about it before history starts sometimes." She cupped her hands over her mouth and exhaled into them to stay warm.

Had Talia been noticing *Rose* these past months, too?

"Sorry you missed it," Talia mumbled, maybe with a little guilt, Rose couldn't be sure. "So does your mom, like, disapprove of me?" Talia asked through her fingers.

Rose looked right at Talia. How did Talia know that? Did she think it was funny? Did it bug her?

Before she could ask, Talia's muffled voice said, "Seemed like you didn't want her to see me the other week when we walked downtown."

And Rose wanted to protect Talia's feelings and say the truth about that night, which was that Rose couldn't stand getting caught in a lie with her mom. But at the same time, Talia was right. Her mom didn't approve.

"I think she just doesn't know you," Rose said.

Talia nodded, wordless and shivering. Her bare hands fell to her lap.

"You need mittens," Rose told her.

"Well, I don't care what your mom says—I'm glad you're with us." The corners of Talia's mouth turned up, and her pupils loomed large in the shadows of the night. "Your mom's probably almost here, right? I'm gonna hop up and go. Don't want to get you in trouble. Ha."

As they said bye and Talia disappeared for a moment

behind the pine trees that decorated the library's front lawn, Rose's mom pulled up in the bike lane.

Why was Talia walking? Why wouldn't her parents pick her up on a freezing night?

As their car reached the nearest light, Rose looked back out her window toward the library, and in the darkness, she could still make out the teeny silhouette of Talia walking on her own in the direction of Cove Lake Towers.

After the other Scouts left the monthly meeting at Charlotte's house, where they had completed the first step toward earning their woodworker badge, Rose and Charlotte sat back-to-back, cross-legged, ripping and tying strips of old T-shirts to make dog toys.

The room they worked in once held the playroom where they had led Charlotte's hand-me-down Barbies on incredible quests to battle dragons and win national singing competitions. But now it was some kind of study area with a craft space in the corner.

On a table by the window rested Charlotte's dad's tool kit, which he'd used to get them started on the bench they planned to make for the schoolyard at Cove Lake Elementary. The whole thing was Charlotte's idea.

And she was full of even more. "I've been thinking," Charlotte said as she braided. "Maybe we could collect old shirts from the whole school and create a huge supply to sell at the fundraiser."

"That would be great!" Rose cheered.

Charlotte always had new plans for how to make the world a better place.

And while she could feel Charlotte's satisfied, round-cheeked smile without even seeing it, because she knew her so well, Rose wanted to tell her about the book club *so* badly. She wanted to tell her that she'd started her scanned digital copy of *She Wore Red*, and for two nights in a row the pages had flown by until her eyes couldn't stay open anymore. Charlotte liked reading more than Rose did. If Charlotte read it, she'd probably finish it in a day.

And there they sat, leaning against each other... Maybe Rose could just casually bring it up—talk about it like they talked about everything else.

Except Talia. Except Rose's secret outings with other kids. Except maybe some of the things that mattered most—things that might make Charlotte angry.

A half hour into their hangout, Jennifer knocked on the door and brought in some carrot cake cupcakes she'd made.

Even the frosting swirl on top was perfect.

"Gaah, I am so happyyy!" Charlotte croaked in a wacky voice, and she grasped for the tray.

A couple of the Holmes family's four rescue dogs clawed at the door, trying to come in.

"How's it going, Rosie Posey?" Jennifer asked. She gave Rose a little peck on the head, and then said, "Don't think you can escape the same cruel treatment," and kissed Charlotte as well.

Rose's full mouth stopped her from answering so she gave a thumbs-up.

"Glad to hear it, sweets," Jennifer said as she turned to leave. "You guys have big Thanksgiving plans?"

Rose shook her head, her cheeks still stuffed, and Jennifer chuckled.

"Enjoy your veggies!" she said as she closed the door.

After Rose swallowed, she didn't know if it was her guilt for secretly deceiving Jennifer by joining the club, or simply the truth she really felt, when she said to Charlotte, "I love your mom."

Rose wanted to add, *And I really think she'd like* She Wore Red. *She loves tough-girl stuff. And the girl in the book is so tough!*

But she didn't, of course.

"She's the greatest," Charlotte agreed. "But she should really send Ava to military school. That kid is out of control."

They spent the rest of that Sunday making flyers requesting T-shirts, organizing activities for the fundraiser in May, and scheming about how to make sure they got a room together for the March trip to Toronto.

And a part of Rose never wanted to leave and go back to her quiet, cupcake-free house.

But the other part desperately wanted to run home to her bedroom, huddle up by the lamp, and learn what happened to Grace at the end of *She Wore Red*.

o ✳ o

The Banned Books Brigade met for the first time over Thanksgiving break.

That morning, Rose took a pair of her mom's fabric scissors and grabbed an old shirt that would probably end up in the Goodwill donations pile soon. She cut it right beneath the rib cage. Over it, she threw on her dad's black zip-up hoodie. It was so long it went below her backside.

"Mom, can I borrow your jeans?" she yelled out. Maybe her mom wouldn't ask anything about this new request. Maybe she wouldn't think a thing of it. But Rose couldn't wear another pair of black slacks or tightly fitting boot-cut jeans. She'd look so out of place with the kids in the club.

Her mom opened the door to her room slowly, like she didn't want to spook Rose, and said, "Honey, why would you want my pants? They don't fit you."

She stood with her back against the doorframe, taking in Rose's hoodie.

Thank goodness her mom didn't know what was under there. Her mom didn't mind *all* crop tops—she was fine with the kinds they sold in Target in the kids' section. The ones that hardly even counted as cropped. But she did *not* approve of the styles Rose wanted to try wearing.

Rose took in her mom's glance at the folded, untouched outfit she'd set out on Rose's desk chair the night before.

"I like looser pants." Rose shrugged as she gathered lip gloss and a wallet and stuffed them in her purse. "I could always wear a belt." Rose paused. "If I *owned* a nice belt."

Her mom paused. "If you want to spend your allowance money on some extra clothes, maybe we could go shopping together?"

Why did her mom have to say they would go together? Why was her first thought always something like that, and never that Rose might *want* to be separate? To go with Charlotte? Or whoever else? Talia had told Rose they could go thrift store shopping together.

Her mom just couldn't get it.

"Okay, Mom. Sounds good."

Her mom was not going to lend her the pants. Fine. It was worth a shot.

Rose slid past her toward the stairs so they wouldn't be late.

Talia had texted Rose earlier with instructions to tell her mom it was a hangout with only Bree. So Rose had asked if she could meet Bree for a hot chocolate at Starbucks. She thought she might be out of luck, but her parents said alright. All her mom had asked was, "Not with Charlotte?"

Thank God her mom was okay with Bree.

Would her mom have said yes if she'd told her Talia would be there, too? Rose bet on no.

Be careful with that girl, her mom had said about Talia. But why?

Her mom got out of the car when they arrived and walked Rose to the door. She could tell her mom was peeping inside as Rose walked in.

Bree sat at a table, drink in hand, and waved, and Rose's mom went on her way.

As Rose went to a buy a drink with the ten her mom had given her, Talia popped up by her side.

"She didn't see me, right?" Talia asked. "I hid by the milk over there. I know she thinks I'm gonna turn you into a school dropout or something. Ha!"

Talia said it like a joke, but Rose had no way of knowing if her feelings were hurt or not. In that sense, she just couldn't read her new friend.

As they made their way to the table, Connor rolled in, face pink from the outdoors, and got in line to order.

The Starbucks sat on a small strip down a busy roadway on the border of Cove Lake and Fenwood Township. A physical therapy place, a liquor store, and an office building filled with who knew what neighbored the café. Out the window, a steady stream of cars sped by.

Once Connor arrived, Talia announced it was time to officially dive in.

Rose scanned the place. A few people typed away on laptops, and two women leaned into one another speaking in quiet tones by the window, their hands wrapped around cups.

She didn't recognize anyone. Good.

Talia began by reading a quote she'd found. She said it was from this guy called Salman Rushdie, who was "straight up *stabbed*" over his books. He said, "A book is a version of the world. If you do not like it, ignore it; or offer your own version in return." Rose didn't quite understand it, but she nodded and mmm-hmmed like Connor did.

"Deep!" Bree piped up, playing with a bracelet.

Connor, far from school grounds, wore black nail polish, a scarlet collared shirt with a bow tie, a purple skirt over leggings, sneakers, and a long pendant with some kind of symbol on it.

She wanted to tell him he looked incredible, because he did. But she kept the thought to herself, and she couldn't help but wonder what Charlotte would say. Maybe she just didn't like his style because she always hated it when people did stuff "for attention." Maybe that's what she thought he was doing it for.

Glancing down at her unzipped hoodie and the little folds of her tummy visible under the table, Rose figured Charlotte would say she was just dressing for attention, too.

And was she?

Why was *everything always* so confusing?

"So . . . we just talk about it. Right?" Connor asked.

Rose leaned in, hoping if her body directed its attention on the group then maybe her mind would stop its self-conscious drifting.

Talia nodded. She was clearly their leader.

"Okay. *Why* was this challenged again?" Connor asked, but it was a question he knew the answer to. They'd all seen the video.

Even so, Talia answered, swigging from her cup, "It's just, like . . . there's only one story they want us to know, right? And it's not this one."

"It's basically a true story, right?" Bree blew on her drink.

Talia told her she thought so, based on what the author's note said.

"I want to write a book one day," Bree announced. "About my life. I relate to this." She tapped her phone, which held the Connor-made copy.

Rose didn't know what to contribute. She had *nothing* to add. So maybe she could ask a question.

"Um, so . . . how do you relate?" Rose attempted eye contact, though she still felt like she was playacting at being one of Bree's friends.

Bree sipped her drink and waved a hand in front of her mouth. "Too hot." After recovering, she shrugged and said matter-of-factly, "The stupid stuff people say to her. The kid who makes fun of her eyelids? Because she's Chinese? Like . . . in that way." Bree bit the insides of her cheeks, then let her jaw relax and added, "Obviously."

Rose had no words. They'd left her completely.

Rose wasn't one of the only Black kids in school, like Bree. She had no idea what that would be like. Also, *who* said stuff to her? And how often?

"Yeah, dude," Talia responded to Bree. "I can see that."

Connor jumped in to say, "I like when they copy off Grace because they think, like, 'Asian kids are smart,' and then she bombs the test because she's not good at math, so they all bomb, too. Just like me." He laughed. "Do not copy off me, okay? You will fail."

"Did you know one time, when I was standing outside this Starbucks with my brother and cousin, someone inside complained?" Bree's mouth tightened. Her fingers drummed the sides of her drink.

"Wait, what do you mean?" Rose asked. Maybe she was the question asker. Maybe that was how she could join in. She really *did* want to understand. Even though she knew she should probably understand it already. Why did the world have to be like this?

Bree's leg jiggled under the table. It shook their drinks slightly.

"They said we were 'loitering.'" Her nostrils flared, but the rest of her grew still, and she didn't look at any of them. "We had *Starbucks drinks in our hands*. It's crazy. My mom was in PT right there—" She nodded her head toward next door. "She came in and told the manager what's what."

Who in her town would complain about some kids hanging out by the Starbucks? Would Jennifer? No way. Would her own parents? No . . . Right?

"Anyway," Bree said. "I liked the book. It's also, like, a page-turner." Her smile returned, as did the twinkle in her eyes that Rose had thought never left her. But now Rose wondered what Bree was stuffing back down inside.

"It is!" Talia pounded the table in passion. "Oh, I just loved the stuff with her crush, and how her family was so close to getting the business, and the ending? Like, it broke my heart and healed me at the same time!" She performed a chef's kiss and took another swig of her drink. "I think I'll get a refill." Talia hopped up.

"They do hot chocolate refills?" Connor asked. Close behind him, three old men took a seat at a table, eating something that smelled of banana and chocolate.

"Oh, no," Talia said. "It's coffee. Can I borrow a couple bucks from you guys?"

Bree pulled out a few dollars.

Talia marched back to the line, eyes on her phone, thumbs flying.

Bree, Connor, and Rose all recognized that they were thinking the same thing and fell into giggles.

"Coffee!" Connor put his hands on his heart.

The three of them watched Talia order. Rose wondered who she was texting. Some other group of friends? That boy again?

When Talia came back, she saw their faces and rolled her eyes. "It's no big deal. Try some."

They all shook their heads.

"No, thank you. I'm naturally energy-sufficient," said Connor.

"You guys . . ." Talia smirked in a way Rose knew Charlotte would hate, like they were all littler than her, and she said, "Cultures all around the world let kids drink coffee. Trust. The family that lived below us in Brooklyn was Egyptian, okay? Their kid was drinking espresso at five. Try it."

She held it out, and no one took a sip.

"Rose," Talia said. She pushed it in Rose's direction.

Rose grabbed the cup. She smelled it. It reminded her of her parents in the mornings, her dad rushing to get ready, roasting a pot, handing a cup to her mother as he ran out the door. Her mom always spread her fingers around the mug like it could heal her.

Rose picked up the black drink and swallowed.

"Agh! Ugh, no!" she sputtered, and they all broke into hysterics.

"Wait, wait." Talia sprang up with the drink and filled it with milk. She took six sugar packets and emptied them in one by one, swirling the concoction until it was light tan. "One more try . . ."

Her parents would kill her.

Her nose wrinkled. Rose put her lips to the cup once again and took a sip.

And it wasn't bad. She shouldn't have been doing it . . . But it wasn't bad.

"It's okay," Rose said. She looked at Bree's and Connor's skeptical faces. "No, it's actually okay. Like . . . sweet. Try it."

They passed the cup around, and Bree nearly barfed

while Connor gave a "Mmm, wooow," to the obvious delight of a beaming Talia.

They continued to talk about *She Wore Red* for the next forty-five minutes, until Rose's phone alarm dinged, reminding her that her mom would be outside in fifteen. She needed to wait outdoors so her mom didn't see Talia. Maybe Bree would stand out there with her to bolster her case.

Rose and Talia shared the rest of the coffee as they talked about the book's take on immigration, and Talia reminded them of the words by the Statue of Liberty—the ones she'd quoted to Rose when they'd first talked: *Give me your tired, your poor / Your huddled masses yearning to breathe free* . . . And then they all discussed their own backgrounds.

On her mom's side, Bree's grandparents had been born in Haiti, but on her dad's they couldn't trace very far back even if they wanted to, and her dad said he didn't want to know. Connor was half Irish "going back to forever," he said, and the rest of him was split into "Europe stew," he joked.

And Talia and Rose . . . well, they both had slightly different stories of when the great and great-great-grandparents they knew about had arrived in the United States from unnamed, unknown villages in Eastern Europe. And, in this case, Rose finally had something to add to the discussion. Not about her mom's side of the family, of course, but her dad's. When Rose told them about her dad's great-great-grandpa and his family and their village's fate in the Shoah, the kids got really quiet. And then when Talia told them about *her* grandma's grandparents and how her parents were so close to never being born except for a lucky break getting fake papers in Romania in World War II, Rose worried maybe the two of them were going overboard. Maybe they were making everyone uncomfortable.

"It's okay. We should be thankful, yeah?" Talia tapped the table a couple of times in emphasis.

And with that, they fell into a discussion about how life might be for people who had *just* arrived in the US, like Grace's parents in *She Wore Red*.

They strayed far from the book, but then came back to it. And somehow, even the tangents felt like they were a part of *She Wore Red*. Like how a symphony could be based on one set of chords but hold a dozen movements within it as the melody and tempo shifted and expanded.

13

Once they ended, Rose stood outside with Bree, and her thoughts drifted to how her dad might feel about the book. With his history, how could he just sit by and be okay with the story of an American immigrant getting kicked out of their school library? And not just *She Wore Red*, but *Fateful Passage* even more so? How could he shrug it off? It was so messed up. Maybe if he just *read* it—

Her angst was interrupted by Bree saying, "It's funny we haven't talked much before. Do you remember when we sat next to each other in choir in fourth and fifth grade?"

Of course Rose remembered. But she hadn't known Bree did.

"I was always trying to hear you because you got every note right in our terrible alto parts," Bree said.

"They *were* awful," Rose said with a soft chuckle, remembering. "They still are!" And a touch of daring came to her as she added, "I was just hoping you wouldn't mind being stuck with me."

"What? Why would I mind?" Bree gave Rose's shoulder a tiny, playful push.

Rose's entire being felt like it could break out into tap dancing.

"So you're still in choir?" Bree lifted the heels of her black Converse shoes up and down.

"Yeah. It's pretty boring," Rose admitted. "But, like . . . I like singing when no one can really hear you." Why was she sharing so much? Her mouth couldn't stop moving.

A car swerved into the lot, but it wasn't her mom yet.

"You into K-pop at all?" Bree's whole expression lit up.

"Um, I like . . . like, old stuff? Like singer-songwriters? Have you heard of somebody named Jewel? She's my mom's favorite, so we listen to her a lot. I don't really know any K-pop," Rose admitted.

"Oh, let's fix that." Bree stopped her calf lifts and pulled out her phone, face in screen. "You're gonna love Twice. I can tell from"—she swished a hand in front of her—"vibes. You're totally one of us."

At Rose's blank expression, Bree explained, "The Once fandom. We're truly the best—don't let anyone tell you different. I can even see the Brigade *as* Twice. You're like Sana, kind of shy and real cute, and Talia's like Momo, all spicy, and I'm obviously Nayeon, the one who went solo first—she's my bias, and Connor is probably Mina, because she's graceful and really, like, poised, and he's this incredible dancer, basketball player, soccer player . . . You should come with us to his game this week!" Bree practically shrieked. "You on Spotify?" She went back to her phone. "Oh, and send me some Jewel!"

Rose said yes, and eagerly awaited whatever Bree was sending her. Bree thought she was cute? That she would be part of a group with her? Bree was so friendly. Why hadn't Rose just talked to her before?

She pressed her lips together and still couldn't hide how hard she was smiling.

Rose couldn't *wait* until the next book club, and it was a whole month away. Would they talk to her in between those times? From the way Bree was chatting with her, like it was a normal part of everyday life, Rose thought they really might.

Because as old as everything and everyone had seemed in Cove Lake, Rose saw that Talia wasn't the only new kid. Everyone she'd never talked to was entirely new as well.

When Rose's mom arrived, Bree gave Rose a little hug. And Rose tried not to squeeze her back. It was like her limbs were electrified.

"What book are we reading next month? Did we decide officially?" Rose asked as her mom waited. "We have to decide if Connor is scanning this one, or should we take turns? Also—is that . . . *illegal*?" she whispered. "I shouldn't even be talking about this near my mom's car. I just—"

"Someone had a *lot* of coffee." Bree laughed, patting her back.

Was that what was going on? Rose felt like her torso

held a whirlpool that would eventually shoot out of her in a geyser.

"Hey, Ms. Stern!" Bree hollered, waving her arm back and forth. "Can Rose join us for Connor Roadson's basketball game next week?"

Her mom took this in for a moment without answering, and Rose wondered what she was thinking. Was her mom happy she was making other friends? Nervous?

Rose had never been to a sporting event at school before. Was that a thing people really did? One time her dad took her to see a Spartans game at his alma mater, Michigan State. The athletics part was pretty boring. But she liked how the crowds cheered and booed and grew excited in unison.

"That's so sweet! We'll see!" her mom answered as Rose hopped into the car.

"It's nice you're hanging out with Bree Ryder." Her mom steered them out of the lot. "I've always loved her mom. How'd it go?"

"Great!" Rose answered, way too enthusiastically.

She texted Talia: That was the best!!!!

And Talia wrote back: Thanks for helping me make it happen. We all love you!

Talia sent a selfie of the three of them together, blowing Rose a kiss.

Rose should've asked her mom if she could stay longer. Maybe she would've said yes!

A text from Charlotte sat there waiting for her: You still coming over tomorrow?

Yup, she wrote back.

If Rose was going to go to Connor's basketball game, she had to invite Charlotte. She *wanted* to. Right? If it weren't for Charlotte not liking Talia, or really any of the kids, she would. But before meeting Talia, she'd never gone anywhere without immediately knowing she'd invite Charlotte, and usually she wouldn't go if Charlotte couldn't. Because without Charlotte at an event, there was no one to be with.

But Rose didn't want to think about all that right then. She wanted to think about *She Wore Red* and what everyone had said about it.

"Mom?" she asked. "I know you're Irish, right? But when did your family come here?"

Her mom didn't answer. "Oh, geez. I'd have to talk to Pat."

He was her cousin—the only person in her family she spoke to.

But her mom didn't say any more.

Why did her mom only talk to her cousin? Why didn't she have a relationship with Rose's grandparents anymore even though they were still alive in the upper peninsula somewhere? Couldn't she just ask *them*?

Maybe it was the coffee, but all of a sudden Rose had a million questions—about others and about herself.

14

Charlotte couldn't be mad because *technically* Rose had invited her.

The weekend of the basketball game, Rose had texted Charlotte to tell her she was going, and Charlotte had asked, Why?

She hadn't even asked *With who?* Maybe a part of her had a good guess.

When Rose told Charlotte she was going for fun, Charlotte answered, Sorry, not my thing to sit in that smelly gym more than I already have to lol.

So why did Charlotte seem like she was stewing over something when they met in front of the school the Monday after the game? No hug, no smile, just a "hey" before turning on her heels to get going. Had someone told Charlotte who Rose was with? Was she mad because Rose didn't come over to her house that weekend, and she felt like Rose had chosen the game over her?

Whatever the reason, her frosty greeting at school didn't seem fair.

The game had been *so much fun*.

Rose's dad had dropped her off at the school, assuming Rose would meet Charlotte there because she always went places with Charlotte. Bree and Talia high-fived Rose when she arrived and led her to the seat they'd saved for her on the bleachers. Bree immediately told Rose "So I love Jewel!" and sang a line of her song "You Were Meant for Me" in a hilariously off-key belt. Addie and a couple of her friends had forced some little kids to scoot over so they could join the three of them. And every time Connor scored, they'd hoot and holler at the top of their lungs.

And he scored a lot.

"Has he always been this good?" Rose had asked Bree.

Addie jumped in to answer for her: "You didn't know? Bruh, he's the best one." She leaned into Rose to add, "How else did you think he survived in this school?"

Talia had heard this comment as well, and she and Rose locked eyes.

"Connor wouldn't have to worry about getting bullied in New York," Talia had told Rose at halftime as they moseyed toward the fold-out tables that held free lemonade.

"Really?" Rose couldn't quite believe that. But from what Talia had told her about the place, it did sound a bit like a unicorn in the stable of American towns. She'd told Rose that New York had a place called Jackson Heights, where there were more than 160 languages spoken! She said that almost everywhere in the city there were spots called bodegas, where you could go pick up anything you needed, even in the middle of the night. A lot of them had cats called "bodega cats" that everyone in the neighborhood got to know. Talia claimed that sometimes you'd be walking down the street and you'd just randomly come upon a parade or a street festival or even a rally.

But with regard to the bullying, Talia amended her original remarks as she took her first sip of the watery powdery drink, saying, "Well . . . I guess it would depend where he *was* in New York. That stuff happens everywhere, I think."

The second half of the game had been long, but it was worth it when the Cove Lake Ravens won, and the entire crowd burst into hoots and hollers, and Connor came up to them afterward to give them all big, sweaty embraces.

Maybe Charlotte had seen a pic of Rose at the game on someone's feed. There was no doubt that if one existed, she looked happy in it.

And so that day, when Charlotte and Rose took their daily walk together from lockers to history, the lost weekend hovered between them.

When Rose sat down for class, she saw the day was bound to go from just plain awkward to most definitely terrible.

They'd reached the point in their World War II unit

in which they'd have to learn about what Rose had been absorbing since second grade. Mrs. Paterson had warned them that what they read would be "disturbing." She said it "required sensitivity" on the part of all of them.

Rose could not look at the pictures. She'd seen so many before. For years and years. She didn't need to see them again. Rose couldn't quite believe that these images were new to some kids in her class. They'd all had to read Anne Frank's diary in fifth grade, but that was it.

She splayed her fingers over the photos of the people in the camps and counted the little lines on her knuckles. How many were there? Seven. Why did people think that was a lucky number? Maybe the answer was hidden in a book she wasn't allowed to read...

Was it just her imagination, or were some of the kids glancing over at her? They didn't know Talia was Jewish, probably, or they'd gawk at her, too, to see her reaction.

Maybe Talia purposefully didn't let anyone know.

That's what Rose's dad had done for a while, but of course, everyone figured it out eventually. He didn't like discussing the bullies he'd faced at school. All she knew was they'd called him "Christ Killer" and then claimed every time that it was a joke. *They weren't joking*, he would say before he retreated back into himself, which he did whenever the topic of bullies came up.

Mrs. Paterson didn't go on and on. Instead, she said she

was going to show them a clip from a documentary. More pictures. More "evidence," she said. Rose turned back to check in with Talia, who gave Rose a look of *Here we go . . .*

Mrs. Paterson headed to her laptop and began to set up the film. "As you're watching," she added, "if you need to take a break, I'll allow you a moment outside in the hall."

"I'm triggered! I can't take it!" whispered a kid in the back. Another snickered alongside him.

"Hey—shut up!" Talia said.

They did.

Jerkwads.

"Excuse me!" Mrs. Paterson scolded Talia.

She fiddled with a frozen screen. "You'll find one aspect of the tragedy is that no one knew the extent of what was going on here," she continued as she tried exiting and reopening the film to get it to work. "The Nazis systematically hid their actions, and the Allies only learned too late what had been happening to the Jewish population. Veterans often told of their shock at the state of the prisoners. So remember as you're watching, this footage came much later. They didn't have the kind of twenty-four seven news we do now."

She continued to tinker with the tech.

What on earth was Mrs. Paterson talking about? No one knew what was going on? Sure, the soldiers were stunned and traumatized by what they saw, but there was plenty of information being printed about it for years. Mrs. Paterson was plain *wrong*. Rose understood this from years of religious school! And then there was the government, and what *they'd* known . . .

Raizel from *Fateful Passage* rushed to Rose's mind; Raizel, age thirteen, turned away, sent back, finding that at the end of a war she never asked for, almost everyone she'd ever known was gone.

Rose should say something.

But how? She didn't have facts and figures and old newspaper headlines sitting in front of her. Worse than that, she couldn't stand the idea of Mrs. Paterson giving her the look Rose imagined she would: that look that said *I see you now for what you are—a bad kid.*

"Hey, Mrs. P?" Rose heard a familiar voice from the back.

It was Talia. She was doing it.

Mrs. Paterson didn't answer. She worked to stop the glitching in the film, her long pink nails clicking again and again. Addie came up front to help her.

"Mrs. Paterson?" Talia said again.

Out of her peripheral vision, Rose saw Charlotte's fingers curl under her palms.

"Um, hey, I just want to make sure everybody knows that, like, America did *not* do all it could to help the Jewish population," Talia stated, plainly and simply. "And people definitely *did* know about it. The president, for *sure*. But also, like . . . anyone who read a newspaper."

Mrs. Paterson took a step forward. She let Addie address the technological issues behind her.

"My dear." Mrs. Paterson sounded tired. "The United States let in more refugees than any other country in the world. And that's that."

That was true, too. People ran there. They let many of them in. Eventually. Rose knew this land was the land that allowed the lucky ones of her dad's ancestors to stay safe.

But Rose also knew about girls like Raizel. They didn't let *her* in. Why didn't those 937 people on that boat count? It didn't make sense!

"They could've done more, though," Talia muttered. "They *knew*." She paused, and some chatter rumbled around her. "I'm just sayin'."

"This is an extraordinarily complex topic." Mrs. Paterson let out the long exhale she'd been holding in. She spoke firmly, each word a warning. "It is very easy to judge the actions of the men of the past. Thank you for bringing up such a helpful question to ponder, Talia: What will students in the future think of *us*?" Eyeing the clock, she added, "And with that, we have to start now." She slicked her hair back with a palm as she returned to the laptop and smiled politely to Addie, who gave her a thumbs-up and said it was working now.

"But if it's complex, let's talk about it!" Talia called out.

"Oh, for crying out loud, will you *stop talking*?" Charlotte whipped around and scowled at Talia.

Oh no. Rose slowly reached out to tap Charlotte's arm and get her to take it easy, but she paid Rose no mind.

"Everyone—let's settle down. The issue up here is fixed, and we're going to begin..." Mrs. Paterson started the film, but even that did no good.

"You just can't stop yourself, can you?" Charlotte went on, her whole body swiveled around, her face twisted up in what looked an awful lot like hatred. Or maybe disgust. Her head bobbed back and forth, shaking in anger. She didn't look Rose's way even for a second—she just beamed a death glare toward Talia.

Talia leaned back in her chair and blew her off with a "Psssh, yeah, okay."

"You think you know everything, but you *don't!*" Charlotte held on to the sides of her desk like she might jump out of it, and Rose remembered the Charlotte who could smack someone upside the head. She pulled on Charlotte's sleeve.

"Yeah!" Paige jumped in, too, backing Charlotte. "Just stop it, for once."

"Catfight!" a boy hollered.

"Yeah, but I *do* know what I'm talking about!" Talia yelled back. She slammed a fist on her desk.

Rose needed to say something. She had to. But she didn't know what the fight was about anymore. So she'd say the one thing she knew was true:

"Talia's right!" Rose spoke up, loud enough to be heard by the room. "She knows what she's talking about, okay?"

A couple of "ooohs" flurried through the desks, and Charlotte went quiet.

Rose tried to slow down her breaths. She wondered if people could see her rapid breathing.

Would Mrs. Paterson hate her? Would *Charlotte*?

"Enough!" Mrs. Paterson clapped her hands twice. Thankfully, she didn't seem focused on any one person. "*Not today!*" she warned them all. "Of *all* days!" She pursed her lips and scanned the room, staring down any dissent. "*Respect* this film. *Enough*," she repeated.

Mrs. Paterson pressed PLAY again and sat in her chair with her arms crossed, her attention glued on the students.

Then Charlotte turned to Rose. She shook her head and slumped back in her seat. She played with the wisps of fake teal fur surrounding her pencil's eraser and refused to look at Rose for the duration of the class.

When a few kids giggled at the nude bodies in some of the images of the camps, Rose attempted to turn to stone.

She dreamt of escape.

After class, Charlotte and Rose walked silently through the halls together.

What was there to say?

15

They pretended it hadn't happened. Any of it. The basketball game. The fight in class.

A few days into December, and they'd managed to never speak of any of it.

And Rose wondered . . . If they were both so good at acting like everything was normal, were there other times in their friendship that had been fake as well?

Meanwhile, that month, Rose had finished reading *Riley Johnson*. She didn't know how she would tell the other members that she didn't really like it . . . It was slow and, honestly, a little boring. Did that mean she thought it shouldn't be available to kids? That she was on the side of people Talia called ignorant? Rose didn't think so. But she wasn't sure if Talia would agree.

Itching for more reading that she could fall into and enjoy, Rose looked up other books by the author of *Fateful Passage*. Tirzah Wolf had also written about French resistance fighters, four women in a refugee camp, and the imagined life of Yocheved, Moses's mother. They were all books for adults.

But Rose had asked Talia to pick some up for her on one of the many afternoons she spent at the library, and now Rose was halfway through another Wolf novel.

As she sat at lunch with Charlotte that day, she fought the urge to pull it out of her backpack and dive back into chapter twenty.

"Ho ho ho! It'll be Christmas before you know it! You guys ready?" Bree announced to the entire cafeteria as she sauntered into lunch that day, greeting dozens of people. "I'm bringing the cheer!"

Before going to her usual spot, she made her way over to Rose and Charlotte's corner.

"How's it going, Charlotte?" Bree angled her head to the side like she was trying to get a read on her.

"Good!" Charlotte gave a closed-mouth smile as she drank her ginger ale.

"You gonna do youth group in the spring, too?" Bree asked.

"Yeah, of course," Charlotte answered in a syrupy voice.

Rose kept quiet. Why did she feel like she had to pretend to not be friends with other people? It was some unspoken rule, and Rose couldn't figure out who'd created it or when.

After an uncomfortable pause, Bree broke out a wide smile and said to Rose, "Did you see my last video?"

Rose blushed and nodded. Of course she had. She'd been sneaking past her parents' phone restrictions and watching them all. Bree had recently performed the dance to Twice's "Fancy" and racked up six thousand views.

"So good," Rose assured her.

"Thanks!" Bree performed a little spin and faked throwing her hair back behind a shoulder, even though her tight curls were too short for that. "Love that necklace, Rose." She pointed at Rose's little dove, which was visible above the shirt she'd picked for herself, ignoring the ones her mom had laid out. "You guys wanna come sit with us?" Bree asked as she walked a step backward, like she had people to see and places to be.

"We're okay, thanks!" Charlotte sang before Rose could answer.

"You can always join if you change your mind!" Bree shot Rose a look that was somewhere between disappointment and pity. And she was off.

Art club had decorated the cafeteria walls with paper snowmen in bright yellow scarves and blue hats. White paper snowflakes hung from the ceiling's rectangular, room-length lights and floated a few feet above their heads. In the corner closest to the door stood a big plastic Christmas tree.

It was a little annoying. Not everybody celebrated Christmas, after all.

Rose and Charlotte unwrapped their lunch bags.

"Want to give it a try?" Rose asked her while peeling an orange, nodding toward where Bree sat. "It might be nice. Something new, you know?"

"Bree thinks she's the queen of youth group at church just because she's a queen here," Charlotte grumbled.

That was a no.

Rose wished she could tell her about the Banned Books Brigade.

Charlotte might *love* it if she gave it a chance. If she gave those kids a chance.

Charlotte loved to read, right? She'd read every Ranger's Apprentice book, like, three times. She loved the Warriors series. And ever since her dad had read her all of *The Hobbit* when she was a kid, she would talk about *The Lord of the Rings* to Rose like it was a language Rose should know. Maybe if they read a fantasy book for the Brigade, then that would be a good "in" for Charlotte.

Charlotte didn't have to agree with her mom, right?

Should Rose tell her?

But then Charlotte announced with a harsh bluntness that took Rose aback, "I think we should just officially kick Paige out of the troop."

Rose scanned the room for Paige. She was now sitting next to Piper. Wow, she'd really made her way into that group. Rose remembered them as kids, running around in Paige's enormous backyard after meetings led by Jennifer. They'd bounce so high on Charlotte's trampoline they practically flew, and then they'd tumble, curling up like roly-polies. They could've jumped for hours.

Those days were gone.

"It's her choice, no?" Rose asked.

"Meh," Charlotte said, her face blank.

Next to Charlotte sat her sequined backpack, filled with flyers about the T-shirt drive for the dog toys.

After five minutes of eating in silence, Rose said, "Hey, why don't I pass around some flyers?"

"You? You're, like, Mrs. Social Butterfly now? Okay..." Charlotte handed her a stack.

Charlotte was clearly furious at her. And if it was for making other friends, that was not okay. And if it was for agreeing with Talia in class, that wasn't alright, either.

Rose decided she would be furious right back.

So she hopped up and went table to table, saving Bree's for last.

All the way at the other end of the cafeteria sat Bree, her friends, Addie, Connor, a few theater kids, and Talia. It looked like a quarter of the school had gathered at those two enormous tables by the lunch line.

"We're doing this drive..." Rose pitched it to them.

And before she knew it, they were all making a space for her to sit and tell them about it and show them pictures of the dogs at the rescue. George got the biggest "awws" of them all, and Rose told them how hopefully she'd get to adopt him at the end of the school year because no one else wanted him. Then, as one of Bree's friends started telling this wild story about how his old babysitter now worked as a dog walker for Beyoncé's financial advisor, Rose found herself staying in the seat.

Talia didn't really join in much. She was on her phone. When Rose leaned in to say hi and ask what she was up to, Talia made space for her to sit and showed her some memes Dillon had sent her. They were funny, but Rose still didn't understand why it didn't bother Talia that she'd never met him in real life.

When the bell was about to ring, Rose hopped up to grab her stuff and found Charlotte had already left.

But Bree stopped Rose before she could go searching for her. "Why doesn't Charlotte like me?"

"Huh?" Rose said. She couldn't hurt Bree's feelings with the truth. "I'm sure she does. She's just kind of funny sometimes."

Bree's face fell, and that—Rose had come to find—was rare.

"I just hate when people don't like me." Bree spoke to Rose's feet and fidgeted with the clasp on her beaded bracelet.

"Everyone likes you," Rose assured her before they parted ways for class.

In choir that afternoon, as Rose sang her alto harmony, she thought of Bree sitting next to her back in elementary school, and how intimidated she had been by her popularity even then. She never would've guessed Bree Ryder worried about people not liking her. As Rose sang four measures of middle C, it hit her that maybe Bree worked so hard at being nice and appearing so sweet *because* of that worry.

And it left her feeling even more frustrated that Charlotte wouldn't give Bree a chance.

After that day, Rose started asking Charlotte if she wanted to sit with the other kids, but after she said no a couple of times, Rose explained, "They've invited me, so I'm just going to go for a bit."

Not long after, Charlotte moved her spot to be next to a girl who was also in her youth group at church.

Rose stopped checking in with her and just went toward the table with the Brigade.

Even though they were working separately to get donations at school, and not together like they'd always planned, they were still able to collect a ton of old T-shirts. Charlotte, Rose, Paige, and Addie began stuffing their lockers with them and carrying them home in tote bags. Their plan was to craft all of them into dog toys and add them as money makers for the eventual fundraiser. About six of the T-shirts belonged to Rose. She figured if she gave away a bunch of her clothes, her mom might let her get new stuff ... Stuff that felt a bit more like the new her.

Whenever Rose did have a moment to chat with Charlotte and brought up their typical weekend hangout, Charlotte always seemed to have something. First it was a youth group activity. Then Noah had a basketball game.

One day Charlotte told Rose she had to switch her time

at the rescues from Wednesdays to Tuesdays so she could start sewing lessons. "Addie can go with you on Wednesdays instead. I've been on the wait list forever, so I have to take the spot," she'd explained.

As December rolled on, it was like she was hardly seeing Charlotte at all.

16

The synagogue hosted their Hanukkah party after sundown on the fourth night. After the Havdalah ceremony where the braided candle dripped wax and sizzled as it hit the wine, and the lighting of the candles on the menorah with dozens of families surrounding it, a warmth and light filled Rose up. The bright lights in the darkness made the cold, outside world disappear. They felt like protection.

Talia had said she'd be coming with her grandma. But Rose didn't see her.

Cara and Ariella hung out by the grape juice, discussing what gifts they'd gotten so far. Rose's parents had given her a book on dog training. "Keep it up, and your dog will be here before you know it, angel!" her mom had cheered, kissing Rose on both cheeks. They'd also gifted Rose the dress she was wearing that night, which sat on her body like a long-sleeved purple potato sack.

She tugged on the tight neckline.

"Hanukkah, Oh Hanukkah" blasted through the temple's speakers as the hordes of families danced and played with

Hula-Hoops and ate sufganiyot and meandered from table to table. Grandpa Jacob and Grandma Adele sat together, watching the kids play. Rose's uncles attended with their wives and her cousins. They came to events with her family sometimes, even though both families lived forty-five minutes away.

Rose needed to ditch the B'nai Tikvah kids and her cousins to find Talia. She must have been there somewhere.

But Rose's cousin grabbed her, and they danced to yet another version of "Hanukkah, Oh Hanukkah," this time sung by the cast of *Glee*.

No Talia yet.

After a few more dances, Rose collapsed at the table where her aunts sat chatting with one another.

Rose eyed her dad, who was debating with his brothers about something.

"Has he always been this, like, uptight?" Rose mumbled to Aunt Laura, thinking of his lecture to her about Roosevelt.

Aunt Laura had colorful tattoos up and down her arms—a big taboo at their synagogue—and she'd traveled all over the world. Because she'd been with her dad's oldest brother since forever, she knew every story.

"As long as I've known him, yup," Aunt Laura said, digging into her latke. "But, hey, he's not so bad. He did okay if you consider who raised him . . . Sorry. In-laws humor. Ha!" Her laugh reminded Rose of Talia's.

Where *was* she?

Aunt Laura took another bite and shot Rose a tiny smirk.

"So you got in trouble for some kind of book-banning thing, right? Geez, this stuff is everywhere, huh? Even Cove Lake . . ." She tut-tutted the town and took a sip of her wine.

"That was a while ago!" Rose defended herself. Did all of Rose's family know about her getting caught with *Fateful Passage*? Rose didn't like her family seeing her as a kid who got in trouble.

Rose slumped into her chair with her legs rested straight. She could trip someone. She should pull them in.

"Oh, it's okay, Rosie. Like mother, like daughter, right?" her aunt said, raising her glass. "Cheers. We love a rebel."

"What?" Rose asked, wishing her aunt hadn't had so much wine, so she could talk to her straight.

Her dad did always say, "When your aunt Laura drinks too much, she can be . . . a lot."

Then, finally, she spotted Talia over in the corner by the exit. Her hair covered her cheeks. She was all alone.

"Oh, come on, no one's ever told you? Your mom was a renegade." Aunt Laura leaned back, one arm crossed comfortably across her chest and the other holding the drink.

"Oh, yeah, sure. Uh-huh," Rose murmured.

The screen Talia was holding slightly lit up her face. She was texting something furiously.

"Before your dad? She was wild. Out there with a hundred boyfriends, partying like a . . . I dunno. She was nuts. I loved it." She let out a pensive sigh. "She *deserved* that fun, too," her aunt said into the glass's rim, barely audible.

"That's somebody else." Rose pulled herself up to sit straight. "Not Fiona Stern."

"I guess it was Fiona *Joyce* then!" Her aunt hollered her mom's maiden name too loudly as Rose shot up and made a zipline toward the exit.

Rose checked to make sure her mom was busy. She clocked her by the sour cream and applesauce, stuck chatting with a lady who was known for telling long stories about her grandkids. Perfect.

Rose made her way to Talia.

A huge crowd of people gathering around a limbo stick blocked Rose and Talia from the view of her family.

"Hey!" Rose greeted her.

Talia had been crying. Her eye makeup looked like it had been wiped with a sleeve, leaving tiny streaks on her upper cheeks. When Rose approached her, she tucked her phone into her bag and said, "Come here."

Talia pulled her into the hallway and downstairs to the Gan Katan room. Toy blocks covered in Hebrew letters, huge cardboard cutouts of Stars of David and menorahs surrounded them.

"I saw you with your family." Talia sniffled. She circled around the room, through toys and art projects.

"They're so weird," Rose said automatically, like that was what you were supposed to say about your family.

"No." Talia stopped walking and fixed her eyes on Rose,

like she tended to do, and as always seemed to happen when Talia did that, Rose felt immobilized. Talia looked at Rose like she desperately wanted something from her, but Rose never knew what.

"No, you're *lucky*." Talia drew in a big breath. "You're lucky," she repeated with a sigh, dragging her feet toward a toddler-sized chair.

"What's wrong?" Rose took the chair beside her. She worried that her armpits smelled. She'd been dancing a lot, and the sweat stains on her dress probably stood out to everybody.

"Dillon has a girlfriend." Talia's cherry-painted lips quivered, and she sucked in a cry.

"Oh," Rose said stupidly. What was she supposed to say? Why would Talia be this sad about a boy she didn't really know?

"I just . . . I liked talking to him. He's so *smart*, and he really cares about things, and . . ." She shook her head. "But he doesn't care about me, I guess."

"Maybe you guys can be friends?" Rose offered. She heard some voices outside the door. Maybe other people were hiding out, too.

Talia clutched one of her necklaces. She closed her eyes. A couple of tears left trails in her blush. "Yeah. Maybe."

Talia told Rose that she thought she'd meet him in New York sometime, if her parents ever went to visit again. But tickets were, like, millions of dollars.

She pulled out her phone. "Let me show you this girl. That's them."

Rose took in a picture of a boy kissing a girl's cheek as she beamed. *That* was Dillon?

"He looks really old," Rose said. She tried not to sound as freaked out as she felt. He could've been twenty. What was he doing talking to Talia?

"He's only sixteen." Talia took the phone back and stuffed it in her purse again.

"Sixteen?" Rose's mouth fell open. Even *that* was *so old*! Why would she have ever thought there could be anything between them? Her and this mystery sixteen-year-old?

"Ha. You're so adorable, Rose." Talia pulled her chair closer to Rose and cuddled up under Rose's sweaty arm.

Rose tried to respond appropriately. This was a friend going through a breakup, right? Not that Talia and Dillon were actually dating . . . Rose couldn't put a word to what their connection actually was, but *breakup* was the closest she could find as she rummaged through her mind for definitions. In every movie she'd ever seen, when a friend's heart was broken, the girls cuddled up on the couch and watched movies while eating ice cream.

But Talia had called Rose "adorable." Rose acted young. She was ignorant. In the face of Talia's heartache, Rose felt eight years old. So her memories of movie stars eating ice cream together were probably childish, too.

She tried to act mature. Knowing. To sound her age.

She pulled Talia in for a hug and rubbed her back. "I'm sorry," Rose said. "It must feel really awful."

Through whimpers, Talia nodded.

So maybe Rose had done alright. And she truly did feel bad for her friend. How could Talia compete with some high school girl a million miles away?

"She's not even that cute," Rose added, sensing that kind of comment was the right move.

And Talia hugged her tighter, so it must have been.

They stayed there for a minute. Or maybe more. Rose felt more dampness on her dress as Talia's tears drenched her.

"Your mom will probably wonder where you are, right?" Talia said after a while, leaving Rose's arms and wiping under her eyes. She whipped out a mirror and some concealer and went to work disguising the blotches on her face.

Rose sighed and mumbled, "She always does."

Rose's and Talia's eyes met in the compact's reflection.

"That sounds hard." Talia tapped on the makeup under her eyes with the tip of her ring finger.

And Rose felt like it was her turn to cry, but she wouldn't. She didn't have it bad. Her parents were fine, and no one was breaking *her* heart.

"I mean . . . they got mad when you read *Fateful Passage*, right? Are they, like, supporting the parents who want the books removed?" Talia asked casually, but Rose got the sense it was something Talia had been curious about. Because if they didn't support the book ban, why *would* they care so much?

Rose knew. But it still didn't seem right to her.

Into the dark of the classroom, Rose spoke. "They don't, even! They just . . . I don't want to talk badly about them, or make my dad seem like he's a jerk or something, but . . ."

Rose thought of how Charlotte always shut down any conversations complaining about parents. She'd say that Rose's mom and dad were so sweet, like there wasn't room for anyone's parents to be any other thing. Maybe because Charlotte's mom was so fun and perfect, and her family was so happy, she couldn't get it.

"Remember how people were giggling during the movie on the concentration camps? My dad had it *so* much worse than that in school. He won't really talk about it, but he told me he learned to stay quiet, be one of the best students in school, and then if no one noticed him, they wouldn't call him 'Jewboy' and stuff like that. And so he'd shut up when kids joked about Jews being cheap or, like, running the world or whatever." Rose let herself laugh. The thought of her dad running the world was hysterical. If he was secretly in charge, the planet would be a lot more organized and quieter. Everyone's rooms would be clean.

"That's just the stuff he's told me. I think he wants me to . . ." Rose paused. What was it? "He doesn't want anyone to have an excuse to hurt me. Maybe? I'm sorry. It's stupid."

"Don't say sorry, dude." Talia shut her makeup case and put a hand on Rose's knee. "That's real stuff." Her face oozed sympathy.

And Rose felt a weight lift that she hadn't known she'd been carrying, even if it was merely for a moment on a random Hanukkah night.

And she started to tell Talia about how her mom didn't seem to get her, and she didn't even get *herself* because she had always done whatever Charlotte did, and how sometimes she wondered who she was supposed to be and how to make her parents happy at the same time. It was all so stressful.

Talia listened. And she hugged Rose like Rose had hugged her moments before.

Like real friends.

And then they held hands and headed back upstairs.

Back in the dining hall, they made their way over to the Hula-Hoop contest as the Kiboomers' "Happy, Joyous Hanukkah" blasted through speakers and congregants stood in line for the dessert buffet.

Rose checked back in on her aunts, who looked like they'd caught up with Aunt Laura in the drinking department, and her uncles, who were now cracking up with her dad, their hands on his shoulders. She couldn't find her mom.

So when Talia took her hand and threw her a Hula-Hoop, Rose let go of any worry that she had to "be careful." Why would she have to be careful with a person who thought well enough of her to share secrets and tears?

17

The day before winter break, they held their next meeting after school at Starbucks once again.

After Talia ordered her coffee, it was Rose's turn. She looked at the cashier, with his nose piercing and bright eyes, and hoped he wouldn't judge her for her order.

She was already going against her mom by hanging out with Talia, so why not do this, too?

"I'll have the same," Rose said, and Talia flitted over to the milk and sugar bar to teach Rose how to create the sweetest coffee concoction.

"You're the best," Talia cooed at her as they made their way to the table.

Once they'd all taken their seats, Connor deadpanned, "So . . . I thought it sucked."

The energy it took them not to squeal with laughter was so strong it could've powered a city. Bree put her forehead onto the table and her back shook.

"Don't, don't," Rose told them, as their giggles heightened. "People will look."

Thank God they all agreed with her about the book. Her laughter had the same relaxing effect as a deep sigh.

"It's so bad," Talia said. "So let me get this straight. This girl Riley is mad that the lawnmower ran over some littered water bottles on her school's field and shredded them. She somehow sees a turtle die at an ocean nearby because of one of *her school lunch's specific bottles*? Like—how would she even know?"

"I know, right?" Bree fell into hysterics again and hid her head in Connor's shoulder.

"And then—" Connor jumped in. "She decides to *fix climate change*? By . . . doing a *show*?"

Talia shrieked and said, "Stop it, stop it."

Ultimately, Talia declared that although the quality of the book was terrible, it made no sense for it not to be on their school library's shelves.

Rose suggested that if they were banning books for quality, it might be a much longer list.

Everyone chuckled.

Also, Rose wanted to tell Charlotte, or maybe Jennifer, *Hey, look—not every book affects kids as intensely as* She Wore Red *or as other books you're worried about! Kids have loads of different opinions about* everything!

Before they left, Connor reminded them there was a problem. *If* they wanted to read *Ella & Elliott* next, as planned, they needed an adult library card to request an interlibrary loan. And Connor didn't want to ask his parents.

"I know I said they'd be, like, the chairpeople of the Brigade," he said. "But . . . I don't think they'd want to risk me being seen with that book, even if that's, like, irrational? You know . . ." Connor rolled his eyes and groaned. "It's about a girl who dresses like a boy. So . . . not gonna lie, I really just don't even want to have that conversation with them, where I have to get a talking-to about protecting myself, not getting too much notice or attention around here, blah blah blah . . ."

Connor sounded like he was brushing it all off, but Rose noted that as he spoke, he picked up a napkin and ripped it into teeny pieces, one after the other, until they covered his section of the table like brown confetti.

"Maybe we could read a different book?" Rose offered, wishing she could calm whatever tension pulsed through Connor.

Talia seemed ready for something like this. She explained that no, they had to read this book, it was one of the most hated of the pack. And luckily, just that week, through talking to Mariko, she'd discovered there was an app for the library where you could request books to read on your phone.

But that wouldn't work, Rose jumped in. Her parents had access to her card. They could see what she checked out if they really wanted to. And then if they compared those books to the challenged books list, they'd be furious she went behind their back with the Brigade. And trust her, she wanted to add, they'd check.

"Can't your parents do it?" Bree asked Talia.

Talia's answer took a minute. She massaged her temples. Her chin jutted out.

"I'll figure it out," she said.

And as they cleared up their table and Rose prepared to wait outside and get picked up, she saw her worst nightmare coming true: Her mom walked in.

Rose had *asked* to be picked up outside. Why was her mom doing this?

Connor, who had the only physical copy of *Riley Johnson*, flipped the cover down.

So obvious. So clear he was hiding something.

And Bree covered her phone, even though her screen was off, as she smiled up at Rose's mom, like that would make a difference.

But her mom only glanced at what Connor was reading. She seemed much more interested in the kids themselves.

"Oh, hi, Talia." Her mom nodded politely. "I didn't realize you'd be here?"

"Hi, Ms. Stern," Connor said, a friendly grin blooming across his face. Whenever he smiled, his complexion flushed a little ruddier. He lifted himself from the chair and shook her hand.

"Oh, hey, Connor." Her mom laughed a surprised laugh, maybe at his formality. She'd known Connor since he was about three, probably. Connor and Rose had both gone to Jill's House for daycare.

"So did you all have fun?" her mom said.

They talked the smallest small talk with Rose's mom until Rose couldn't take it anymore and said, "Well, we'd better go!" practically tearing her mom from the scene of the crime.

In the car, Rose tried to gloss over the fact that she'd lied by omission about who she was meeting there by going into all the details of how she planned to get a head start on spring semester reading over the break. She talked about how she was looking forward to getting into the 1950s and then the Civil Rights Movement in history class now that World War II was over. She spoke into her fingernails, nibbling on them, to hide the scent of sugary coffee on her breath.

But her mom eventually interrupted her. "So have you been spending a lot of time with that new girl? Talia?" she asked.

"A little," Rose equivocated. She leaned her head against the window. It was ice-cold compared to the heat from the interior of the car.

"Huh. I saw you guys hanging out at the Hanukkah party." Her mom waited, like it was Rose's turn to talk. But she wasn't going to take the bait.

Her mom went on: "You know Cara's dad? Cara Morales?"

Of course Rose did. Why was her mom even asking?

"He told Dad that Talia was kicked out of her school back in New York. And that's why her family moved back to Evie's house." She paused again, putting her turn signal on and muttering as some car passed her when they shouldn't have. Outside it started to drizzle. Rose hoped it would turn colder and colder and they would get sheets of snow.

"Talia's mom grew up here, I heard," her mom kept going. She put some hair behind her ear and glanced to Rose and then back at the road. "Her mom's pretty young, though. Very young, actually. Dad didn't know her."

Where was this going? For some reason, her mom didn't like Talia. Was it the low-cut shirts? The extra-short crop tops? The blue hair? Talia was *smart*. And *passionate*. She wished she could explain that even though in the beginning of the semester she'd just really liked that the new girl wanted her around, Rose was now Talia's friend for the sake of being her *friend*. Why didn't her mom want her making more friends?

Apparently, she and Charlotte wanted Rose to stay one way forever.

Rose couldn't help herself. She knew it would hit her mom like a gut punch, but she still spat out, "Geez. That's some serious lashon hara, Mom!" *Lashon hara* was gossip. The rabbi had just talked about it in a sermon a few weeks earlier. Her mom hated breaking the moral rules of Jewish law. If it had been her dad in the car, he'd have laughed and said, *Oh, so you're a rabbi now?* But her mom ... Maybe she cared so much because she converted, and was insecure— who knew? But she'd slammed her mom where it hurt.

They drove past a lone Dairy Queen and a couple of churches and into Cove Lake proper in silence.

"You're right," her mom said eventually. "You're very right."

Rose turned on the radio. A SZA song played. On the mist of the passenger window, Rose drew a moon and a star.

As they reached their neighborhood, her mom piped up again. "I just worry, that's all. You know me." And she smiled this sad smile that Rose wished she hadn't seen.

She shouldn't have said that about her mom gossiping. Wasn't Rose the gossip queen whenever she hung out with Charlotte? Or rather, when she *used* to hang out with Charlotte.

Thinking of Charlotte in the past tense was so strange . . . Were they really not going to see one another anymore?

"How's Charlotte been doing lately?"

How did moms mind-read like this?

The drizzle morphed to a hard, cold rain, and the windshield wipers turned on. "She's not there on Wednesdays anymore, I noticed."

"She's super busy these days." With a sleeve, Rose wiped away what she'd drawn and looked out at the Christmas decorations that adorned the town . . . A blow-up Santa. A house with a projector that showed reindeer prancing across a top floor.

Rose's mom didn't give *her* much information, so why didn't it go both ways? For example, now that she was thinking about it, why did no one ever fully explain why she didn't even know her own grandparents? All she heard was "They fought a lot." They didn't tell her anything!

Why did *all* these adults get to do that to her?

When they arrived home, Rose ran upstairs and googled "how to access banned books" and "how to hide elibrary requests" before deleting her search history.

She turned on "Feel Special" by Twice and followed what her body wanted to do as it moved to the melody all around the room. She swayed by the desk, spun next to the bookshelf, and let her hips move side to side in front of the door, mouthing along to the parts she knew. She couldn't speak Korean, so most of it was "la la la" until the chorus: "*You make me feel special* . . . la la la la la . . . *That's what you do. Again I feel special* . . . la la la la la . . . *I feel loved, I feel so special!*"

Soon enough she forgot how embarrassed she usually was if anyone in the house heard her sing—really sing, like she was a star on a stage—and she let her voice emerge from some hidden cave in her gut and pour out, unafraid.

18

Hours after Chinese food and their annual viewing of *Remember the Titans*, a Christmas tradition no one could remember the origin of, Rose lay in bed on Christmas night lost in her phone. A part of her felt the call to pick up their next book and read, but after looking up fan accounts of second-generation K-pop groups like Wonder Girls, she'd stumbled upon an article about Britney Spears. It led her down an internet rabbit hole about the breakup between Britney Spears and another singer and how Britney had been made the villain of the story even though that wasn't the whole truth.

A loud *clang* woke Rose up from her Britney deep dive.

And then another.

She put the phone down.

The sound came from her window.

Was someone trying to get in? Should she call for her parents?

Rose turned off all the lights so that whoever it was couldn't see her. She crouched down on the floor and crawled to right below the windowsill. She peeked up and down in a flash to see if anyone was there. She half expected some floating monster, or robbers in cat burglar attire, ready to attack.

But there was nobody. No flying ghouls.

She pressed her whole face against the panes and looked down.

And there was Talia, holding a huge rock.

"*No, stop!*" Rose whispered. Talia couldn't hear her . . . Rose hurried to unlock the window and pulled it open halfway. A freeze rushed in.

"What are you doing?" Rose prayed her parents didn't hear her. "Are you trying to break my window?"

Talia beamed up at her. "Hi! No! I'm throwing pebbles at it! To get you down!"

"That's no pebble!" Rose pointed at the palm-sized stone in Talia's grip.

"This one is a little big, yeah." Talia spoke in a stage whisper.

"Hold on!"

Rose, wearing nighttime sweats and a Cove Lake Middle School Choir sweatshirt, tiptoed down the hall toward her parents' room. Light off. No noise.

She threw on some layers and crept down the stairs to grab her coat and winter boots. In the dark of the house, she made her way toward the kitchen and opened the door that led into the backyard, hoping against hope that no one could hear her. Talia was already there, waiting, hopping from one foot to the other in the cold. Under the awning, no one could spot her if they looked down from an upstairs window.

"Were you really throwing rocks at my window?" Rose whispered, giggling, motioning for Talia to come toward the warmth.

But Talia stayed in place. "It's so cringe, but I needed to reach you!"

"Why wouldn't you just text me?" The icy air rushed in through the doorframe where Rose stood.

"Aw... Would that have been as fun, though?" A sly smirk broke out across Talia's face.

"You could've broken the window." Rose took a step out of the door and shut it, leaving it unlocked behind her. She pulled her red wooly mittens out of her coat pockets and slipped them on.

"Oh my God, what if I had? I would've run away and never said a thing. For real."

"I thought I was gonna get murdered!" Rose whispered so forcefully she felt a scratch in her throat.

"Why would a sound on your window mean you're going to get killed? Is that where your mind goes?" Talia let her back fall against the wall. "Your mom's anxiety has messed you up so bad."

"That's true." She leaned back with Talia. "I'm a head case."

Rose wished that for just one night, for just one moment

even, she could be someone else. A totally different type of kid. Somebody with no anxiety, no nerves, no voice in their head always telling them to never do anything wrong. Someone who could let it all go and just . . . enjoy the world.

"Hey, hey, no, I didn't mean it like that. Mental health is a real thing." She shifted to a more sober and serious Talia. "Grams always calls people 'worrywarts,' and I'm like no, Grams, they have generalized anxiety disorder."

"It's freezing." Rose checked back and forth between Talia and her house. "What's up?"

"We have a date," Talia whispered.

Rose had no clue what she meant.

And Talia must've seen it on her face. Her gums showed, and she rose up and down on her tiptoes. "It's Christmas School Day."

"Oh!" Rose laughed and then her hand shot to her mouth, eyes wide, searching for her parents as if they'd magically appear in the snow and scold her.

Talia shushed her. "Come on." She took one stride toward the fence's gate.

"No!" That had been a joke. What was Talia thinking? This was a step too far. "I can't do that!"

Talia inched closer to Rose and into the slice of light coming through the window from a single bulb above the stove.

Had Talia been crying again? The skin under her eyes

appeared both dark and pinkish-red at the same time, like she'd had sleepless nights, crying into a pillow. It had to have been about Dillon, right?

Talia appeared so small and sad that Rose wanted to take her inside for a cup of tea.

Rose faced out toward the light purplish-gray sky.

Could she leave? Could she just walk three quarters of a mile to school and do . . . what exactly?

·"It's our special thing, though. Isn't it?" Talia stepped side to side, tapping a toe on the inside of each foot again and again. "And," Talia pleaded, her voice raspy and low, "isn't it just amazing to think of doing something so *special* and *just ours*? Let's go. Don't let me be alone . . ." She widened her eyes, begging Rose.

Charlotte had practically ghosted Rose overnight. Her lifelong best friend. Talia had stood up for Rose at times she didn't quite mesh with the Brigade. She'd brought her into the fold. She'd shown her that not everything against the rules—like a list of books—was something to be afraid of. Maybe Talia understood what to *actually* be afraid of better than anyone else Rose knew.

Rose nodded, moved shoulder to shoulder with Talia, and together they strode into a freezing Michigan midnight.

"Lots of bad things could happen, though," Rose said, feeling the familiar nerves settle in upon their first half a block. But she felt like she could say these things around

Talia. She could let out any thoughts she was having. Talia didn't seem to mind.

"Alright." Talia linked an arm around Rose's and upped their pace as they passed a thousand rainbow Christmas lights on Milkwood Avenue and Clayton Drive. The night twinkled like a fairy world. "List them for me. Let's talk through every one!"

As they walked, Rose told her of scary strangers, falling into something they couldn't see that resulted in broken bones, and, worst of all, her parents waking up and finding her not there and then taking away her future dog, maybe the Toronto trip, and potentially her whole life as she knew it.

Talia told her she'd learned some Krav Maga and could attack the stranger, that if Rose broke her bones they'd use a tree branch as a splint, and if her parents caught her, Talia would simply explain she was a CIA operative and had needed Rose's help on a mission to save Michigan from microchip-controlled enemy raccoons who—obviously—only came out at night.

It was Rose's turn to let out a loud "Ha!"

Rounding the corner to the street with the fancy houses, where elaborate displays of silver reindeer surrounded the biggest house's pond, Talia said, "You're gonna laugh at me, but I'm rereading *Charlie and the Chocolate Factory*. I grabbed it at the library the other day."

Did Talia blush? Rose couldn't tell in the dark, but the

way she let out a laugh-at-myself type of breath and kept her head down made Rose think maybe she had.

She told Rose that she was curious about it because there was an attempt from some people—people who were actually *against* the school board book challenges—to cut out language from Roald Dahl books that were offensive now.

"I want to see for myself. You know?" Talia explained.

Rose didn't know—was cutting the offensive stuff good or just as bad? Maybe she should read those books, too.

Crossing the empty street that took them from the mansions to the school parking lot, Talia said, "I think I'm for free speech always. No censorship. Ever." She paused and added, "I *think*."

So Talia didn't always know what she thought, either.

"Also . . ." Talia hopped over the curb and wrapped one arm around a SPEED BUMP sign's pole at the entryway. "If we change the stuff that offends people, aren't we just protecting some old British guy's image? Couldn't we read more books from authors who, like . . . never wrote that kind of stuff instead?"

Talia seemed like she was thinking out loud—asking these questions to herself.

"Anyway, Roald Dahl sounds like a dude I would *not* want to hang out with." Talia took one spin around the pole and added, "He was an antisemite, for one! But I would take a golden ticket if I had the chance."

"I used to love *The BFG*," Rose piped up, following Talia into the empty lot.

Once they arrived at their school, Rose shuddered. The lights were all out except for the ones illuminating the entrances. They made her think of floodlights that helicopters used to find criminals. The parking lot and fields stood empty. The occasional car flew down the street in front, though mostly the road remained quiet. The American flag fluttered here and there in spurts of wind.

"Here we are." Talia stopped in place and surveyed the grounds ahead.

"Now what?" Rose asked, and a terrible gnawing took over her gut. She was far, far too far from home.

"If you're worried I'm going to sneak us in, I have bad news for you. I'm not a supervillain. I *wish*." But still, Talia hopped up to several windows and jumped to look inside them, like maybe she'd find an opening.

"There's the library." Rose pointed.

"Let me get on your shoulders," Talia directed her.

"But we can't—" Rose heard the whininess in her voice.

"We're not sneaking in! I just want to look..."

So Rose propped her up as best she could, and Talia climbed on, her hands holding on to the windowsill.

"It's the librarian's office!" Talia reported. "Oh my God."

Rose felt her legs petering out. "You done?"

Rose swayed one way and then the next, and down they both fell.

After a shocked silence, they cackled.

Once they recovered and made their way to their feet, Talia said to Rose, to the air, to the window, "Hey. I figured it out."

"What?" Rose found herself checking their surroundings as if someone might pop out at any minute.

"How we'll get the books."

As Rose asked, "How?" it started to snow. The purple clouds let loose. Speckles of white floated down onto the soccer fields.

Within less than a minute, it sped up, coming down in loads like the clouds were pouring flour onto earth.

"It's so beautiful." Talia ignored her question and headed, dazed-like, toward the field.

"It's so cold," Rose added, joining her.

They walked and walked until they stood in the center, with the woods on one side of them, school ahead, and the path of neighborhoods to back home off to their side. And on top of them, the world swirled.

Talia held her face up toward the sky.

"In New York?" Talia whispered. "The snow is *super* pretty for a day, but then it turns to this gross, dog pee, trashy slush. Here? It's clean for so long. I used to love visiting Grams in the winter."

Rose liked to think that at least one thing in Cove Lake sounded nicer than the famous city of New York.

When Talia returned to earth, Rose saw that snowflakes decorated her hat and the ends of her dark hair and eyelashes.

"Your face is almost purple," Talia said to Rose.

Yet Talia's tan cheeks sparkled like the snow was some kind of glitter.

Talia wiped her lashes, and Rose noted her bare hands.

"You still don't have mittens." Rose took Talia's hands to hold between her wooly ones.

And right as she grasped on, Talia swung her. Their arms stretched out and they spun and spun. Rose saw nothing but Talia's face peeking through in flashes between churning white. The snow clouded the air entirely.

"Come on, faster!" Talia commanded.

And they whirled each other in the snowfall, chins to the sky, until Rose slipped and fell, and they landed on the ground together.

Between heavy breaths, Talia said, "You know how in movies they'll say, 'I think I'm falling in love with you' to somebody?"

"Yeah." Rose lay in snow-angel position, and she imagined her snow print staying there, her body's shape encrusted into the ice like a child's initials written into wet sidewalk concrete.

"If this were a movie, I would say, 'I think I'm falling in best friend with you.'" Talia turned on her side on the increasingly white ground. She held out a hand to Rose and, though it trembled in the cold, Rose could make out an inked drawing of a rose on top it.

A part of Rose, one she tried to throw away as soon as it bubbled up inside her chest, heard Charlotte's voice say something like *Stalker much?* or *You're* my *best friend.* The other almost wanted to sing.

"Really?" Rose couldn't believe it. Why her?

"You don't feel the same way?" The sides of Talia's lips curved down slightly into the first stages of a frown.

And Rose protested, "I do!" She took a breath. "I do."

"Good." Talia jumped up, gummy smile back on. "Come on." She stuck her tongue out to catch some flakes. "We should get you home. I don't want us to turn to ice statues."

It was the most reasonable thing Talia Anderson had ever said.

"But who will walk *you* home?" Rose asked as they trudged back through the field and toward the increasingly dusted sidewalk.

"Girl, I'm fine," Talia assured her as they said goodbye to Christmas School Day and trekked through the year's first snowfall back to Rose's dark house.

19

If you thought something bad could happen and it didn't, did that mean it was safe all along?

Rose questioned herself as she returned from winter break to an expanded life. Besides the Hanukkah presents Jennifer and Greg had dropped off for Rose and her parents, she'd had almost no contact with Charlotte over the break. The only exception was their emails with Jennifer, who was supervising the hours at the rescue and the steps toward their badges. That was it.

"Such sweethearts," her mom had said about the gifts, which they brought every year, with dreidel wrapping paper and everything. Rose figured that if Jennifer knew what Rose was secretly reading, she'd probably cut off the yearly Hanukkah cheer.

The Brigade was in full swing. That first week back, Bree grabbed her in the hallways to join her friends, and Charlotte had disappeared from her side, so there was no reason to feel bad.

What had done it? What specifically had put her and

Charlotte into this odd, nebulous place of not even speaking besides a "hey" or a brief catch-up on the status of the dog-walking schedule?

Besides everything else, Charlotte was probably also annoyed with Rose's new style. For Hanukkah, Aunt Laura had gifted Rose a hundred bucks, and she wanted to spend it on clothes. Her mom insisted on taking her but did let her go to the thrift store instead of the outlets. And, after some negotiating, they'd agreed on a few outfits. No short tops with short bottoms, her mom said. Nothing that broke the school's dress code.

Fine.

Rose could swear a boy or two looked at her differently with these outfits on. She didn't know if she liked it or hated it . . .

That Wednesday, Talia texted the group that they had to have a meeting, this time about logistics.

Downtown after school? Bree asked.

So cold. Starbucks? Connor suggested.

Rose's mom came in last time, Talia answered, protecting Rose as always. Plus Rose has dog walking today.

Oh yeah! With Addie, right? I wanna walk the dogs! Connor wrote. We could tell Addie about the Brigade. Ngl I trust her 100. And Rose I wanna meet Bill!

Lol it's George, Rose answered, after finding the messages on her phone between English and math. They all agreed they'd invite Addie to join. It was only right as she was Connor's best friend. Honestly, he'd probably told her about it already.

It'll be great! a text from Talia read.

Rose knew the other kids texted during class, but she wasn't about to get caught dead doing that. In some classes that could mean a call home.

Talia didn't just *text* during class. She read entire books, both on her phone and in paperback, always labeled on their bindings with COVE LAKE LIBRARY. Rose was pretty sure their teachers had noticed and just given up. Rose had caught her racing through two books by someone named TJ Klune and a couple of Jacqueline Woodson novels, and one time she saw Talia turning pages slowly, like she had to read every sentence twice, as she made her way through a novel called *My Antonia* by Willa Cather. "I want to name my future daughter Antonia, I think," she'd announced to the lunch table that week. "It's a name like a poem."

Rose didn't even have time to think about whether Mariah, who might be tired after another long day working at the rescue, would be okay with them joining, let alone if Charlotte would, when Addie approached her in the hall. The jewelry that bedecked her all over shimmered as she said, "I hear we're having guests at the rescue today!"

And, before she knew it, at 4 P.M. Rose's mom dropped her off at the rescue. Hopping out, Rose instinctively checked for Charlotte before remembering Charlotte had switched days. Every Wednesday, when she had to remember that all over again, her eyes tingled with the rise of unwanted tears, before she took a breath and made herself forget.

The Brigade arrived five minutes after her mom had parked. They were all bundled up for winter, happily heading toward the rescue building, which was decorated with mounds of snow out front.

It turned out Mariah *didn't* care she'd brought her friends. "It's probably actually good for these guys to get the attention," she told them. Because the new kids hadn't been trained, they weren't allowed to walk a dog, but they could accompany Addie and Rose.

So they set off around the block, walking in lines of two between the three feet of snow on either side of the pavement, Rose making paths for George and his wheels. Addie led the way with a rambunctious pit mix and a sweet boy that was some kind of poodle.

Surrounded by new kids, and under the beauty of the bare trees that held both ice and droplets that occasionally splashed down onto her nose, a daydream overtook Rose. What if they told more and more kids about the club, and then the whole school was in it, and then everyone was reading the books? There wouldn't be a point in challenging those titles anymore if every kid dared to go out there and read them, right? And then no single kid would get in trouble.

With her breath visibly pouring out in white puffs, Talia explained to Addie how she'd given Rose *Fateful Passage*, and Rose hadn't even known it was challenged, and it had made Talia realize that not enough kids even knew what the school board was doing. She told her how the rest of the Brigade members had been brave enough to "buck the system."

As the pit stopped to mark a tree, Addie said, "Aren't they trying to ban the one on Wilma Rudolph, too?"

Wilma Rudolph, Rose had researched when she'd first seen the list, was a Black track runner who'd faced the mammoth discrimination of her era and gone on to win gold medals in the 1960 Olympics.

They told her yes, it was on the proposed banned books list.

"And Roberto Clemente!" Addie and the pit walked on.

"That's a different school. In Calhoun County," Talia answered.

"My parents told me about it. They agree with the challenges," Addie said.

Rose held her breath, and imagined maybe Bree and Talia did, too.

"So I'm extra excited to join!" Addie slipped the poodle a treat when he managed to not bark madly at a biker struggling in the slush, and Rose exhaled.

Then Rose felt George pull. He yowled. His wheels had caught on a stick, and he was crying. She hadn't been paying enough attention. "I'm so sorry, so sorry," she said to George, and she picked him up and cuddled his tan, wet fur against her cheek. She checked for any injuries—he was fine. Just scared. He visibly relaxed as Rose comforted him.

"That li'l guy is just *meant* to be yours, Stern." Bree patted her back.

Talia announced to them that she had a plan. "Rose helped me come up with it," she said, smiling at Rose. And Rose remembered hiking Talia up to peer inside the library's windows. Talia had been planning on explaining something then, hadn't she? But then the year's first snowfall had arrived.

Talia told them she noticed loads of boxes in the librarian's office. Mr. Lawrence was a mess in there. Either he had a serious organization problem or ... his boxes held books. And what had happened to the copies of the titles that had been challenged? Remember, she told them, *none* of the banned books were actually *on* the curriculum of what was taught in class. They were simply books that could be found in the school's already small library.

Was Ruby Bridges hiding in those boxes in the back, Talia asked them? Wilma Rudolph? The most-reviled books from the local school board recording? Like *She Wore Red*?

Nearing the rescue, Rose spotted her mom's car. Watching and waiting.

No need to rock the boat ..., her mom had said back in October.

Rose hated that. She absolutely hated it.

And here she was, for better or worse, strategizing how to rock it.

"So this is my plan ...," Talia said, grabbing a low, thick tree branch and using it to pull herself up and propel forward. It shot back and banged the other branches, bits of ice falling to the ground. "For every book we need, one of you will distract the librarian, and I'll sneak inside his office and grab as many copies as I can for us."

Bree clapped her hands, Addie squealed, "Diabolical!" and Connor said he'd wished they'd thought of this before he'd spent hours scanning.

But Rose could not do this. She could not *steal* from the library! From school property! Could they get expelled? Was it against the *law*?

Her mom looked up from her phone screen and caught their crew making their way indoors.

Mariah greeted all the kids with warmth and let them cuddle with a few of the friendlier dogs. She groaned as she knelt down to return George to his kennel, and Rose saw Talia ask her, "Is your back okay?"

"Oh, sweetheart, far from it," Mariah answered.

"I'm so sorry. I wish I could help," Talia said, and Rose could tell she meant it.

When all of them left, Rose hopped into her car and watched all the kids pile into Addie's mom's van, on to some second half of the early evening that she knew her mom wouldn't let her be a part of. She had homework to do.

Only a few weeks ago, when she and Charlotte had said their goodbyes at the rescue, she'd known they'd text or FaceTime later that night. Back then, leaving the rescue felt a lot less lonely.

But poor George got left by them every time they ended their shift. And he'd been left by someone else months ago, forever, dropped off at some shelter even in his old age. Dogs must feel lonely, too.

Bree was right. He was meant to be hers.

With her chin on the sill of the car window, Rose said to her mom, "Why didn't you guys let me get a dog before?"

Her mom gave her usual answer that it took a lot of responsibility and with her fibromyalgia and nerve damage, it was tricky, so she wanted to wait until Rose could take on caring for a pet herself.

Rose interrupted her. "I'm an only child, Mom. You never worried I'd be lonely?"

"You always had Charlotte." Her mom changed lanes and tinkered with the heat.

"She's not a sister," Rose grunted.

"I was an only child, too," her mom answered almost inaudibly.

"So you thought you'd torture me the same way?" Rose lifted her head, but kept her body pressed against the door.

She couldn't believe how she was speaking to her mom. She didn't even really care that she was an only child. But she did care that they dangled a dog in front of her as a prize. It was too much pressure! Rose pressed her hands onto her knees, and her fingernails dug into her jeans. Her volume rose. "You don't even *talk* to *your* parents."

Her mom took a long breath in through her nose. She

gripped her hands on the wheel and took a sharp turn onto their street. Then her mom spat out in the closest voice she had to yelling, "And if I end up being anything like my parents, then you are *freely* allowed to not talk to me, either! Okay?"

Rose sputtered out a "Fine!"

But she didn't know what her mom's parents had been like. And no one would tell her. And she was so happy to be in the Brigade, but she didn't want to break into the librarian's office. Maybe if her parents had told her some things, and pushed her to make new friends, and not made her feel like she had to be such an angel, then she wouldn't have been in this whole situation in the first place.

They pulled into the driveway and got out without speaking.

Rose slammed her feet up the stairs to her room.

Her phone lit up with a text. It was from Charlotte:

First you're ignoring me and then you BRING TALIA TO THE RESCUE???? HOW COULD YOU DO THAT?

What? What was Charlotte talking about? Rose paced back and forth in her room. She tilted her face up toward the plastic stars on her ceiling. One of them was peeling off. They were supposed to get their light from the window and then glow in the dark at night, but they didn't even get that bright anymore. They were duds.

How did Charlotte even know about Talia? Did Addie tell her?

Rose would find out soon enough. Little dots let her know Charlotte was writing more . . .

> Yea your little friend texted me just now. Apparently she has aaaall these plans on how to make our fundraiser better???

Oh no. Why did Talia do that?

Charlotte sent Rose a screenshot of the conversation.

Talia had written to Charlotte: Hi! We haven't talked much and that's stupid. Are we really gonna let wwiii stand between us lol. So hey, I went to Cove Lake Rescue today with Rose and I can totally see why it's so special to you. So I was thinking, what if we take the fundraiser to the next level? Instead of the street market sale you guys are planning, what if we organized a huge GoFundMe?? And if it reaches a certain goal we promise a PARTY for the school!!! Anyway lmk!!!!! We should talk!!!!

What was Talia thinking? Wasn't she supposed to be the one who always knew what to do? How could she not know this would infuriate Charlotte?

Rose sat next to her bed and cradled her head in her hands with her phone on her knee. The screen lit up again.

> Congrats on your new bestie. Is she in our troop now??? Maybe give her a heads up that we can't take donations and spend them on a party. As usual she doesn't know what she's talking about. Bye.

Rose couldn't bring herself to respond.

Why did Charlotte have to be so . . . *possessive*?

Why did everyone want to tell her what to do?

Charlotte must have responded to Talia because Talia texted Rose, omg I am so sorry. I know you love charlotte and I just didn't want to be the reason you guys weren't friends. I messed up.

And there it was. *Talia cared about Rose.* This was more proof.

Rose wrote her back to tell her it was okay, and she knew Talia was just being kind.

Because Talia was her best friend now.

Talia told her things and let Rose tell *her* things—things that usually sat deep beneath the surface.

Everyone else just wanted Rose to be the same girl she'd always been, unknowing and unchanging.

If Talia needed someone to help steal the books, Rose would be that person. She'd get the Brigade what they needed.

Putting her phone on the floor, Rose grabbed her desk chair and piled thick books high upon it. She balanced on top of them on her tippy-toes and ripped off as many ceiling stars as she could reach.

Maybe you didn't have to keep things the same way forever.

20

"Go," Talia whispered. "Go!"

As Mr. Lawrence left his desk to grab the stray book cart, Rose watched him stride aisle to aisle, lightly humming to himself, placing every title back. She played lookout as Talia ducked down and made her way behind his desk and into his office.

Talia would have to look over multiple boxes. Would it be easy to find *Ella & Elliott*, the next Brigade pick? Or would she take whatever she could find? How many copies would there be?

Mr. Lawrence turned the squeaky book cart back toward the desk, and Rose played her part. She took the hoodie wrapped around her waist and threw it on to cover up a crop top that was dangerously close to getting her dress coded.

"Mr. Lawrence!" She touched his arm and guided him away.

He'd been their librarian since seventh grade, after the lady who'd been there since their parents attended the school retired. Mr. Lawrence was a young man. He was Black, wore square-rimmed brown glasses, had a light layer of hair that revealed a tiny bald spot in the back, and walked with a bounce in his step. He had an unassuming, lilting voice that perfectly fit the style of a librarian. When he helped them find a book they needed, he'd talk to himself with a long, running commentary over every few books he passed by.

"How can I help you?" He held on to the end of the cart but leaned over it toward Rose.

"I'm in choir, see." She enacted the plan. "And I was told there's sheet music here, and I need to make a copy for a solo audition. Can you help me?"

Rose knew very well that the sheet music was toward the back, as far from the desk as one could get. And also that she would never, in a million years, audition for a solo. Seeing Mr. Lawrence light up at the prospect of showing her something and helping her, she felt ashamed. And when the shame grew, it morphed into dread. If they got caught, would he feel used?

But as he said, "Come on, come on!" and she followed him past encyclopedias toward the bins that stored the sheet music, she just couldn't believe she'd succeeded. New Rose had completed her task and was fighting the book ban. With action this time. Now she just had to keep him there.

"Can you explain how it's organized? Alphabetical but . . . Is there a difference in time period or style?" she asked.

Mr. Lawrence broke down the system for her, explaining why such a system was created and when . . . elucidating every detail like she'd hoped he would.

When Talia appeared before them, her backpack bulky and heavy, panting slightly, it was time to go.

"Thank you so much, Mr. Lawrence! I've got to head out, but I'll grab it another day!" Rose tried not to run out of the room, though a coffee-level energy surged through her legs.

"That was so easy!" Talia and Rose jumped up and down once they got to the stairwell.

Talia unzipped the top of the backpack, and Rose saw two copies of *Ella & Elliott* and three of *All the Things I've Seen Before* peeking through.

They had not been caught. They'd gotten away with it. Rose was both terrified and exhilarated, and she wanted to grasp the books like they were trophies.

"This was what he had," Talia reported. "We'll share them."

She told Rose the books were all stuffed together in three boxes off in the corner by the window, exactly where she'd spotted them.

"And it's not like he's going to go looking for them, right?" Rose said, almost to assure herself, as they headed to Talia's locker to drop off the cargo. "They're just there until the school board officially announces the decision, right?"

"I guess so. I doubt he's up at night memorizing each word or something. Ha!"

"I wonder how he feels about all this stuff...," Rose heard herself say out loud. She hadn't even thought about how this might affect Mr. Lawrence. Were people mad at him for any of it?

After the drop-off at the locker, they ran to gym class.

"Slow down!" a hall monitor yelled, so they walked so fast it was almost a jog and giggled the whole way.

They made it to PE and waited in line to climb up a knotted rope.

Sitting against the wall, Talia wrote on Rose's arm with a pen.

"Are you getting excited for the Toronto trip?" Talia asked as an athletic boy heaved himself up the rope and banged on his chest several times once he got down. They inched farther up in line.

Rose nodded, her eyes tracing the swoops and curves of Talia's pen on her skin.

"We should ask for rooms together," Talia said. She paused. "I think you're allowed to list two requests."

Rose didn't answer. They both knew her mom didn't approve of Talia. So they just let the daydream hover between them, unresolved.

The pen tickled, and Rose squirmed.

"Stay still!" Talia commanded.

Almost every kid struggled to pull themselves up the bright yellow rope. Some of them whined as they slid down and burned their hands.

Charlotte sat two kids down from them. Rose had never responded to her text about the dogs. They weren't really talking, right? That fact was official. So why would she answer an angry text?

It was Talia's turn. She clapped her hands once and said, "Let's do this!" Her pen dropped to the floor.

Rose looked down at her inner forearm to find an anime version of herself: straight hair down to her breastplate, which held her dove necklace; a freckle-covered nose with a teeny bend to it; her arms two sticks. The drawing somehow made her appear . . . What was the word her mom or dad might use? One time her dad had seen a video of a rescue dog bound through a snowbank and he'd called that Lab intrepid. The portrait, with its huge anime eyes and thin, curling smile, made her look *intrepid*. A girl on a quest. Someone brave.

"Hey," Charlotte's voice said in her ear, and Rose almost jumped.

She'd switched with another kid in line and moved next to Rose.

"Nice tat," Charlotte grunted. "Imagine what people's tattoos look like when they're ninety. Like you're covered in pictures of melting stuff. And then people will just think you were always into melting-looking stuff for some reason."

Rose couldn't help herself—she let out a snicker. She really missed Charlotte's sense of humor.

"I told Talia to back off the rescue. Did she tell you that?

You guys obviously talk about everything, yeah?" Charlotte twirled the ends of her yellow shoelaces.

"So what? You act like I don't exist now," Rose whispered, trying not to get the PE teacher's attention.

"Me? You abandoned me at lunch for those pick-me girls and their sidekicks." Charlotte was clearly straining not to yell. "And what's with those clothes? Your mom allows that?"

"What? What am I supposed to do—make sure I never have any other friend but you?" Rose knew it was mean, but Charlotte was being mean, too.

"You sided with Talia in Mrs. Paterson's class!" Charlotte dropped her laces and slammed a palm against the gym floor.

It was almost Rose's turn at the rope.

"I just said what's *true*!" Rose whispered. How did Charlotte not get that? It wasn't about Charlotte versus Talia, it was about something bigger, more important. "And by the way—" Rose's whisper felt like a scream as she said something she'd wanted to for months now. "I don't like the way you talked about Connor Roadson!"

"What? What are you even talking about? You know what?" Charlotte clicked her tongue against the roof of her mouth and shook her head. "Forget it. Go have fun with your new friends doing whatever weird thing you're up to together. I'm not stupid. I know you have some kind of little secret with them."

Before Rose could respond, it was her turn.

Talia slid down the rope and held up her palms to the

class to show how red they were. "Modern-day child abuse," she declared, and the teacher told her to stop it. She moved back toward the end of the line, and Rose was up.

"Always ranting about something," Charlotte said loud enough to hear as Rose made her way to the rope.

As January ended and February kicked into high gear, and the homework increased and the new sports season overtook the school, the Banned Books Brigade dominated Rose's thoughts more than anything else.

They'd read *Ella & Elliott* in January, using one of the rescue dog walks for a meeting, hoping it wouldn't look too suspicious.

Rose had wondered if Connor would share any personal response to the book. Ella is the only girl in her school who wears "boy clothes" like her brother, and Connor was the only boy in school who wore things like skirts and nail polish.

And he did have things to say. But he didn't talk about *himself*. Not really. As they strolled through the snow that had now melted into mere patches of crunchy ice on dead grass, Connor had a lot to say about the character of Ella. He told them that he really felt for her. He said she was just trying to be herself—no box, no label. He told them he was scared for Ella the entire book. He thought somebody might hurt her—beat her up or something—and he was relieved when the author didn't go there. He said that not every story about a kid being different should end with them getting "hate-crimed." He said that could end up feeling like punishment, even if it wasn't supposed to, which Rose had literally *never* considered before. And he told them he understood why Ella didn't want to be alive anymore after Elliott died, because Elliott was the only one who accepted her as she was.

Rose had wondered then, listening to him with all her might like his words might seep into her brain and allow her a tiny taste of his life, if he'd ever wished he wasn't alive, too. He seemed like the most confident person in the world. She knew his parents were supportive of him and didn't care what he wore. But still . . . Did he ever want to disappear?

With a shudder, she thought of Charlotte calling him a weirdo. But even though Charlotte and she were fighting, she knew Charlotte wouldn't want to hurt anybody. She called *everybody* weirdos. Didn't she? Even her own self and Rose.

But so what? Charlotte might not *want* to hurt anybody, but her words were hurtful ones. Especially when they put down someone so many other people in the world put down, too.

The rest of the Brigade had some issues with how the story sort of plodded along, and how not much happened that wasn't inside the character's head and feelings. But maybe that was the point. They couldn't be sure.

By the end of February, they would be ready to discuss *All the Things I've Seen Before*.

Rose had started it. And stopped. And started again. There was something familiar about the story, even though it was nothing like her own life. And that unsettled her. Instead of ripping through the pages, she took that time to read some of the other books on the list that they wouldn't get to for months.

Rose read a graphic novel about a boy who morphed into a mermaid, and a novel about a Black family in 1950s Alabama trying to get their own business off the ground.

She'd never read so much in her life. It was a habit, she found—something you naturally did more of the more you did it. But reading so many stories was more than that . . . It was like owning a telescope, pointing it somewhere far-off in the world, and zooming in to watch the most private, extraordinary happenings unfold before your eyes.

But before any more Brigade meetings could take place, Talia brought them earth-shattering news. It arrived in a text message on the night of Rose's parents' anniversary, the first night they ever let her stay home alone.

Rose had suggested the idea. They never went out, and it was their anniversary, and she was thirteen, and it was about time Grandpa Jacob and Grandma Adele got released from babysitting duty . . . And they said yes!

They left her armed with a list of numbers and asked their neighbor, the sweet and sometimes-confused

Mrs. O'Connor, to check in on Rose at least once. Her parents would be gone for three hours only, not even enough time to binge more than a couple of episodes of her favorite show, but they prepared for it like they were going off to war.

"And if this happens, you'll . . . ," they'd say. "And in case of this, you'll . . ." And she nodded, assuring them all was well. "No big parties while we're at East Wok!" her dad joked.

At freedom hour when her parents left—6:45 P.M. on the dot—Talia texted the group a link to an article:

School Board Approves Partial Removal of Challenged Titles in Cove Lake School System Book Battle

Emergency, Talia wrote. Code red.

Propped up on her couch's comfiest pillow, taking in the silence of her home, Rose read it. Almost all of the fiction books were officially banned from the school grounds. The nonfiction books were allowed to stay. *Fateful Passage* had not been saved. Neither had *Ella & Elliott* or *She Wore Red*.

Rose could have screamed.

Of course they're banning my girl Ella, Addie responded.

I guess since we're learning about the Civil Rights Movement they knew they'd be too big of hypocrites if they didn't let us read about Ruby Bridges. SMH! Connor wrote.

We have to fight this, Talia said. We have to make a plan.

What can we do? Bree asked them.

Petition. Protest. My friend Dillon says we could try to circulate a petition and get enough signatures from students to fight it, Talia wrote.

Talia was talking to Dillon again? Huh?

My parents would kill me. I can't get in trouble at school, Bree wrote.

Another text came in. Rose's mom.

We forgot to remind you. If for some reason you need it, the extra key is under the white rock by the herb garden.

Rose gave the text a thumbs-up and returned to the list.

What if she brought it up with her parents? Would they agree with not allowing all thirty titles? How long would it take them to read those books and make a decision for themselves?

A need to yell rose up in her again, but this time she wanted to direct it toward her parents, her mouth wide open, the sound waves of her screech thrusting them away like a strong wind.

This is how it all starts, Talia wrote. Book burning. Taking away access to information. I can't believe these people. We should've done more. We should've fought this harder. I hate living here.

There wasn't a response for a while. And then the kids jumped in to tell Talia it was okay, it was good she lived there now, and they'd figure out a way to handle it.

Talia hated living there? But all of *them* lived there *with* her.

Talia never talked about her friends back in New York. Only the people Dillon introduced her to.

Were her friends back home so great?

Rose couldn't walk around with a petition. It was one thing if everything was secret, but to open herself up to the world and all those angry parents? To undo her standing at school completely? The robbery of the library books would almost definitely get discovered.

Rose did the one thing that she could handle right then. She pulled out her stolen library copy of *All the Things I've Seen Before* and tried to force herself to read the next chapter. The mother in the story was crying in the bedroom after a big fight with the dad. The daughter was at the door, knocking, and her mother wouldn't answer.

And then Rose heard a knock on her own front door, and the sound in life matched the sound on paper.

It would be Mrs. O'Connor, completing her check-in. Rose left her phone on the couch, took a breath, and prepared herself for a friendly conversation with her neighbor, who was very sweet but repeated a lot of stories that could go on for a long time.

But behind her door's windowpanes stood Charlotte.

Those pesky worry spiders exploded in Rose's insides as she opened the door.

"Where are your parents?" Charlotte asked. She didn't come in. She just stood there in her fluffy white jacket and white earmuffs, making her look like a cold marshmallow.

Rose almost laughed. Her love for Charlotte rushed in as she thought about how if life were normal, she'd tell Charlotte what an adorable marshmallow she made. But Rose kept quiet about it.

Rose explained her parents were out, and Charlotte joked, "Oooh, big step for the Sterns!"

Rose didn't respond. She thought of the book list. The way Charlotte had blamed her for the awkwardness between them. The heavy weight of it all.

"Rosie . . . ," Charlotte started, her mouth opening and shutting a couple of times, the words not coming to her. "I . . . I miss being friends." And she started to cry. Big, heaving sobs. "I don't want to fight!"

Instinctively, Rose put an arm around her, pulling her inside from the cold.

Charlotte's brother, Noah, her ride, sat out in their car, and Rose could hear his music blasting.

Rose motioned, *One second!* to him.

Charlotte automatically slipped her boots off, and she let Rose take her over to the couch.

"I'm sorry," Charlotte sobbed.

Rose's mind flooded with memories, like when they started an Are Aliens Real? club in the third grade and how they'd decided aliens were indeed real, and all of them were teachers at Cove Lake Elementary. She thought of when Charlotte had taught her how to use a pad after she got her first period at school and almost fainted. She remembered when Charlotte's family took her to Lake Michigan, and they'd dug a hole so deep in the sandy mud that it became a hot tub and they'd charged Charlotte's siblings a quarter to use their "spa." The good times with Charlotte were never-ending.

How was it possible they'd fallen out so badly?

"I'm sorry, too," Rose said, hugging Charlotte tight and taking in that cinnamon scent. She didn't know which precise thing she'd done that most needed apologizing for, but she knew she'd hurt her friend. She knew she'd missed the last two Scouts meetings. And she hadn't sat with Charlotte in two months. And she'd seen that Charlotte felt replaced, but she hadn't fixed it.

"And I'm sorry if I was rude about Connor." Charlotte breathed slow, shaky breaths. "I'm *not* like that."

"I know," Rose said. "That's why I didn't like it. But, even if you didn't mean it like that, it's still hurtful."

"Yeah." Charlotte paused. "You're right." Her nose was runny, and she took sniff after sniff. "I've been trying to figure out how to talk to you about everything."

Rose hopped up and went over to their clear glass coffee table to grab Charlotte some tissues.

"You know I don't like Talia. I'm sorry, but I don't." She rubbed an eye until it turned red. "I can't help it. She thinks she's better than me."

"Look, I hear you, but—" Rose tried to jump in, but Charlotte cut her off.

"*But.*" Charlotte lifted a finger in the air and then let her hand fall onto Rose's lap. "You're my *best friend.* I promised you a hundred years ago that I'd be there for you forever, and I keep my promises."

Rose wanted to say, *You're my best friend, too*, like she had a million times, but she could picture Talia's declaration in the snow, and she didn't know if you were only allowed one best friend at a time. Some people, like Bree, seemed to have truckloads.

"So," Charlotte went on, "if Talia is a part of your life now, I'd like it if we didn't pretend it wasn't happening." She blew her nose. "Whatever you guys are really up to? That's made you less into . . . our stuff? Can you just tell me?" she pleaded. "It's the worst feeling when your best friend has a secret with someone else."

"I'm not less into—" Rose protested.

But Charlotte stopped her with a raised hand. "Just tell me."

Charlotte was right—it was the *secret* that had started it. It was Rose hiding from Charlotte that she was reading the challenged books. If she hadn't hidden it, then she could've tried harder to make all of them friends. She could've not given up when Charlotte pushed back. But the lies broke everything.

Rose studied Charlotte's pink, wet face. She'd always been trustworthy. She might feel defensive of her mom, but there was no way she'd care *that* much. Not if she read the books! Or heard their conversations! In fact, she'd love to give her own opinions on the books if she ever joined. Thinking of

Charlotte joining the Brigade, and of how easy that would make everything, filled Rose with a calm she hadn't felt in months.

But still. It was a secret for a reason.

"You'd tell," Rose said, feeling herself test Charlotte.

"Oh my gosh, is it a murder or something? Otherwise, no," Charlotte insisted, slamming her tissue-holding hands in her lap.

If she read *Fateful Passage*, she'd know why Rose loved it, and why she'd joined the club—how it had shown her that one story always had unseen parts, sometimes darker, more difficult ones. And maybe Charlotte would understand why Rose couldn't stop there. Why she had to learn more.

"Okay. I'll tell you," Rose said. "But first—I'm sorry I've been a bad friend." A choked cry jumped into Rose's throat, but she stuffed it down. Her abdomen gripped itself.

"No, it's okay," Charlotte said unconvincingly. "I get it."

"I really did want you with me," Rose maintained. "I *invited* you to come sit with us."

"I know, I know, I just—" Enormous tears rolled down Charlotte's cheeks. "I like it just us. I liked it the way it *was*."

Rose nodded. She didn't know what to say to that. Everything had changed. Even her *outfits*. But she could give Charlotte one thing: the truth. End the secret. It would solve everything. Rose knew it.

"You can't tell *anyone*. Here's what happened," Rose began.

Charlotte wiped under her eyes with another tissue, and Rose told her Talia had given her *Fateful Passage*, and how she'd felt when she found out it was on a banned books list.

Charlotte nodded to show she was listening, and Rose took a couple of deep breaths before she continued.

Then she told her the idea for the Banned Books Brigade came out of it. Just saying the words loosened a knot inside of her that had been there since she first lied to Charlotte.

So she went on. But she made sure not to mention Charlotte's mom or anything about the school board.

By the time Rose finished, Charlotte's crying had ceased. "I get why you didn't tell me. Kind of. You know my mom's deal." After a beat, Charlotte said with a sniffle, "I just don't like the word *banned*, I guess. It feels a little dramatic to me." She pulled some ChapStick out of her coat pocket and rubbed it on her lips.

Charlotte was talking to her. She wasn't freaking out. This was good! They *could* make everything right between them.

Rose thought of what Talia had told her and responded, "Well, if they're not in the library at school, then not every kid can actually get them. *We* couldn't get some of the books."

"But," Charlotte started, her mouth tightening in that way it did when she was frustrated, "the thing is? My mom said they're just trying to protect kids. Like . . . how could that be bad? And I don't want to know about everything scary or sad in the world!" She let out a laugh. "I don't need to read something that's going to, like, give me nightmares!"

Rose was starting to feel nervous about how worked up Charlotte was getting. Okay, so Charlotte might disagree with the Brigade, but she'd keep the secret, right?

Rose glanced out the front window. Noah was still parked there.

"So what do you mean you couldn't get the books? How'd you read them, then?" Charlotte gave Rose her full attention. Every now and then, she patted under her eyes, recovering.

"Eh, it depends." Rose swallowed hard. She didn't want to think about how they'd done it. And how they would do it again. "I need to be able to trust you," Rose said.

Charlotte adjusted her long waves. Some of the strands were wet and had stuck to the edges of her face. "You can."

"Okay." Rose grabbed Charlotte's damp hand. She had an idea. "I'll tell you if you promise me something else, besides keeping it secret."

Charlotte nodded. "Okay."

"You have to get *Fateful Passage* from the library and read it. So you'll see what I mean. Or the one we're doing now, *All the Things I've Seen Before*. If you swear to do that, I'll tell."

If Charlotte read them, she'd get it. Rose was certain.

Charlotte paused.

She had to. She had to promise.

"I swear." Charlotte clasped Rose's pinky.

So Rose told her about the stolen library books.

Charlotte gave a little gasp.

"You *have* to keep it secret," Rose repeated. "If I get

caught—there's no George. No dog at all. And that's just me. I don't know what happens to everyone else."

Charlotte hugged her. "Yeah, totally. And now everything can be normal again, right?" she said into Rose's ear.

Rose tried to picture a school day in which she was the girl she was becoming with Talia and the girl she always had been with Charlotte at the same time, and she couldn't. But she'd try. "Right," Rose answered.

As Charlotte walked to the door, she said, "So we can request rooms together for the Toronto trip, yeah?"

Rose opened the door and said yes. Of course. That had always been the plan.

Returning to her phone, Rose saw a dozen texts from Talia. The last one read:

> Bree, Rose, we can protect you for right now, but we have to start fighting harder. Next week, we meet at the site of the conflict—the school library. We won't get caught, not until we're ready with a plan for what comes next. But once we're ready to holler it to the rooftops . . . I want to show them we did it there, under their noses.

Rose didn't know what that meant or what would come.

Charlotte would read *Fateful Passage* and understand everything. At least that was something good.

But Rose couldn't show her face at some kind of protest. No way. Talia didn't get that.

Her thoughts wouldn't stop swirling. She had to escape her own life, even if it was just for a little while.

Rose turned on the lamplight beside the couch and dove into the rest of *All the Things I've Seen Before*. Stories, it turned out, could offer some escape when you needed it the most.

22

Had Rose betrayed Talia by telling Charlotte? She tried not to think about it.

And she tried not to think about Talia's idea for a petition. Or how they could get caught at the library. Or her parents taking away George. Or being on Mrs. Caputo's "bad kids" list forever. She ignored those thoughts. *Ignore, ignore, ignore.*

"Okay," Talia whispered as they sat at a library table the Monday after Rose had told Charlotte. On the shelves surrounding the room, books chosen by Mr. Lawrence for display stood perched and proud. "The Banned Books Brigade commences."

"So what'd you guys think of the book?" Bree drummed on the table.

But Rose didn't know what she thought of the novel. It was . . . dark. In the story, Myra and Cyrus live with a nice mom, and a dad who talks to them like dirt. He says Cyrus is weak, and Myra is a "bad girl." He controls what they say and eat and do, and the mom doesn't stop it. It was banned for the b-word and a scene where he hits the mom.

The book made Addie really sad. She said it made her think that maybe other kids in school had parents like that and she'd never know.

Talia agreed. "You *never* know."

Connor told them he thought it was a little over the top. Like, is any parent really *that* cruel to regular kids in a regular place?

Bree asked him what he meant by "regular."

And Rose, speaking without thinking, said: "I don't know much about my mom's parents? They don't really, like, talk?"

Everyone leaned in with their elbows on the table and their necks craned toward her.

Rose averted her eyes toward the tabletop and let the story she'd been told take her over, the memory pouring out. "But I remember *one* story. My mom told me that one time she was complaining about wanting dessert, but she wasn't done with her dinner. And it was really annoying her dad. And so he got up and grabbed this chocolate Hershey's Syrup? And . . ." She paused, the imagined face of her unknown grandpa looming over a tiny version of her mom. "And he poured it all over her macaroni and cheese. And he said, 'If you want it so bad, eat up.' And he did it to her mom's plate, too. And he didn't let anyone leave the table until they'd finished. My mom said she threw up."

No one spoke, and then Talia whispered, "Watch out.

Librarian." And they all sat up with perfect posture and pretended nothing was going on.

Mr. Lawrence strolled by. He stopped. He looked at the group. His eyes may have fallen on the top of the book sitting in Connor's bag.

They held their breaths.

Mr. Lawrence smiled in greeting and kept on walking.

They let out a collective sigh.

"That's a wild story, dude," Talia said, redirecting the attention to Rose.

They sat quietly, no one else adding anything.

"So he was, like, emotionally abusive?" Bree asked.

They all stared at Rose. Her flesh turned blotchy. She could feel it. Ruddy clouds covered her skin.

"I . . ." Rose thought of her mom. The way she always said about Rose's dad, *I picked such a good man.* The conversations Rose had overheard of her dad whispering, *Just call them!* and Rose's mom insisting, *No!*

"I don't really know," Rose answered.

She hadn't even realized it, but the whole time she'd been reading the book, she'd been picturing her mom as the little girl.

"You gotta ask her. Yeah?" Bree intertwined her long fingers.

"Yeah . . ." Addie jumped in. "Maybe *I* should ask my parents more about *them*." She traced the shape of a heart someone had carved into the table.

"I should, too," Connor added, scrunching up his nose. "It's weird to think of our parents as kids, right?"

Talia didn't say anything.

A couple of minutes of silence passed between all of them as they sat surrounded by noises of papers shuffling, Scarlett and Zion giggling by a shelf, and the pounding of keys at the computer center.

Talia moved on to the topic of petitions. She pulled a printed document out of her bag and dove into her protest plan.

But an outside voice interrupted them.

"Can someone explain to me what is going on here?" Mrs. Caputo asked.

She stood, arms crossed, two feet away from them—stout, her white blouse tucked in, and her nostrils flaring.

Before they could respond with any excuses, Mrs. Caputo stalked over to Bree's backpack and poured it out on the table.

"Hey!" Bree moved to snatch it back. Her copy was on her phone, so Mrs. Caputo wouldn't find anything.

Then Mrs. Caputo reached for Connor's bag, dumping its contents out next to Bree's notebooks, pencils, makeup bag, and pads.

She picked up *All the Things I've Seen Before* and held it up, a long, mulberry fingernail running across the school library name wrapped around its side.

Talia's head fell into her palms.

Rose couldn't keep her eyes off Mrs. Caputo. She gripped her own fingers so no one could see them shaking.

And then a thread from an old book club meeting wound its way through Rose's mind and out of her mouth as she cried to Mrs. Caputo, "Wait! Why did you go to Bree's bag first? Why would you pick her? Why did you do that to her?"

Besides Zion, Bree was the only Black student in that library. Had she charged at Bree first because that stood out in Mrs. Caputo's mind, whether she knew it or not? Because of some type of prejudice? Maybe, maybe not, but it didn't seem right.

Rose didn't want to speak for Bree. She caught Bree's eye, and Bree challenged Mrs. Caputo, adding, "Yeah, why?"

"Yeah!" the other Brigade members protested.

"Excuse me!" Mrs. Caputo fumed, shutting them down. "We will have *none* of that." She surveyed the kids at the table, then grabbed each of their bags like maybe one of them held some secret or a dangerous substance. But no, all that was dangerous were the words. The stories.

"It's exactly like you said," Mrs. Caputo growled, assembling the books under her arm.

"Exactly like *who* said?" Talia stood up. She, too, crossed her arms, which, even in February, were bare. She wore silver bracelets that wrapped around her biceps. She'd told Rose she got them from the New York Renaissance Faire. "Who?"

And then, several feet behind Mrs. Caputo, Rose saw her.

Charlotte played with the bottoms of her hair. Her mouth took the shape of a small, angry circle, and her stare did not break with anyone's at the table. She held her head high. No wincing or hiding.

Rose's tummy spiders morphed into tarantulas. Scorpions. They wanted to crawl out of her and sting.

As the other kids handed their books over and answered, "I don't know," to questions of how they'd received them, and Mr. Lawrence headed to the table to see what on earth was going on, Rose stormed toward Charlotte.

"How could you do this to me?" Rose fumed.

"I did it *for* you." Charlotte's fists smacked against her thighs.

"You're all coming with me," she heard Mrs. Caputo say behind her. "Let's go. Hustle. We're handling this in the office."

"You guys had a banned books club without me?" Scarlett asked from over at another table. Zion, seated beside her, pulled out a cell phone. He started filming the unfolding scene.

Before Rose could respond to Charlotte, Talia's voice boomed throughout the library.

"This is *censorship*!" Talia hollered.

Did she notice the phone directed right at her?

Mrs. Caputo edged closer to Talia, her finger aimed right

in Talia's face. "I told you not to do this," Mrs. Caputo raged. "I *warned* you kids. You are *choosing* to disobey."

Talia moved the inch forward that resulted in Mrs. Caputo's finger touching her, and Mrs. Caputo dropped her hand immediately.

Connor snatched a chair and—with the exchange of a look—Talia knew to stand on it.

"Librarians all over are getting *threats*. Because of *books*. They say they're a *bad influence*. Do you know what a bad influence is? Taking away books from kids!" Talia hollered from atop the creaky wooden library chair.

"*Down*," Mrs. Caputo commanded. "Right. Now."

"For free speech!" Talia shouted, fist up, like she was speaking to a huge crowd.

Scarlett and Zion clapped wildly. Addie, Connor, and Bree joined in.

Talia hopped down off the chair with a "Come on, guys," and the Banned Books Brigade dragged their feet toward the exit. "We'll be fine," she assured her small army.

But Rose couldn't move. She turned her focus to Charlotte once again.

Hadn't Charlotte *just* been on her couch, assuring her she was trustworthy? Hadn't she made her think that everything between them was *going to be okay*?

"You promised me." Rose felt her shoulders and chest sag to the floor like something was pulling her down. This couldn't be happening. How could she rewind time? Untrust Charlotte Maria Holmes? Could she go back to kindergarten and, when Charlotte claimed her as a friend, reply, *I need to assess my choices—let me get back to you*?

"You're getting brainwashed." Charlotte held her palms together like she was praying. "This isn't you. Getting yelled at by Mrs. Caputo? Are you serious? This is more important than being a Silver Award Scout? Than George? Rose, you *stole*!"

Charlotte blinked hard and fiddled with her hair until she'd created a tangle.

"*I'm* brainwashed?" Rose exploded. "You haven't even *read the books*!"

Mr. Lawrence tiptoed over to Rose and Charlotte and his hands hovered over both their shoulders. "It's time to leave, you two," he whispered, ever the librarian.

"I didn't *need* to! I went home and read the Goodreads reviews of *that* one!" She pointed toward the table where the book had just been, smattered among the private belongings of Rose's friends. "People said there's cursing and violence, and it's literally for high schoolers, if that!" Charlotte pulled on the tangle like it was what she was angry with.

"We're in *eighth grade*, Charlotte!" Rose raged at her, even though she saw that Charlotte was beyond reasoning with or convincing.

"It is *not appropriate*!" Charlotte sounded like a mom. Maybe like her own mom.

"You know what?" Rose's jaw clenched. "I don't care what you think."

The Banned Books Brigade walked away from the table in a pack, moving past chairs, trailing Mrs. Caputo.

"Enough!" Mrs. Caputo yelled back toward her and Charlotte.

And Rose knew it was time to follow them—her people.

"I will never—not in a million years—forgive you," Rose raged at Charlotte as she turned her back and walked away from her old best friend.

23

Principal Thomas sent them all to "study hall," which was essentially a detention room. Their parents had been informed, and they would be picked up at the end of the day as usual, but the suspension had technically begun already.

They sat scattered in desks in a room with enormous windows looking out on the field. A group of sixth graders did running drills for PE among orange cones and mud.

Rose tried to catch Talia's eye, like the first day they met, or like in synagogue, or all the times they'd had a secret between them, but Talia remained face forward for the whole hour. She rested her chin in her palm, looking toward the dry-erase board, ignoring everyone.

Connor and Bree scribbled away on homework, and Addie sketched something in a journal. They were not allowed to speak.

Rose couldn't tell how anyone felt, and it was all she wanted to know. She wished they could go around in a circle and each say one word that described their state of being. That way she'd have a clue as to who was angry with her for ruining everything by trusting the wrong person. Rose knew that Addie's parents would be furious. They approved of the school's book ban. And Bree's parents wanted her to be in "good standing" at school, Bree had said. Maybe especially because of things like getting her bag searched first in a group where there was no reason to single her out at all?

What had Rose done?

She could see from Bree's foot tapping on repeat that she was anxious.

Rose had to talk to her. To truly apologize.

At one point, Connor turned to Rose and mouthed, "Hey, bud, it's okay!" with his earnest, kind face.

But that wasn't all there was to it. What if Connor had to miss future sports games because of her?

At the ring of the bell, Talia practically ran out.

Rose popped up and bounded to Connor, Addie, and Bree. Addie assured her she didn't care if her parents got mad. Connor told her it was understandable—people make mistakes. Bree, who mumbled toward her feet, seemingly unable to look at Rose, said, "Maybe next time make sure you're thinking of *everybody* before you do something like that?"

Rose apologized over and over.

As they got shooed out of the room and Connor and Addie split up to head toward their lockers together, Rose stopped Bree and said, "I owe you the biggest apology of all. Your parents worry like mine do." Rose paused and grabbed the ends of her backpack straps, rubbing the tips on repeat so hard she would probably get a blister. "And I can see why," she added.

That snatch of Bree's bag hovered between them.

"Not everybody gets the same consequences." Bree said each word with equal emphasis, her tone sad and firm.

Rose had been *so* selfish. Like Bree said, she had only thought of herself and relieving her guilt with Charlotte, not the others in the group.

Bree didn't offer forgiveness to Rose, not that Rose expected it, but Bree did put a hand on her shoulder and say, "I'll let you know how it goes at home, okay? And you tell me, too," before jetting off.

And, with dismay, Rose made her way outside to the pickup line, looking for her mom's blue Honda. Maybe she should just run and not turn back.

A couple of cars down the line, Rose saw something that made her hold her arms in front of her stomach like they could hide or protect her. She never prayed except for a whispered Shema as she lay in bed drifting off to sleep, but she was about to pray right then and there. What could she say?

Please, God, if you're real, don't let Jennifer see me, don't let Jennifer see me.

"Hey, Rosie Posey!" Jennifer Holmes hollered out, rolling down her passenger window.

Rose frantically checked the area for Charlotte. No sign of her. Thank God. That was one unspoken prayer answered.

Had Charlotte told Jennifer?

Jennifer made large *come here* motions to get Rose to move closer.

When Rose arrived at the window, she saw Jennifer was in her scrubs with her hair in her usual messy bun. She'd probably come from a shift.

"How're you hanging in there?" Jennifer asked.

But how much did she know? What information did she want to get from her?

"I didn't have the greatest day," Rose reported. What she wanted to say was that she wished she could evaporate into thin air, and it was all because of Charlotte.

Jennifer leaned as far as she could over onto the passenger seat, so Rose dragged herself closer in response and put her head in the window frame.

"Honey, I don't want to stick my nose into Charlotte's business," Jennifer said, doing the same Charlotte-check of the school grounds that Rose had just done. "But what's been going on with you two?"

To her total surprise, Rose's voice trembled. "I'm sorry, Jennifer."

"Hey, hey, hey, it's okay," Jennifer said. She reached out to grab Rose's hand.

Rose's torso fell further into the window, her backpack hitting the top of the car.

"It's about the books, right?" Jennifer said. "Charlotte told me."

Of course she did. Had Jennifer convinced Charlotte to tell on her?

"Wait," Rose asked, still afraid of upsetting her second mother and forcing herself to speak politely even as she had the sense she could erupt at any moment. "Is that why she reported us?"

Jennifer's look of total confusion told Rose that Jennifer didn't know what she was talking about. Charlotte had made that choice all by herself.

"I'm not looking to get anyone into trouble, honey." Jennifer smacked her lips and looked up to the roof of her car. "Sweetheart . . . ," she said. "You don't have to agree with me."

"I—" Rose wanted to run to her mom, despite the punishments she knew awaited her there.

"All any of us want is to create a safe, kind world for you kids. There are things out there . . . that are . . . Oh, sweetie, they are *dangerous*. And you don't even know about them yet . . ." Jennifer shook her head. She had the look she'd had in the school board meeting, like a cry was on its way out, but she wouldn't allow it to take her over. "We're just doing our best to keep you safe." Jennifer squeezed Rose's hand hard, and Rose saw that Jennifer meant it. She meant it with every bit of her heart. She loved Rose. She wasn't mad at her.

"I thought you'd hate me," Rose admitted, wiping at her eyes with her coat sleeves.

"I could never—*never*—hate you," Jennifer said.

And Rose knew Charlotte would be coming soon, because too much time had passed for her to still be far off . . . She wanted to say something nice to Jennifer, to thank her for not being angry at her. But was the most important thing to make sure no one was angry at you? To not "rock the boat"? It couldn't be.

"But . . . ," Rose said, forcing herself to speak. "How does it keep us safe to not read swear words? Or, like, read about a kid with two dads? That's just . . . the *world*. Right? And what's *wrong* with that world?" Rose gently took her hand from Jennifer and pulled it out of the window.

Jennifer sat back up at the wheel and took a deep breath. "We miss you, honey," she said.

"I miss you, too," Rose replied as Charlotte jogged toward the car like she was trying to catch Rose, and Rose booked it, heading to her mom.

She wanted to shake Jennifer's words off her. They were sweet, and she knew Jennifer meant well, but at the same time they gave her this feeling that everything between people on this earth was broken and there was no answer to mending it. She hated it.

When Rose made it to her mom's car, she threw her backpack into the back seat, and nodded her head even before her mom said, "Well, we need to talk. Don't we?"

24

Will you ever forgive me for telling Charlotte? **Rose texted** Talia on the ride home from school with her silent and seething mother.

It sucks. I'm ngl, Talia wrote back immediately.

Rose wondered where Talia was that she could respond so quickly. Was she already on her phone, texting Dillon all about the trouble Rose had caused? Or, even worse, complaining to the other Brigade members?

But I think maybe I get it. Talia followed up.

Sorry I ran out before we could talk.

You're my best friend.

Rose was so thankful for Talia. The only person who could be that kind.

"Who are you texting? Put down the phone," her mom snapped, reaching over like she'd snatch it away.

"One second!" Rose pleaded with her mom.

You're my best friend, too. My REAL best friend. **Rose tried** to write as fast as the words were coming to her in her mind. I wish we could just run away. Hop on a train and go to New

York. You could show me the Statue of Liberty haha. Just get OUT of here!!!

That would be amazing, Talia wrote back, and hearted Rose's message. Such a good idea.

Her mom successfully grabbed the phone and put it in the cup holder between them.

o ✳ o

As they waited for her dad to come home, Rose heard the sound of her mom's steps around the lower floor. Her mom groaned or moaned occasionally as she prepared a frozen meal, her muscles obviously aching, as usual. And the whole time, she was undoubtedly thinking up a way to punish Rose.

Rose put on her headphones and let the melodies of Nayeon and Jeongyeon carry her away to another place.

Despite what she might have hoped, her parents did not hear her. Even after she explained everything over dinner, they still weren't on her side. Her dad yelled over her when she tried to tell him about why he might appreciate *She Wore Red*. Her mom shut her down when she tried to question if some rules needed to be broken. No, it was just:

You were doing this the whole time?

You're lucky you're suspended now and not right before the school trip!

I do not want you to be a target! I'm trying to protect you! Why don't you get that?

Just like with Charlotte, she'd thought if only they could

see her point of view, they'd get it. But her point of view didn't matter to them.

The more they spoke, the less Rose could make out their voices. She felt like she was disappearing.

But as her dad stood up and paced around the dinner table, Rose heard her mom say, "This is that girl. Talia."

Her mom was bringing up Talia? The only person who *did* care about Rose's point of view? Who valued it and brought it into the Brigade, letting her speak and protecting her and making sure she shared her thoughts? *That* Talia?

"Who?" her dad asked, speaking over Rose's head to her mother. "Evie's granddaughter?"

Of course her dad didn't even know who she was. Rose's life was a series of grades and polite dinners to him, wasn't it?

The dining room suddenly shrunk. Like the cabinet with the china and the picture frames and the small window seat a few feet away from the table were closing in on them.

"It's her." Her mom's entire body remained still except for a finger tapping on the edge of the table. "All of it. The club. The outfits. And I don't want you seeing her anymore."

"It's not her fault!" Rose hollered at them. They didn't even *know* Talia. "And I *love* my new clothes!" she added, as if the two topics were of equal weight. "Who wants to wear what their mom chooses after they're ten years old?"

"It's enough. You're not seeing Talia again," she said.

"If she's at B'nai . . . then fine. That's unavoidable. But it's done."

"No!" Rose screamed. "Just over these *books*? You guys really think she's so bad because she loves to *read*? Because we had fun talking about *books*? Are you *serious*? Talia's, like, the smartest friend I've ever had!"

"Honey!" her dad yelled. "You *stole* the books! You *lied*! You kept *secrets* from us! This is what's best for you!"

He was just repeating what Charlotte had said. They were all the same.

"Those books were stolen from the *students first*, Dad!" she shouted. And it was true.

It took everything in Rose not to shriek *I hate you* or pick up something on the dinner table and just *throw it against the wall*. Against those stupid old pictures of her. But she didn't.

"You're both, like . . ." What was the word she was looking for? She couldn't find it. "*Not brave!*" she shouted as she ran out of the room and toward the stairs.

"We're something, alright!" her dad yelled after her. "We're nice enough to let you go on that school trip, aren't we?" She could hear his voice hollering up to her as she made it to her bedroom. "Because that's your job when you're a kid, honey! School! Being a good student!"

"I don't care what you think!" Rose croaked from the top of the stairs.

"You're so grounded!" her dad hollered back. "And *no dog*!"

"Fine!" she shouted, like she didn't care.

But how could he do that?

Rose slammed the door shut to block them out.

She thought of George, that perfect little dog, and she screamed into her pillow.

Then she flipped onto her back, face hot and soaking, and tried to think.

She still had her phone.

If they blocked Talia's number, she'd find a way around it.

She texted Bree, told her what her parents said, and asked how she was doing.

Bree wrote: they're, like, proud of me?!? But mad I got in trouble. But proud I did. Lol

Wow. They should be! **Rose answered.**

Rose wanted to beg for forgiveness, but that wasn't fair to her friend, was it? Bree was allowed to be mad.

The guilt churned in Rose's stomach.

Rose wanted to take off to San Francisco, where Grace from *She Wore Red* grew up. It had rolling hills and cable cars and spring weather all year long and no parents or betrayals.

And then a text from Talia popped up. It was a link:

The AmeRail Midwest Express

She opened it.

The AmeRail Midwest Express was a rail line that started in Chicago, stopped in Detroit, Toledo, Cleveland, Pittsburgh, and ended at a place called New York Penn Station.

> I did it. I bought them. A ticket for each of us. Bye, bye Cove Lake.

> You coming?

Rose opened Talia's next message and saw a screenshot of two tickets to New York, set to leave on the morning the eighth-grade class left for the trip to Toronto.

> And this time, tell no one.

25

Talia said they'd only go for a week—an adventure. They'd break free when the class left for Toronto and then return at the same time. They'd tell their teachers they were grounded. "It's a week away to get us out of here. To give you a taste of a *city*," Talia had said to her in the hallways, with that persuasive gleam in her eye, like she knew how magical life could be and she wanted to share it with you.

But Rose couldn't go. Right? The list of negatives was infinite: an even worse grounding (for life), never finding a way back home, getting expelled for faking that she was on the Toronto trip, making her parents ashamed to talk about her, getting lost on the train, and getting mugged and attacked by violent maniacs on the streets of a city.

And as the days went by post-suspension, she'd sit in class adding to the list in her mind. What if she ended up homeless? Got arrested as a runaway? Fell into a body of water and drowned and no one ever found her?

But her ex-best friend had betrayed her. *She'd* betrayed *her* friends. Her parents had taken away the promise of a dog, which she'd wanted and begged for since she was four. The school officials looked at her as a problem kid, and she could swear she saw it on the faces of her teachers, too. And if her parents and her teachers thought of her as a problem now? Then why not *be* one?

Addie was grounded "for infinity," she said, though she announced it with some relish, telling them at lunch, "I liked sticking it to the man. And the man is my parents!" Bree was grounded for lying, but her parents were supportive of her. Her brother had told her she was his hero. And when Bree reported to them how her bag had been searched first, her family grew furious. With her family's backing, Bree was more fired up than ever about the cause of the club, and no longer worried about getting into trouble at home.

Why couldn't Rose's parents be like that?

Rose wasn't speaking to her parents anymore. They tried to talk to her, but it was pointless.

"Honey, what I was trying to explain to you is that, well you know I had a hard time in school in this town," her dad said to her a couple of times—once while she did dishes and one time as they drove to get groceries. He'd told her this a thousand times. When would he realize she wasn't him? "So I know things are better now, but I just . . . I just wanted you to keep your head down. You see?"

If he really thought things were better, why was he so protective? It made no sense. And he couldn't see it.

He was a coward.

And her mom brought up other things that had nothing to do with the drama that had taken place, like, "I saw you took down your stars, sweetie. Do you want to make any other changes to your room?" And she said stuff like, "I saw in your folders that you're really acing those long answer quizzes in history" and "Do you think you'll join choir in high school?"

Rose responded "yes" or "no" or "mm-hmm."

She wouldn't give them anything.

And whenever Rose *wanted* to say more, she thought of George. Of how she couldn't face him at the rescue anymore. She couldn't stand to see him, knowing she'd lost her chance at giving him a home. She stopped with Girl Scouts altogether.

And all this over her breaking rules that weren't fair, anyway!

The angrier she got at her mom and dad, the more she thought the New York City trip might be a surprisingly great idea.

Who cared what they wanted? Who cared what they thought?

Even as Rose went back and forth inside, she moved forward with the plans. Talia and Rose told everyone that their parents had punished them by not allowing them to go on the Toronto trip. They never handed in the final financial installment. The check Rose's parents had signed was now long gone in tiny pieces scattered throughout the trash bins at school. Rose was to get dropped off at school on the morning of the trip and ditch the scene before any-one noticed—difficult, but not impossible. Talia would be waiting for Rose by the gates of the mansion with the pond, and they'd make their way to the bus, which would take them to the Detroit train station, where their ride left at 2 P.M. They'd arrive in New York at 6 A.M. Friday morning.

"And from there?" Talia would say. "We'll have a whole week of pure freedom."

Freedom. Dressing up like a pop star and walking down the streets like one. Reading whatever she liked. Going places new and unknown.

She had to go.

And Talia had people there. Friends. Family. She could take care of Rose.

So when that Thursday arrived, Rose woke up with her backpack and suitcase packed. She'd stuffed extra food inside it, like Talia had suggested. Talia promised she'd bring cash, but Rose had stashed all the allowance she'd saved up into an inside pocket of her suitcase. Sixty-four dollars and fifty cents. The rest of her money sat in a Bat Mitzvah account somewhere that she couldn't access without suspicion. Especially right then. And her parents gave her seventy-five bucks to spend in Toronto. She'd probably have a good amount to get by.

"I'm meeting my group by the soccer fields. They split us all up into separate buses." The lie slipped easily from her lips as her mom dropped her off on the side of the school.

Rose saw kids with backpacks and suitcases meandering about, but nowhere too near her.

"Please don't wear those shirts that show your whole tummy. You're going to get cold!" her mom fussed, zipping up her jacket for her.

Her mom's concern filled Rose with a shame that physically ached, low in her gut. Or was it terror?

"I love you," her mom said, stroking Rose's hair back to settle some frizz. "So much." She paused and added, "It's all going to be okay. You're going to have a wonderful time!"

Her mom pulled her close and kissed the side of her head. "And don't forget—text me right when you get there!"

"Goodbye," Rose said, and she waited on the school's curb to make sure her mom drove away.

And then she ran, her suitcase bouncing on the uneven squares on the sidewalk. No one could see her. If she was spotted by the wrong person, they could ask where she was on the bus. If someone called her mom, she was toast.

Was she really doing this? Could she really run away?

There was no other option now. She'd already ripped up the check. Her teachers hadn't included her on the roster, since she'd told them she wasn't going. If she turned back, she would have nowhere to go for a week unless she admitted she lied.

But maybe she and Talia could think of some excuse. Maybe they could say they had a miscommunication at home or tell their parents the school decided to keep them off the rosters as punishment.

Talia stood in front of the mansion, wrapped up in a long black puffer jacket, a gray beanie, and a ring on every finger, waving. Talia only had a backpack, and Rose wished she'd found a way to pack lightly. But she had to make it look like how she would have packed if she was going to Toronto for a week. And her mom had an extensive checklist that Rose had to fulfill.

"Come on," Talia said, bounding onward.

Maybe instead of going to New York City, they could hole up at Talia's apartment for a week. She'd said her parents were cool with everything she did. They might understand and let them hide away together.

The bus stop was half a mile away, down Michigan Avenue toward the outlets.

Rose's heart beat at record speed.

"I can't believe we're doing this." Talia's smile revealed some crimson lipstick on her front teeth. "I am the luckiest person in the world to have met you. No one else would be brave enough to do this with me."

Rose deflated.

Talia thought Rose was brave, and all she'd been doing that morning was questioning the journey more with every step.

She started to feel ill.

As they hustled onward, Rose and Talia both checked their phones at the same time. It was Bree.

We'll miss you guys! it read.

Rose was so relieved that Bree hadn't held on to her anger, even though she had every right to.

They turned onto the busy strip of road.

"Um, Talia?" Rose peeped. "What's going to happen to us when we get there?"

Talia paused for an instant, then strode forth. "I have a plan."

"But," Rose heard herself saying, the worried piece of her taking over, "maybe we are overreacting. Maybe it's just too dangerous. You know what I mean?"

Talia halted, but did not turn to face Rose. "You're not backing out. Right?" She spoke toward the vroom of the many-laned street they'd reached, filled up to the max as people made their way to work.

"I—" Rose tried to say something, to know what to do. The moment had arrived, and she was too weak for it.

"I'm going whether you want to or not," Talia declared, her head held high. "I won't live another day here."

Rose knew that was true. Talia would get on that bus and that train with or without her. But what did she mean by "another day"? According to the plan, they'd be back in Cove Lake by the next week. She was probably just talking in her dramatic Talia way.

They arrived at the bus stop, and Talia set up Rose's suitcase so Rose could sit on it, while Talia hummed and swayed back and forth beside her.

"It's your call," Talia said with a shrug. She turned her back to Rose and headed to the fare machine.

And even though Rose couldn't see Talia's face, she knew she was angry.

Rose had to go, or she'd be backing out of what felt like a pact.

And if Rose didn't go, Talia would leave anyway. Alone.

Every fear that Rose had named for herself could happen to *Talia*. Would she get mugged? Kidnapped? No one would be there on the trip to keep her safe.

Talia handed her a bus ticket, and Rose slipped it into her back pocket.

Rose couldn't let Talia go on her own. Could she? A good friend wouldn't abandon her friend and let her travel all alone to New York City. But at the same time . . . a good *girl* would *never* run off. On the other hand, being a good friend *made* you a good girl. Didn't it? Rose's thoughts did somersaults.

"Anyhoo, I have a gift for you," Talia practically sang, reaching into her backpack and pulling out a piece of cloth, so tightly folded that it was almost a ball.

Rose took it, and the fabric fell, revealing the emerald-green shirt she'd tried on at the Silver Selkie.

"Oh my gosh." Rose held the soft cloth up against herself in awe. "Thank you so much, Talia."

"You'll fit right in in the city." Talia's eyes crinkled at the edges.

And the bus rolled up.

Rose quickly unzipped the top of her suitcase and stuffed the shirt inside. Talia stepped up to greet the driver, and Rose stood on the curb in front of the open doors.

Her breaths sat all the way up under her collarbone. She could feel streams of sweat in her underarms.

"You coming in?" the driver, tired and having none of it, asked.

Talia looked back at Rose. Her eyes pleaded, "Please."

She'd told Talia she'd go. She couldn't let her down again. And if Talia had taught her anything, it was that fear wasn't always the right messenger to listen to.

Rose heaved her suitcase up the first step. "Yup," she answered as she fumbled for the ticket stub and followed Talia toward the back.

26

The train to New York was already packed with people from Chicago.

They had to walk down four train cars to find seats next to each other.

It might've been her imagination, but Rose swore every other person looked up at them like there was something strange about two young girls roaming for seats together.

Rose had changed at the Detroit station bathroom into her tight-fitting crop top. Maybe the adults were thinking it was inappropriate.

"In here." Talia found a spot and picked up Rose's suitcase like He-Man, throwing it on bars packed with luggage above the seats. She nodded for Rose to take the window seat.

"'I can show you the world'..." Talia sang from *Aladdin*, teasing her.

It was only 2 P.M. They had sixteen hours to go.

Were her parents already looking for her?

She whipped out her phone and texted her mom: At the hotel. All is good.

A few seats behind them, a woman spoke angrily and loudly into her cell: "And you're saying I'm at fault for this? Me? No. Listen. You *left your kids* for a *month*. No—no, shut up! Will you shut up!"

"Will *you* shut up?" a man somewhere in the train car hollered, and a few people clapped.

"It reminds me of history class," Talia grunted.

The woman didn't stop talking.

A man strolled by shouting, "Tickets! Tickets!"

Rose felt her breath quicken again. "You're sure you have them? You're sure?" she whispered to Talia. "Wait, don't our ages mean—"

"I made sure we got parental approval covered. Chill," Talia almost snapped at her, but not quite.

As the man came toward them, Talia held out her phone and the man scanned it.

Rose attempted to look mature and collected, and then remembered with dread the breakout she'd had that week, and how scrawny she looked compared to everyone around her.

But the man hardly seemed to notice her.

"You're so funny, dude," Talia said, relaxing into her seat.

Through the window, the view shifted from broken-down buildings to broken-down houses to cows and graffitied walls and then to cows again.

Rose wondered how close they had to get to New York for there to be no more cows.

Talia had told her all about "the city." How every neighborhood had an entirely different feel to it, like, Little Italy wasn't anything like Chinatown, and Spanish-language music boomed out of cars in a place called Washington Heights, whereas if you went to Borough Park in Brooklyn, it was like you'd stepped into a Jewish village in nineteenth-century Lithuania. She said the beautiful thing about the place was that everyone, from all over the world, was trying to navigate the same streets and neighborhoods and subway cars, and sometimes in the right moment, you could feel like you were all in it together.

When she listened to Talia describe it like that, Rose could take the breaths she needed.

Rose pulled the shirt down a bit. She was getting cold. She zipped up her gray hoodie and the jacket she wore over it, like a bubble of protection against the unknown of the train.

"Hey—how'd you afford the top?" Rose asked. "Do your parents give you cash?"

Talia shrugged. "I just borrow my parents' credit card sometimes. They might notice, but hopefully not."

Rose sat forward and gasped. "Are you serious?"

"We're *family*. Why would it matter? Anyway, you look gorgeous in it." Talia pulled out a small mirror and redid her eyeliner.

Rose wished she could say she couldn't believe Talia did something illegal, like steal her parents' money. But ... she could. She really could. Rose watched Talia apply makeup, and she wondered if there was anything outrageous that Talia *wouldn't* do.

"What's that smell?" Rose sniffed again and again to try and figure it out. "Like ... sewage."

"The bathroom," Talia said. "Probably. That kind of old-pee thing mixed with sanitizer? That's the one."

"Eeew." Rose giggled.

"Glad to see you finally smiling," Talia said.

It was a gut punch. Not only was Rose doing something so, so wrong by going to New York, she wasn't even doing it well. She wasn't fun.

But Talia fixed it. "I know you're afraid, okay? Let's do what we did on Christmas School Day. Tell me every single thing you're scared of, and I'll tell you how we're gonna handle it." She tapped Rose's knee signaling for her to begin.

Rose leaned into Talia and, in a little huddle, they dove in.

Once they made it through the whole list, Rose added more. "What if there are rats? I've seen videos of rats in New York carrying entire pizza boxes. Can they attack people?"

"If a rat attacks you, I will challenge it to a duel," Talia assured her.

"Are there alligators in the rivers there?" Rose made a little snapping motion with her hands.

"No, but we can avoid the water. Rose," Talia said, interlacing her fingers with Rose's, "we are on the adventure of a lifetime. It'll just be you and me in the greatest city in the world. No one can tell us what to do. It's going to be incredible."

Rose could feel the cold metal of Talia's rings between the flesh of her own bare fingers. And, gripping palms, Rose chose to believe her friend.

The train rumbled on and on, and Rose rested her head on Talia's shoulder, scrolling on her phone, while Talia read a book called *The Haunting of Hill House*.

After a while, Rose reached in her backpack under the seat to pull out a protein bar.

"Wait." Talia stopped her, letting the book, held open by a thumb, rest on her lap. "Just make sure you're really hungry. We'll have to save our food in case we need it later."

Rose put it back. "But . . . once we make it to one of your friends' houses, we'll be okay foodwise. Right?"

"Yeah. Maybe. Yeah, I think so," Talia half answered, returning to her novel.

Rose watched out the window again. So many horses. So many barns. So many little houses filled with people living lives she couldn't imagine. What would it be like to live by the railroad track and hear that roar multiple times a day?

"So what are your friends there like?" Rose asked her, and Talia put the paperback down on her lap but kept her finger in her spot.

"To be honest, I didn't really click with that many people there. Like, I have the kids I know from school. But they're kind of, like . . . Not all of them are my biggest fans?" Talia played with her moonstone earring.

The man in front of them snored, his head of thick black hair resting against the window in front of her. His earbud had fallen out, and Rose could hear the light drone of a podcast go on and on.

"I'm sure you know the stupid rumor that you got kicked out of school." Rose attempted to sound casual, because she'd never wanted to bring it up before, but it *was* something everybody said.

"I didn't get kicked out," Talia said with a *tsss* laugh that didn't sound like she thought it was so funny. "But yeah, we partly left because things got so rough there for me."

Rose tried not to sound as interested as she felt, like that might scare Talia off from sharing. "Oh?"

"Yeah. Mom and Dad were already out of work, and just kept getting more and more behind on payments and stuff, and the crappy little jobs they got didn't do the trick, so when the girls at school decided I was Public Enemy Number One or whatever, that kind of pushed them over the edge to want to move back home. I guess. I dunno! Who knows why parents do the stuff they do?" Talia spoke into her fingertips. She rearranged each ring so it faced up. The hamsa. The star. The mood ring that looked like it had been won at a Chuck E. Cheese.

"But..." Rose couldn't take her eyes off Talia. What was she hearing? "You, like, instantly made a million friends at Cove Lake. You..."

"What can I tell you? Kids from Michigan are easily impressed."

Rose saw Talia shut down.

Rose wanted to ask why no one liked her at her old school, and why her parents lost their jobs. And as the train made a brief stop in Toledo, Rose wondered if she was going on an adventure with someone she might not know very well after all.

27

They ate their protein bars and bags of grapes for dinner. The sunset outside the window brought tranquility. Rose wanted to melt into its orange.

Genius that Talia could be, she'd suggested they go to the sixth or seventh page on Google Images of Toronto and save some tourist site photos to send to Rose's parents.

"Are you sending, too?" Rose asked.

But Talia said, "Naw." She was almost finished with her novel and didn't want to stop until it was done. "Plus," she added, "they'd be even more weirded out if I *did* send them pictures. They'd be, like—something's wrong! She's talking to us! Send help!" She snorted.

"That's so weird." Rose laughed along with her. "So, like, what did you tell them about the Toronto trip?"

Rose couldn't imagine parents caring this little. It didn't even make sense.

Talia let out a puff of air that was sort of like a chuckle and sort of a sigh of annoyance before saying, "No offense, but can you pleaaase let me get to the end of my book?"

She plastered a pretty-please smile on her face and batted her eyelashes before opening up the pages again.

Why wouldn't Talia answer about her parents?

And why hadn't Rose ever met them—this freedom-loving, cool couple who let their kid stay for hours at the library and walk all around town doing whatever she wanted?

As the view outside the train darkened, Rose thought back to when they'd gone to the library that first time in the fall. Talia had waited with Rose and said her parents would pick her up . . . But she'd just walked home alone.

What was life really like in Talia's grandma's home?

A huge contingent of the crowd got off in Cleveland, and snoring earbuds man was replaced by a small woman whose silver hair was swept up into a tight ballerina bun. Rose could smell her perfume from there and was grateful it covered up the mounting stench of the bathrooms.

What were her friends doing right then? Were they done with dinner and settling into the hotel? Watching movies on their laptops? That's what Rose should do. She pulled up her favorite romantic comedy while Talia remained glued to her book.

By 10:30 P.M., Talia was fast asleep on Rose's shoulder.

Rose shut her laptop, plugged her phone into its portable charger, and helped Talia's head and torso fall onto her lap to rest.

At some point Rose must have slept, too, because the

next thing she heard was "PENN STATION! NEXT STOP NEW YORK PENN STATION!"

In the darkness, Rose had to cup her hands around her eyes with her forehead glued to the window to catch a view. She thought she caught glimpses of the buildings—the mountainous skyscrapers growing out of a river and then disappearing again behind the train's turns and its dips under tunnels.

Right as they got there, the sun began to rise, yellow beams peering out from the edge of the earth.

But Rose lost her view as they made their way into a dark tunnel. People around them started to stand up, stretch, and gather their things. Even as the train jostled, riders inched their way toward the front of the car.

Rose looked down at Talia, who had left a tiny pile of drool on Rose's jeans.

Fast asleep, she looked so much younger, with her makeup smudged and faded from a long night.

Rose tapped her. "Wake up, Talia. We're here."

Talia rustled awake and stretched her usual cat stretch. "Home," she yawned.

Rose worried they weren't moving quickly enough and they wouldn't get off the train before the doors closed again, but Talia told her it didn't work like that. They were at the final stop, and it was okay.

"But," Talia warned her, pulling Rose's suitcase down, "it's going to move fast out there. It's intense. Don't leave my side."

Fast was an understatement. On the rush out the door, she let Talia pull the suitcase as she tethered herself to Talia's other arm. Even at 6 A.M., half the people bounded forward like they were going to be late getting somewhere, while the other half dragged their feet, trying not to get caught in the stampede.

But then, at the end of the walkway by the train, they arrived at a huge escalator and a set of stairs that appeared never-ending. The crowd slowed, groaning and mumbling all around her. The other passengers were so close to her she could smell cologne and bad breath and hair spray. Someone must've been scarfing down a sandwich, because she caught the scent of mayo, too.

As they stood in place on the escalator, they rose up, up, up into bright, blinding lights.

Above her an enormous glass ceiling came into view, like she stood beneath pure sky. Rows of escalators brought throngs of people up to the same sleek floor Rose and Talia stood on. Above them, right beneath the view of the sky, a giant, ticking clock hung like the room's moon.

"Pardon." A woman in a pantsuit sidestepped Rose and her suitcase. She was scarfing down a muffin as she zoomed by, a few crumbs tumbling down onto the ground.

"Is there food here?" Rose asked, feeling her stomach groan.

"Yeah, but it's, like, eighteen bucks for a frickin' sandwich," Talia grunted. "Later."

"Are we almost..." Then it hit Rose that she still didn't

know their final destination. It was Talia's friend's house, right? So did they walk to it? How did they get there? Were they going outside?

She spotted enormous lit-up boards with numbers and times listed on them, and people crowded beneath, coffees in hand, staring up.

A few feet away from them, two women in beautiful, colorful saris looked to be debating something in a language Rose didn't know.

She felt a tug from Talia. "Don't get too distracted, girl—look straight ahead," Talia commanded. "We're following the signs to the 2 train. It's red. Look out for it."

"Hey, Talia, which, like, neighborhood are we going to?" Rose asked, wishing she had a map, and she wanted to pull one up on her phone, but then she'd lose her line of vision as she dodged various people walking at full speed right by her.

"You'll see," Talia said. "I have a surprise."

She couldn't glance at her phone. What if, back in Michigan, this was the moment her parents found out? What if something in their plan had gone awry and they were on the hunt for her? Would police be looking?

They followed signs with big red numbers on them and eventually arrived at a set of machines where Talia told her they'd buy "MetroCards" to get on the subway.

"I thought when we got to Penn Station we were there?" Rose said, fumbling with the cash she pulled out of her suitcase.

After Talia led her through the screen's directions, a little card popped out, and she followed Talia to the subway's entryway. It was all metal with a bar in front of it and a little slot you had to swipe your card through. Rose walked. The bar hit her in the stomach.

"You have to be smooth with it, but not slow," Talia directed her from the other side.

"*Come on!*" a man bellowed at Rose from behind. "Jesus Christ," he cursed.

"Hey! Just use the other one!" Talia yelled at him.

"It's broken!" The voice roared at Talia like she was stupid.

Rose could not believe that a grown man was talking to a kid this way. A stranger.

"Just use your phone!" he snarled.

"I don't know how!" Rose tried again and again to swipe it, but nothing was happening. A crowd was growing behind her. She could hear frustrated mutterings. It felt like ten minutes, but it had probably only been a few seconds.

Saving the day, Talia leaned forward over the bar and did the swipe for her. Rose thrust her body past the metal.

"Finally," the man behind her grumbled.

As she rushed out of his way, she saw he was a six-foot, balding, middle-aged man dressed in a fancy suit. He moved at cheetah speed once he got through.

"Okay." Talia picked up her pace again as Rose rushed to keep up. "That was a bad first example of a New Yorker. Most of us are nice. We're just . . . *busy*."

They reached a train platform, but it was a different kind of train. Not the large, sturdy AmeRail Midwest. A thin, dirty silver one shot by them on the other track. When it thundered by, Rose couldn't hear a thing Talia was saying, but she was pretty sure she lip-read her yelling, "I'm so happy to be home!" and then "But I need a coffee!"

When their subway train arrived, Talia practically leapt onto it, holding on to the fabric of Rose's coat to make sure she didn't lose her. "Coming through, coming through!" Talia nabbed them a seat.

Rose didn't know if she'd ever in her life been so relieved to sit down.

Then, checking her phone and seeing the time was 6:30 A.M., she let her head fall back against the subway's wall and tried not to descend into total horror.

"Ew, don't let your hair touch that." Talia tilted Rose's head up from behind.

Rose popped up.

"We'll be there in, like, twenty. If there are no delays." Talia balled her fingers up into fists like she was cheering at a sports game. "Yay!" She took in Rose's face, undoubtedly flooded with dread, and said to her, "Hey. It's okay. Look around—there's a lot of other kids on here, too."

So Rose took it in. A few seats away from them, on the long blue seats that looked like benches attached to a metal wall, sat two boys around their age. Above them stood a pack of girls holding on to a metal pole. They must've been around thirteen or fourteen. They wore clothes that reminded Rose of Talia—hoop earrings, teeny tops covered by baggie sweaters, and loose pants or skirts that ended high up on the leg. One of them had three different colors in her hair. They were joking and yelling and cursing up a storm.

The grown-ups around them sat still, their bodies jostling a bit with the train's movements, but their eyes glued to the screens of their phones.

And then, at the next stop, where Talia put a hand on Rose's thigh to stop her from getting up, a huge group of kids came in. They had a stereo and asked everyone by the doors in the wider middle section to step aside. Two of the boys were shirtless, even in March. One of them held a baseball cap upside down.

"Are you readyyy?" one of them whooped, his head bouncing to the beat. He cracked his neck left and right, then handed the stereo to another, younger boy. He hopped up onto the pole with his two hands and he held his legs out so he made a ninety-degree angle with the pole.

"Oh, this is perfect," Talia whispered to Rose, tapping her knee again and again.

A couple of people across the seats from them put on headphones.

One of the guys took the hat and started bouncing it on his head, his shoulders, his feet, his stomach . . . It reminded Rose of the hacky sack some kids played outside the school now and then.

"And here he is!" one of them hollered, clapping. "Only eight years old!"

And a little boy jumped up onto poles hanging from the ceiling and placed his whole body on the top of the train car, then jumped down, walked on his hands through the uneven subway. He flipped back up.

By the next stop, they were holding out the hat, and a few people pulled out cash.

Rose smiled at them and searched in her pocket for money.

"No," Talia said, stopping her. "We need that."

So Rose just gave them a smile and clapped along with some of the other passengers.

"Pretty smile," one of the boys said as he passed by and moved toward the end of the car.

Was he talking to Rose?

Talia lightly bopped Rose's shoulder with hers. "He means you."

And Rose hated herself for blushing.

Talia laughed.

"That was amazing." Rose watched the boys go.

Eventually, Talia told her it was about to be their stop. The train had grown crowded. Two men in suits stood right in front of Rose, up against her suitcase, holding on to the bar above her seat. They spoke about some guy at work. Rose couldn't help listening in.

When the doors opened, she popped up as fast as she

could and said, "Excuse me, excuse me," in what felt like a very tiny voice as she rushed out of the train. The doors seemed to close so fast. She couldn't lose Talia.

A black sign read PARK PLACE in white letters, and she followed Talia down another long hallway and up two flights of stairs. At the top of the stairway, Rose stopped, looked around at the bright day, which seemed much warmer than Michigan, and whispered, "So many people."

Talia snatched Rose by the arm and pulled with considerable force.

"Rule number one in New York," Talia told her. "You don't stand on the top of the subway stairs. Blocks the way."

"What are the other rules?" Rose murmured as a woman rushed by her practically hissing, "*Excuse me!*"

But Talia had found her way a few feet over to a man in a cart selling bagels and coffee. She got them drinks, telling the man, "Lots of sugar!" for Rose's.

"Are we almost there?" Rose asked with a touch of desperation, though now she wanted to look at everything. They were finally out of a station, in the world, in New York! Soon, she hoped, she'd meet Talia's people.

"Come on," Talia chirped. "Isn't this the best?"

The buildings were . . . Well, there was no other word for them but *beautiful*.

They walked by a café with an Italian name and opera music blaring from it. People spoke into cell phones, and Rose noted multiple languages—one of them might've been

French? Some hipster-looking guys skateboarded down a bike lane. She saw yellow taxis and also some weird green cars. Racks of blue bikes lined some of the streets. A large group of women in full-body scarf coverings—she didn't know the name of them—walked by laughing and looking at their phones as if they were trying to find something. A couple of women scurried by the group in yoga pants with yoga mats on their backs. One of them carried heels in her hand like she was going somewhere to freshen up. Every block or so, she saw men hauling large boxes out of trucks and talking to managers in their storefronts.

As they turned a corner, while Rose found herself lost in the maze of buildings and people and smells, she saw a man with no coat, lying on the ground. He had something—maybe clothes?—and a few bags behind him, pressed against the wall. And he groaned over and over again, clutching his forehead.

Rose stopped. "Talia," she said. "Call 911."

"Huh?" Talia had been lost in the sights, too, it seemed.

"This man needs help," Rose said. She wished she remembered the skills she'd learned from when the Scouts spent a day shadowing nurses.

Talia put an arm around Rose, her hand resting on her shoulder. "Keep moving, bud," she said.

Behind them, she heard the man retch, maybe throwing up.

"But that guy needs help!" Rose pleaded.

"Rose," she said. "You gotta get used to that. Every big city is like this. That's the world."

And they kept walking. But now Talia had a topic.

"There's just no real mental health or drug rehabilitation program that *works* in this country. I swear, they give the money to the wrong stuff," Talia said as she took great strides down the sidewalks, complaining about the mayor of NYC, her comments going right over Rose's head.

How could that man just be left lying there? Would he be okay?

Talia led her across a busy street even though the pedestrian light was red. "We're here."

Rose, her feet aching, looked up and saw what might be described as a park. Or a sprawling boardwalk. There was a seemingly endless strip of cement next to a huge body of water. People jogged and strolled along it. Or maybe it was a play space, because she also saw toddlers balancing on concrete ledges surrounding bushes. Benches dotted the grounds.

"Come with me. We're going to the Esplanade," Talia told her. She marched with a purpose.

Rose didn't know the word *esplanade*. It seemed like she meant the boardwalk, the one with a bench every few feet by the waterside.

They survived the bikers zipping by them, and Talia collapsed onto one of the bird-poop-speckled black benches.

Rose crumpled beside her, somehow more tired and more awake than she'd ever been at the same time.

"Look." Talia pointed out toward the water.

And there, across the sun-rippled river, Rose saw her: the Statue of Liberty, raising her torch to touch the New York clouds.

28

"I can't believe it." Rose wanted to cry.

Talia let out a breathy laugh. "It's funny. When you live here, you just get used to it."

"I know you said it's touristy, but..." Rose spotted boats in the water, some of them maybe going toward Lady Liberty.

"It's still cool, yeah," Talia agreed.

"Grandma Adele told me some of her family came to Ellis Island," Rose said in an awed whisper.

"That's awesome."

They stared out at what Talia had informed Rose was the Hudson River.

As life unfolded all around them, they sat for several minutes in silence. The world surrounding them had sound enough. Rose saw why Talia wanted to come back.

But who did she come back to?

Rose didn't know when to bring it up. She looked at her phone, and it read:

Good morning, honey! I hope today is great.

And at the thought of her mother, and how far she was from her, Rose's mouth went bone-dry.

She took a big gulp of coffee, but that made it worse.

The muscles in the back of her neck tensed up.

One week. She could keep up this lie for one week. It was *possible* to never get caught.

And then, for the rest of her life, she would've done one wild, unbelievable, courageous thing.

But she had to know what was next. She loved sitting there, watching the people, taking in the water and the enormous bluish-green statue that people flocked from all over the world to get a glimpse of, but she couldn't live hour to hour. And she wanted a bed. Somewhere to rest and think everything through. Talia had last lived in a place called Sunset Park, Brooklyn. Rose remembered that because Talia had told her about the views of Manhattan from the top of Sunset Park, the park the neighborhood was named after. Rose pulled up her phone. They weren't anywhere near it. The thought of another subway made her want to twist up into a ball and fall asleep right there.

"So what's our plan?" Rose felt like she'd asked it a million times, but maybe she hadn't. Maybe she'd just let herself be led.

Talia bounced her pointed toes up and down like a ballerina, put her hands under her bottom, and swayed back and forth, like she wanted to burst. Smiling, she bit her lip.

Then she exploded: "Dillon is going to pick us up!" Her hands flew up in the air. "He's going to come get us, and he has a place for us to stay. Get this: It's in *the West Village*. Can you believe it?"

Rose stared at her. She could feel her lips twitch. "Dillon?" Rose could hardly get the sound out.

"Don't worry, dude, I told you." Talia blew off her concern. "He has a girlfriend. It's nothing romantic or anything. He won't be creepy. We're just friends. I'm telling you, the Brigade and Dillon and a couple of the kids he connected me to are the only way I survived the year." She rocked some more like she wanted to bounce out of her seat.

"Um . . ." Rose fidgeted with her jacket's zipper. "You guys just chatted, though? You've never, like, met?"

Talia rolled her eyes. "That's not a big deal. Trust me."

"Could you show me his picture again?" Rose asked as a man hobbled in front of them on a walker with a woman in scrubs helping him along. A pack of bros strutted by him so fast they could've knocked him down.

Talia handed her the phone.

Photo after photo showed Dillon, mostly in selfies, posing in front of colorful graffiti, digging into some perfect-looking food at a restaurant, and throwing up a peace sign in front of a group of guys with tags like #TheFam.

"I don't like this." Rose held on to the phone and kept scrolling down. He definitely looked older than sixteen. And even if he was sixteen, that was way, way too old! Just like she'd told Talia on Hanukkah! And why did everything on his feed look so . . . manicured and perfect? So shiny and put on?

"You're kidding me, right?" Talia's voice lowered a register. She leaned forward with her elbows on her knees and shook her head. "Don't be crazy. You can even read our messages. Look."

She showed Rose the DMs between them.

Yesss

one of Dillon's recent ones said.

coming back to the homeland!

Thx so much for helping us out

Ofc, beautiful

we only need a place to stay for a bit. then well figure out our own deal. its just hard because we'll be on our own, you know?

For sure. I know some ppl who can really help you out. Get you settled.

"What am I reading?" asked Rose.

"Huh?" Talia's once-confident face had fallen. Her eyes transformed into those piercing, angry ones from all those months ago when she'd claimed that Rose was ridiculous for not even knowing about the banned books list.

"This doesn't sound like you're planning a week in New York, Talia, it seems like you want us to, like . . . stay here? For real? With *Dillon*! A *stranger*!" Rose's head and shoulders slumped over onto her lap. "Oh no, oh no, oh no . . . ," she moaned.

"Girl. Stop it." Talia reached under Rose's torso to take the phone. "Do you *see* where I got us? Out of that *boring* little town."

"Talia, you're *thirteen*!" Rose sounded like her mom now. But the weird thing was . . . it didn't bother her.

"Yeah, well. Thirteen to me is different than thirteen to you," Talia grumbled. She hopped up and started walking down the path by the water.

"What if Dillon is not Dillon, huh?" Rose grabbed her suitcase and threw her backpack on, leaping up to chase Talia. "What if he's really some creepy old man? What if he's here watching us right now?"

Talia froze, her face drained of all its earlier excitement. She scowled at Rose. But she did glance around. She seemed—Rose hoped—to take in the possibility.

There were men on benches. Men strolling with friends. Men watching their kids on the playground. Men eating breakfast as they ambled by.

"Okay, now you're freaking *me* out." Talia kept walking. "And I'm not like you—I don't make a list of everything terrifying in the world, I just *live* in it. Stop."

"When is he supposed to meet us?" Rose asked, grabbing

Talia's arm and stopping her again, pulling her over to the bars that blocked the water. Her suitcase rumbled behind her as she dragged it along.

Talia glanced at her phone. "Noon," she said.

Rose checked her own as well. It was 11:45 A.M. They'd been sitting there for hours. And the day had hardly begun.

"He's going to take us to get something to eat," Talia explained, her tone faltering a little into something resembling worry, "but we're meeting back there, at that bench, so I should . . ." She glanced toward where they'd come from. "I should go sit. Why am I leaving? Why are you messing with my head?" She turned on her heels and stormed to their previous spot, although a woman sat on the corner of it now, typing on a laptop, headphones on.

Pulling the suitcase in another direction, once again, felt like a chore. Rose's arms and shoulders and feet ached.

Talia sat, arms crossed, while Rose stood above her.

"Don't you have any friends' houses we can go to? Was there any other plan?"

And Rose had the same urge for her mom to hold her that she'd had after she woke up from that nightmare about *Fateful Passage*. She wanted to smell the lilacs. To be cradled. The tension in her neck bloomed into her skull, and a headache came on.

"No, *Rose*." Talia said her name with dripping contempt. "I *don't* have any friends. Not real ones, anyway. People hated me. Okay? My best friends left me for the popular kids because they thought I was stuck-up. Or something stupid like that. I don't even know what it was! *People can turn on you.* I was so depressed. And it annoyed them. An opiniated bookworm who tried to dress like them and couldn't hack it. You have no idea..." Talia took in an enormous breath and let it out as she said, "You just have *no* idea what life can really be like."

An enormous flock of pigeons that had been pecking at the ground a few feet beside them exploded into flight.

"I'm so sorry. And you're right," Rose said. "I'm sure you're right about everything and all the stuff I don't know," she repeated. "But we cannot go stay with a boy you've never met. We have to go."

"I'm not going with you." Talia sat upright and faced the statue. "It turns out you weren't a real friend, either."

Past the trees, a truck honked, and it felt like the sound took up the whole city.

"What do you mean, I'm not a real friend?" Rose had to stop this.

"You *told Charlotte*! What are you—an idiot?" Talia was so angry she practically breathed fire. Her limbs looked like they didn't know what to do with themselves, and her arms shook in front of her. Her knees jiggled up and down. "You *ruined everything*! Don't you get that we're here because of what *you* did? You were my best friend? Yeah, right." Talia pulled at her own hair.

Rose had to ignore it. Of *course* she'd been furious that Rose had shared the secret. She'd been hiding that rage and, Rose was beginning to see, a whole host of other furies.

"You really think you can live here? By yourself? When you're a kid?" Rose tried to reason with her. "What about your parents? How do you think they'd feel?" Rose knelt down and tried to get Talia to move an inch. To face her.

"My parents don't give two craps about what I do!" Talia yelled. Her cheeks darkened to a deep pink, her eyes to near black. "Why do you think I'm at the library for hours after school? My mom spends all day at at this new job that she totally hates, and at this point my dad is too depressed to even keep looking for work, and then they just fight about that nonstop, and if you asked them anything about what I did during a given day, they would have *no answer* because they *don't care*, alright? So just shut up!"

The woman with the laptop slowly got up and moved to another seat elsewhere.

Talia threw her body down along the whole of the bench and let her face collapse into her backpack.

"Someone like you—with your family?—could *never* understand! Must be nice to have a mom who cares so much about you, but you just *complain*!" Talia's shouts came out muffled through the bag.

A boat's horn bellowed across the water.

Rose knelt down lower, speaking close to Talia's ear. "But

we love you in Cove Lake. You're amazing. Why would you want to leave it? Hey—maybe you've made friends who can appreciate you there."

"Appreciate me?" Talia mumbled through the backpack. "You just want me to be Miss Exciting New York City Girl. You want me to lead you guys in some, like, rebellion. I'm . . ." Talia lifted her head slightly. Her lipstick had smudged at the side of her mouth. "I'm just as boring as anybody else. You don't even know me at all."

Checking her phone, Rose saw that it was noon. Dillon could be coming any second. She could not and would not leave her friend there, however cruel that friend was acting.

"There must be someone we can go to," she said, as much to herself as to Talia. "Even an old friend, one you fell out with," she said, thinking of Charlotte and how, no matter what had happened, something within her knew that if she truly needed Charlotte, she would be there.

Talia lifted herself to her elbows, stomach still on the bench, and turned to Rose to say, "I'm not like you. I have nobody." Her head fell like she was a marionette and someone had cut the string at her neck. "Nobody," she repeated.

Rose had to act. Seeing Talia's phone in her back pocket, she grabbed it.

"Okay," she said to Talia. "Maybe you're right. Just show me his pics again? I was overreacting. It's my thing."

Talia sat up, typed in her phone password, and swiped up Dillon's profile.

And Rose took her shot. She grabbed the phone, stepped away, and messaged him:

> we're not there yet. got held up. wont make it today.

Talia jumped up and wrestled with her for the phone.

"No, Talia!" Rose commanded. She grabbed Talia's backpack with the hook of the arm she held the phone in, grasped her heavy suitcase with the other hand, and speed-walked away. She had no idea where she was going, but she had to move. And she had to get Talia to follow. She ran.

When Talia caught up to her—which wasn't hard because Rose was on the go while hauling a suitcase and two backpacks—she grabbed her bag off Rose.

"Why would you do that?" Talia wailed.

"Someone needs to look out for you!" Rose shouted at her. "This is *dangerous*!"

And Talia started to cry.

Strangers stared at them as they walked by, like how cars slowed down to gawk at a car accident.

What story would onlookers imagine had brought these two kids to this place, standing there screaming and crying?

Rose, totally out of breath, every muscle exhausted, hauled their things to the grass.

A tiny group of women in sweaters and tight black pants did squats next to their baby strollers as an instructor belted out instructions. A child barely old enough to walk toddled after a big red ball.

Rose crumpled onto the earth.

"I'm gonna keep you safe," Rose said between breaths, imagining her mother speaking through her. "I'm going to keep us both safe."

Talia collapsed beside her and wrapped her arms around her knees. Her high shoulders loosened.

"Okay," she said, nodding, letting her tears fall. "I'll let you." Her eyes followed the path of the bouncy red ball rolling past them. "So what do we do now?"

Rose, still holding Talia's phone, handed it to her. "You call your parents. And you tell them where we are."

29

"Okay, your mom is on the phone with the car service. They should be right there. Do you see them? Alright, we're going to stay on the phone with you while you get in the car. Keep the phone on for the whole drive. Do you hear me? Rose, do you hear me? Okay. We will meet you at JFK Airport the second our flight from Detroit lands, and we'll fly you home immediately. You should be there in an hour or so. We are heading to the airport now. I will text you the exact pickup time. It's Delta. Stay there. We'll get you and go home from there. If you don't text me every half an hour, I will call the police."

Her dad directed them on speakerphone as they got in the car that would take them to John F. Kennedy Airport.

"Your dad's *intense*," Talia said. Then, as the driver greeted them and took their bags, she murmured to Rose, "It's kind of nice."

Talia's parents had freaked out, and while they were panicking about how to get her, Rose had called her own parents and they'd made a plan.

When they arrived at JFK at 2:30 P.M., where they'd

spend the next four or five hours, they were both so tired out from crying and from the travel and the fear of their parents' wrath that the cavernous terminal in front of them felt like a dreamworld.

"Are we alive?" Talia asked her. "Or is this the afterlife?"

Rose snickered.

"So what do we do here?" Talia asked.

For once, Talia was asking Rose what to do. Not that Rose had any clue. Maybe that was how Talia felt a lot of the time. Like she had no idea what the right answer was to anything, but if people were going to ask her, then she better think up something.

"Step one—coffee," Rose said, dodging families in sweat-pants hurrying by with enormous suitcases. "Step two . . ." Rose took a few strides forward and looked around at the sights before them. She smelled perfume and fake chai tea and pizza. A ravenous hunger overtook her as she realized she'd hardly eaten in hours. "Food. Lots of food. And then . . ." She scanned the bustling scene. And she saw it. The perfect place. "Bookstore?"

Rose didn't even need to check with Talia. She knew it was a yes.

Drinks in hand, they texted Rose's parents their exact location. Then, after scarfing down an entire cheese pie, they found their way to the books and annoyed other travelers as they leaned against shelves to read.

Rose didn't want to have a fight and not talk about it, like she'd done with Charlotte, and her parents, and probably everyone she'd ever fought with.

"Talia?" Rose said as she made her way over to the mystery section where Talia was sitting, her nose in a book. Standing above her, Rose saw that her roots were growing back in between her box-dyes—a little strip of the darkest brown revealing itself above the artificial blue.

"Hmm?" Talia didn't look up.

Rose let her shoulder fall against the wood that marked the end of the shelf. "Talia, you don't have to be some . . . exciting, extra-special person to be my friend. You know that, right?"

"Not really, actually," Talia whispered into the book. She lifted a ring to her mouth and bit it.

Rose hadn't wanted to see Talia as ever being scared or sad or alone or any of the things Rose didn't want to be, either. But everybody was sometimes. Why had she made up this imaginary person when there was a real one standing right in front of her?

Rose knelt down and put a hand on the pages Talia was reading. "Can we just try to be ourselves? Whatever that is? Good parts, bad parts, scared parts, all of it?"

Talia nodded. "Okay. We can try."

They sat in the tiny corner of the bookstore in the huge airport and read together until Rose's parents arrived.

Rose's parents bounded toward her, her mom's purse bouncing against her side as she raced to Rose, like if she didn't get to her right away, she'd lose her forever.

She wondered if they'd yell. If they'd make a scene.

And yet they just embraced her, both at once, like the family hugs they'd fallen into so often when she was younger. And then her mom held Talia's hand and pulled her in, keeping one arm around Rose's dad and the other squeezing both Rose's and Talia's heads into her side. Then she held on to Rose's cheeks and asked, "Are you okay? Are you alright?" over and over. Her dad collapsed against a wall, removed his glasses, and pinched the bridge of his nose.

He took in the scent of Rose's drink and realized it was a coffee.

"Seriously?" was all he said.

Waiting in line to board the plane, Rose read a text from Aunt Laura:

> When I said I loved rebels I didn't mean this, you wild thing. Please call me? Whenever you need to talk? Now? For the rest of your life? Xoxoxo

Rose also had texts from Bree, Addie, and Connor in their group text. They fired off a million questions, one after the other. Rose had no idea how they found out about everything. But word must have traveled fast, because there was also a message from Charlotte:

> Omg I just heard. You faked the trip? You got to NEW
> YORK CITY? Are you okay? Please tell me you're okay.
> I am praying, praying, praying for you.

Rose wrote back to everyone that she was fine.

Thanks, she responded to Charlotte. I'm really sorry if I scared you. I'm okay.

On the plane, Rose took the window seat again. This time, in the dark of night, she saw the glittering windows turn the enormous skyscrapers into candleholders full of flames.

Out of the corner of her eye, Rose noted that Talia didn't touch her phone. She shared a row with a stranger while Rose sat in a three-seater with her parents.

Talia didn't look at them, focusing only on the paperback she'd picked up at the airport.

As the city disappeared behind them and they reached the clouds, Rose heard her dad mutter under his breath, "Ugh. That city."

"Mom?" Rose whispered. "I am so sorry."

Her mom adjusted her ponytail and closed her eyes. "Thank you for stopping it," she whispered back slowly, like she was choosing her words carefully, "before things went even further."

Her parents didn't even *know* about the Dillon thing.

"Mom?" Rose repeated. "Talia told me her parents don't care about her. That's why they just let her do whatever. She said they wouldn't care if she was gone."

Rose's mom opened her eyes and put a hand on Rose's thigh. "I have never met them. But I know that isn't true."

"I think that's why she wanted to run away." Rose was up against her mom's ear, her head nearly resting on her shoulder. Rose took a beat, then said, "I know I made a mistake. But I couldn't let Talia go by herself."

The seat belt sign turned off, and the flight attendant made an announcement that they were free to go about the cabin. Rose saw Talia stuff her book into the back of the chair in front of her and go to the bathroom.

Rose's mom watched Talia go. "Honey, she's not hurting herself in any way, is she? How worried should I be about her?"

"No!" Rose said. But then she thought of the messaging. And how Talia didn't seem like she knew how to protect herself. And, taking the moment Talia was gone and had no chance of hearing her, the words rushed out and Rose told her mom the whole story. And when she got to the part where she took Talia's bag and phone and ran away from her, Rose let her thoughts come out right as they came to her and whispered, "I think you're actually right that I don't deserve a dog. Taking care of something you really love is way too hard."

Rose's mom reached for her head and pressed it down lightly onto her shoulder. "Try to get some rest, sweetheart," she said. And Rose, her cheek against her mother's soft, sweatered shoulder, fell into a deep sleep.

When they got down to the baggage claim in Detroit at

close to midnight, Rose knew right away that it was Talia's parents standing at the bottom of the escalator beyond the sliding doors. They waved and waved like Talia might not recognize them.

Talia's mom was her carbon copy: short, full-figured, with dark hair and an expressive face. And on her hands, Rose saw, she had some type of swirling, henna-like tattoo. She had bags under her eyes like caves. Talia's dad looked equally exhausted. He was small, too, with the same tan skin but a lightness to his features. He wore a shirt with some band name on it, and it was baggy on his lean frame. They were a lot younger than Rose's parents.

Talia came last down the escalator, bowing her head in a shame Rose had never seen on her before, like one of the rescue dogs who wasn't used to kindness yet. Rose and her parents moved out of the way so Talia's parents could greet her.

And they enveloped her entirely. They scooped her up and lifted her an inch off the ground as her mom kissed her forehead over and over and over again. Her mom sobbed, and her dad looked like he was trying not to.

"Why would you do that? Why, honey? Why?" her mom kept saying into Talia's hair.

Talia's dad broke away and came over to introduce himself to Rose's parents and thank them for getting the plane tickets so quickly.

"See?" Rose's mom spoke into Rose's ear. "I knew it."

30

The next day, after the official two-month grounding was established and the geography monitoring app was installed on Rose's phone, Rose had nothing but time. Her class was in a whole other country for another five days.

Before her dad went into his office to do some weekend work, he hugged her extra tight. "Don't ever do that to us again, you hear me? Ever."

Later that afternoon, Rose's mom knocked on her door.

"Can I come in?" she asked.

"Yes." Rose sat on her bed, reading her old favorites from childhood. She was halfway through *Because of Winn-Dixie*, the book that had officially cemented her love of canines all those years ago.

Her mom, wrapped in a knee-length gray cardigan, her auburn hair held up by two long pins, sat on Rose's bed. She smoothed a wrinkle or two on the blanket and said, "You terrified us, Rosie."

Rose nodded. What could she say? She knew she had.

"It's like you and I have been—" Her mom awkwardly

moved her fingers toward one another but didn't let the tips touch. "We can't meet. We're crisscrossed."

Outside her window, some birds sang, welcoming the oncoming spring.

"I know it was dangerous, Mom. Part of me wanted to make sure Talia was okay," Rose explained. "And part of me wanted to go."

As she saw her mom's mouth open to speak, Rose jumped in. She had to say more before her mom got a chance to tell her how wrong Rose was.

"And I know you don't like Talia, but what if she had gone on a train all by herself?" Rose watched her mother for a reaction, but her mom's head was still slanted toward the bedcovers, her expression inscrutable. "I'm making excuses," Rose muttered to herself, knowing it was true. "I could've just told somebody right away."

The birds twittered even louder.

"When you were little, I never let you climb too high on the playground." Her mom methodically flattened every crinkle she identified. "I didn't even leave you with a sitter. And I *doused* you in sanitizer."

"I remember," Rose said ruefully.

"You were just . . ." Her mom turned her body toward Rose and took a moment to search for the words. "This *precious* little thing. *Breakable.* You know?"

Rose stared at her mom. She didn't know where this was going.

"I knew if I let something happen to you? I would just..."
Her mom's eyes shifted from side to side, facing up toward the ceiling where outlines of old stars stained the paint. "I would die."

It looked to Rose like her mom was picturing or thinking of things that . . . *ached*. That was the constant state of her body, but Rose didn't know if her thoughts often ached, too. Her mom kept rubbing her neck, digging with her thumb like there was something worse in there than a knot.

"Mom?" Rose asked.

Rose's voice seemed to snap her mom back into reality, into the room.

"Sorry," her mom whispered.

"Aunt Laura said you used to be a 'renegade,'" Rose said after a second, twisting a strand of hair around a finger.

Her mom laughed. "That's funny."

"What did she mean?" Rose scooted on her knees over to her mom, so she was seated beneath her. It reminded her of story time at school when she was little, when all the kids would sit on the carpet around the teacher to hear the tale.

"You know I met Dad because I was friends with Aunt Laura, of course," she said, repeating a fact Rose felt she'd known since before she knew anything. "Things were different back then. When I met your dad, I was..."

Her mom began to chew on the corners of a fingernail.

Rose had never seen her do that before.

"I was having a hard time," her mom said, nodding, like

she approved of the way she'd put it. But still, she kept nibbling. "Angel, I went through some pretty tough things."

"Like . . . what do you mean?" Rose asked.

"Should I say this . . ." Her mom fretted to herself. "Do I say it?" She closed her eyes.

"Mom, I read this book in the club. One of the banned ones." Rose leaned in, huddling with her mom like they were sharing secrets at a sleepover.

"Mm-hmm?" her mom answered, eyes still shut.

"And it was about this really awful dad who, like, tortured his kids. He was really bad. And I thought of that macaroni and chocolate story you told me?" Rose didn't know why she was saying this, but it felt like a tool. A chisel to break away old clay and get to the fossil beneath.

Her mom opened her eyes and smiled a sad smile.

It might've been Rose's imagination, but she thought she spotted more wrinkles around her mother's eyes than had been there only months before.

"You're so smart, kiddo." Her mom sighed. "It sounds like parts of that book might've been like my dad. Yeah. And that's part of why I don't understand . . . You left, and . . . I didn't think things were that bad? I mean . . ." She swallowed. "This is so hard."

She lifted another finger to her mouth and gnawed on it.

"I left home when I was seventeen," she said into her fingertips. "And finished high school while I lived at a friend's house."

"You ran away?" Rose tried to picture her mom with a backpack stuffed to the brim, sneaking out at night on a bus or a train . . .

"You could say that." Her mom nodded. "Yup." She started in on yet another nail.

And Rose lifted her own hand up to stop her. She took her mom's fingers and held them still on her mom's lap.

"What happened next?" Rose asked, needing to know the story. Needing to know how it ended.

Her mom took in a big breath and said, "I got into a lot of trouble. Out on my own. For a lot of years there, I . . ." With a voice just above a whisper, she added, "I wasn't my best self."

Rose wondered what that meant to her mom, who was so sweet and put together.

"I started spending time with people who . . ." Her mom kept stopping and starting, choosing her words carefully. "They didn't have my best interests at heart," she said.

"What does that *mean*, Mom? What are you talking about?" Rose asked.

"Honey, sometimes when you grow up with something? When the person who is supposed to love you treats you a certain way? You think that's the way love is supposed to be." Her mom paused to wipe her nose. "You don't make the best friends. Or boyfriends," she added.

And something flitted across her mom's face that Rose had never seen before. Rose had no word for what it was.

She took the pins out of her hair and let it fall onto her shoulders.

"I'll tell you all about it one day." Her mom shook her head again and again. "But I can't now."

Rose wanted to know more. So much more. In some of the books, *horrible* things happened to the characters. Like the mom who was getting hit in *All the Things I've Seen Before.* Or the way people treated the characters Ella and Grace.

"And . . . when you're a parent, honey . . ." Her mom went on slowly, like she was carefully pondering each and every word, "You don't want your kid to know the *bad* things. You don't want your kid to get your story in their head and then make it a part of theirs." Her mom lifted a trembling hand and covered her eyes.

She wanted to help her mom escape whatever was taking her over right then. "But then you met Dad, right?" Rose asked.

Her mom took a breath. She smiled a tired smile. "Yes. I was coming out of that time . . . And I knew Laura from school, and one day, I met your dad. And he was so . . ." She was picturing something again. Rose could see that. But this time it was something warm and wonderful.

"So sweet, right?" her mom said.

Rose looked at her with a strong dash of skepticism. "Yeah, I guess so."

"Okay, maybe you don't see it," she said with a light laugh. "But your dad is *very* sweet. He *loved* me. He convinced me I should go back to college . . ."

"Wait, you dropped out of college before you met him?" Rose asked.

Her mom nodded.

Wow. Did Rose know her mom at *all*?

"And I just saw this whole life in front of me," her mom continued, her entire voice calming. Her shoulders lowering. "For the first time in a long time, I saw a *life*. I would raise a beautiful Jewish family. I'd stay grounded and put my faith in something. I would be with a steady person who just wanted a simple, quiet life in the town he grew up in. A lovely life." She paused, holding something in.

Rose didn't know what to say.

Her mom put her forehead to Rose's. "I was in a hole when I was your age and for a long time after, love. And I don't want you to *ever* have to crawl out of any hole. I want you far above the earth."

As her mom pulled away Rose said, "But I can't be perfect."

"I know, angel, I know." Her mom patted her hand.

"Stop calling me angel, okay?" Rose said. "I'm not an angel. I'm, like . . . *on* the earth."

Her mom dabbed under her eyes with the tips of her sleeves.

"Okay," her mom said. "Okay, I'll try."

They sat there and listened to the sound outside the window of a toddler crying and his mom saying, "That was a bad boo-boo," over and over again.

And then Rose muttered, "The ceiling looks really ugly now. With all the goo left from the stars."

"I saw," her mom said. "Hmmm." Her mom bit her lip and stood up, pacing around the room, looking up at the ceiling. "I have some paint upstairs, left over from the porch."

Rose raised her eyebrows at her mom. Was she saying what Rose thought she was saying?

"Should we paint over it?"

"Yes!" Rose squealed. "Will it take all day, though?"

Her mom smiled. "It's okay. We have time."

And together they headed to the storage in the crawl space at the top of their house, searching for something that could add fresh color to old stains.

31

The end of May came with dreamy weather, even warmer than usual for the start of a Michigan spring.

"Now those shirts of yours actually make *sense*," her mom teased her as the days got warmer.

She'd stopped setting outfits on Rose's bed, though she still had a few rules about modesty. At least until high school started. "Then we'll figure out that whole new ball game...," her mom had said.

And finally, after months of being grounded, Rose and Talia were allowed to see each other outside of school or temple.

They shrieked happily as they opened the door and saw they were wearing nearly identical white crop tops, though Talia had on three layers of necklaces and Rose simply wore her favorite golden dove.

They flew to Rose's room, knowing what they wanted to look at together.

From outside in the hallway, Rose's mom hollered to

them, "You two should go outside! You never know, it could be in the fifties tomorrow!"

"No, Mom, these are too funny!" Rose yelled back to no response.

Within seconds they were already on the sixth comment under the video of Talia hollering on the chair in the library. Zion had given his footage to Bree to post, and the thousands of K-pop fans that followed her reposted it until it had tens of thousands of views. Underneath some of its shares, people had attached a link to the Transformation.org petition that Bree and Connor and Addie had put up when they were in Toronto. They told Talia and Rose that if they wanted any traction on a banned books petition, they had to go big and set it up online. People were signing it from all over Michigan. And even from other states.

Some of the comments had them rolling on the floor in laughter.

"Okay, okay, this one says . . . *If you find these books in any store, buy them, walk out the door, and burn them in front of the window display!*"

"Baahaha!" Talia cackled. "Imagine if someone actually did that!"

"Here's another. It's so mean," Rose went on. "*This generation will be its own destruction.*"

"That dude for sure has a bunker hideout in his house," Talia noted.

"Aw," Rose cooed at her screen.

"What? Let me see," Talia said.

The next one read: *I'm the librarian at Cove Lake Middle School, and I'm proud of these kids. The kids are alright!*

"Do you think that's Mr. Lawrence?" Rose asked.

"For sure." Talia rested her chin on Rose's shoulder to look more closely at the words on the screen.

"I hope he doesn't get in trouble." Rose tilted her head so they were cheek to cheek.

"Maybe he's okay with getting in trouble for something like this."

Rose could feel Talia shrug. She was right—maybe he was alright with breaking a rule here or there, if he thought it was the right thing.

"Like the rabbi said," Talia chirped. "It's civil disobedience."

In a happy surprise, their rabbi had been a vocal fan of the video, too. His granddaughter had sent it to him, and he'd recognized "Evie's granddaughter" and Rose. A couple of weeks after the New York fiasco, he'd brought the footage up to Rose's dad after kiddush on Shabbat morning. "There's a long history of civil disobedience doing great good in this country," he'd said to Rose's dad with a kind smile as Rose stood nervously by her father's side. "You must be so proud of Rose."

Rose had tried to turn invisible. She was unable to imagine how her dad would respond to such a claim about an action he'd warned her against.

"Well..." Her dad had swallowed a bite of a bran muffin

and said, "It turns out . . . my kid's a whole lot tougher than I could ever be." And he laughed a slightly awkward laugh. The rabbi shook his hand, beamed at Rose, and went off to greet others.

And that had been that. They had finished their food and went home.

On the ride back from the temple, Rose hadn't been able to stop thinking about her dad's words.

From what he'd told her, he had to be practically made of steel just to get through his years at school. And to stay there and keep being himself with his family for years on end so he could always be near Grandpa Jacob and Grandma Adele? That took guts. Maybe Rose had seen him all wrong.

Rose leaned forward to get closer between her parents and said, "Hey, Dad? I think we can *both* be pretty tough."

She saw her mom check in with her dad, but he was unreadable.

A few moments had passed by and Rose had watched through the windshield as they passed an exit for one of the two towns that stood between their temple and Cove Lake.

Her dad had cast her a second-long look in the rearview mirror, and she saw his eyes smile—and maybe tear up—as he finally said, "Thank you, kiddo."

Then he'd nodded toward their car's speaker, which played one of Rose's playlists. "Hey. What's this new music you're listening to all the time?"

When she'd explained it was from the Korean band

Twice, her dad had said, "Huh. Korean. That's . . . educational. I like it."

After that day, Rose had formed a plan.

Since Rose's rabbi seemed to approve of her "civil disobedience," Rose was going to ask him to read *Fateful Passage*. She told Talia that maybe, just maybe, he'd give them a space at the temple for the Banned Books Brigade to meet up. You never knew.

Talia thought that was genius.

After tiring of reading the comments, Talia hopped up to check her phone. This time it was definitely only texts from friends, not the unknown accounts, who her parents had made her block forever. Her new therapist was helping her through it, she told Rose.

Rose went on her phone, too. She had a picture from Addie. She and Charlotte stood in front of a tiny crafts market in the park, with an adoption information corner to their side, and Addie wrote:

> We made over a thousand bucks, baby!
> Mariah is so happy!

So cool! Rose wrote back before reporting the great news to Talia.

Sometimes Rose missed being a Girl Scout. But she'd always have a lot of good memories from it. And after the year she'd had . . . it was time to say goodbye to a few things, and hello to others.

Rose's mom knocked on the door. "Snacks?"

Rose hopped up to open it and answered, "We're good, Mom. But thanks."

"Fine, fine," her mom said, off to do her own thing.

"She *still* thinks you're ten," Talia teased.

"Yeah," Rose agreed. "But I'm her baby. I get it."

Bree and Connor would be there soon. There was no book meeting or anything; they just wanted to walk to Center Street to get some food. One of the Brigade's newest goals? See Twice on their upcoming North American tour. Bree told them she needed all their brains to get together to figure out how to make it happen.

As they waited for their friends, Talia and Rose showed each other videos on their phones, trying to make the other laugh harder with each successive one.

Eventually, the doorbell rang. And George barked and barked, always alerting them to any visitor.

Rose scooped him up to settle him down.

Her mom had convinced her dad that while being grounded made sense, and consequences mattered, Rose had wanted this for too long to take it away. Especially when the future of a little dog was in play . . . Her mom had said Rose was old enough to take care of something she loved.

"Rose, it's for you!" her mom yelled from down the stairs.

"Who is it?" Talia asked.

"No idea," Rose said before making her way down to see.

It was Charlotte. The door was already open, and she stood on the doormat right outside the frame.

"Hi," Rose greeted her.

"Hey."

Rose saw Charlotte's mom's car parked on the street in front of their house. Would this be an argument? A confrontation? They hadn't spoken in months, except when Charlotte saw her for the first time after the Toronto trip, squeezed her tight, and thanked God she was okay.

"Is George settling in okay?" Charlotte asked.

"Yeah." A big smile broke out on Rose's face, and she found herself stepping forward so that she was standing in the doorframe. "Despite . . . *everything*, my parents felt like it was time." She paused. "But I do really miss the rescue," she added. She'd failed at the Silver Award. She just had to deal with that fact. It was officially Charlotte's thing now.

"Congrats on the fundraiser," Rose piped up after a long pause between them. "Addie sent me a photo. That's great."

"Yeah, I just came from there. So . . . we were thinking about you . . ."

But Charlotte didn't say anything else. She checked back in with her mom and shifted her weight side to side.

Jennifer waved at Rose from the car with a big smile and then went back to her phone.

Rose waved back.

And she spotted a book in Charlotte's hands.

It was *Fateful Passage*.

"Yeah . . . ," Charlotte said when she saw Rose notice. "You told me I had to read it. I only got a copy after the whole . . . thing." Charlotte kept her eyes to the ground as both of them, Rose assumed, thought of that awful day in the school library.

The sun made its way through the branches of a tree and rippled across her small front porch.

"My parents haven't changed their mind or anything," Charlotte went on, taking a big breath and standing up straighter. "I don't really know what I think. But . . . I told my mom how much this one meant to you. And so she read it. And then she let me read it, too. She still thinks it's a little too mature."

"Oh. Wow." Rose was so happy they'd read it. She didn't know what to say.

"She's not . . . whatever you think she is," Charlotte mumbled.

"I love your mom," Rose said. "That's just a fact."

Charlotte managed a small smile.

Without even noticing it, Rose found that they had moved to the inside of the house together and stood face-to-face at the bottom of the stairs.

"So what'd you think of the book?" Rose asked her.

But then Rose heard a voice behind her: "Who is it?"

Talia showed up at the top of the stairway.

Charlotte raised her hand to say hello.

"Hey, Charlotte," Talia greeted her, but stayed put.

Rose expected Charlotte to call the book inappropriate or say it was silly to get all riled up about it.

"It was really sad," Charlotte said. "I think I get why you spoke up in class that day."

"Thank you." Rose blushed. It felt so strange to talk to Charlotte about it, after everything that had happened.

"The whole story is so messed up," Charlotte continued. Rays of light streamed in through the screen door and hit Charlotte's cheeks. She looked so much older to Rose. It reminded her that they would all head for high school soon. Another world.

"I know," Rose said. "It is."

"I just don't know if I can blame anybody, like, any one person, or place, for a big tragedy," Charlotte said.

Rose nodded, not knowing what to say, and up from the top of the stairs, Talia said, "I get that."

"And honestly?" Charlotte went on.

Rose could feel the Charlotte she knew coming out, ready to give the cold, hard truth about her opinions, whether harsh or hilarious. "I thought the writing was pretty mediocre." Charlotte put a hand on her hip. "Like . . . the author just uses the same words over and over. And there's that whole middle section where, I don't know, why was she talking about clothes? Like . . . get to the story!" Charlotte flipped through the pages like maybe she could find it. "So I thought it was just okay. As a book."

"Ha!" Talia erupted. "Well, no one said you had to *like* it!"

"Yeah," Rose said, grinning. "You're allowed to have your own opinions, Charlotte!"

Charlotte paused. "Okay. Well . . . I just wanted to let you know. So, my mom? Well, she thought I should come by—not in a text—and tell you. That we both get why you felt that way about this story. So . . . Yeah."

Rose took in her old friend—her sweetness and her hard edges. She missed her.

She looked back up the stairs at Talia. Was there a way to convey to her new friend, through one small glance, how important the old one would always be?

Was there a world in which these two people could forgive each other? Or maybe even *like* each other one day?

Someone had to take the first step.

Rose turned back to Charlotte. "Hey, what are you doing now? Do you want to hang out?"

Charlotte paused.

Rose felt Talia move a few steps down the stairs.

"Yeah," Talia said. "Some other kids are coming over, too. If you wanna, like, say hi."

Rose could hear the strain in Talia's attempt, but all that mattered was that she'd done it.

Rose smiled, and she let the smile fall onto Charlotte. She wanted it to tell her, *It's alright. We can make this better.*

Charlotte glanced back through the screen at her mom's car, and Rose worried that in one turn of the head, maybe they'd lost her.

Maybe Rose should grab Charlotte's hand. Maybe she should pull her up the stairs and they could all watch videos together or make paper fortune tellers like they always did back in sixth grade or do one another's makeup and take ridiculous photos—history class and blurted-out secrets and warring lunch tables just a blip behind them.

"Sorry. I've got to watch Ava's game today." Charlotte rocked on her heels like she was still waiting for something else to happen, for something unsaid to be said aloud.

The hope in Rose evaporated.

Talia took another two steps down and stood by her side.

"Are you sure?" Talia asked.

And with Talia next to Rose, asking Charlotte to come in, Rose knew Talia could see how important Charlotte was to her. How they had to make it right.

Charlotte shook her head. "No, I've really gotta go."

So that was that.

Rose and Talia nodded in sync to say okay.

Charlotte reached for the doorknob but stopped before she turned it open. She swiveled her head back toward them and said, "Maybe next time, though?"

"Yeah! That would be great. Next time."

And as Charlotte trotted off to the car and her mom waved bye and blew a kiss before driving off, Rose thought that maybe—just maybe—everything between them might be fine one day. Even if it couldn't be easy. Or perfect.

"Thanks for that," Rose said to Talia while they watched the car disappear.

"Of course." Talia followed in Charlotte's footsteps, opening the door to the tiny porch. She took a seat on the concrete step.

Rose joined her, resting her elbows on her knees. A flock of chickadees swooped down onto the growing grass, pecking at the soil beneath. Her neighbor across the street pushed a wheelbarrow filled with bulbs and let it fall by the garden bed, where she knelt down and shoveled.

"Don't worry," Talia said to Rose, shifting until she found the sunlight. "We'll get there."

Rose took in the fresh scent of the newly blooming spring air.

Earth was awakening all around them.

"Yeah," Rose said, hoping against hope it was true. "We'll get there."

DISCUSSION QUESTIONS

1. What do you think it means to have a friend who is a "bad influence"? In your view, what actions would a friend have to commit in order to influence you negatively? Have you ever had a friend who was a bad influence? Have you ever had a friend negatively influenced by someone else?

2. Rose, Talia, Bree, and Connor all have aspects of their identities that have at times led to someone acting—intentionally or unintentionally—in a prejudiced manner toward them. Based on what's in the text, do you think they gain anything of value by reading books in which others face prejudice as well? How so? Do you think identity is important to discuss, do you dislike when it is a focus, or do you have another view entirely?

3. Parents and kids often disagree about what it means to stay safe or how to properly protect young people. Do you think kids need protection from stories, ideas, or fellow peers? Any of the three? How so?

4. Has a book ever changed your life? Has a novel ever altered your perspective on something? In what way?

5. Talia quotes author Salman Rushdie as saying, "A book is a version of the world. If you do not like it, ignore it; or offer your own version in return." What do you think he means by that?

6. Rose, Charlotte, and Talia come from wildly contrasting home lives. They also experience the push and pull of friendships coming together and drifting apart. Ultimately, there is hope that all three of them can bond, along with other new friends. Do you think kids from dissimilar backgrounds can become good friends? Can they hold vastly different views and still connect?

7. Rose comes to believe that none of the books on the list deserve to be taken out of the library, even ones she finds upsetting or that could be viewed as inappropriate by some adults. Charlotte's mom thinks that there are certain library books kids should not be exposed to. Do you think there are limits to what is appropriate material for your age group?

8. If you do think there should be limits, do you have any ideas about who should set them and how?

9. Rose tries to understand Charlotte's mom's point of view, even though she comes to disagree with it quite strongly. How important is it for people who disagree to try and see the perspective of the other person? Is there a time in your life when you tried to do that? How did it turn out?

10. Talia points out that some of author Roald Dahl's books were at one point altered due to words deemed offensive. After a public outcry, it was announced that both altered and unaltered versions would remain available. In your opinion, how is altering outdated text similar to or different from parents requesting the removal of books from a school library?

ACKNOWLEDGMENTS

Thank you to my editors, Connie Hsu and Nicolás Ore-Giron. Connie, you've been one of my greatest writing and storytelling teachers. Nico, you are able to tap into the heart of stories and characters with a sensitivity and artistry that bowls me over. I am absurdly lucky to get to work with you both and could not have told this story without you.

And thank you a million times over to Melissa Edwards! You have been a godsend from the beginning, and I will always consider you my dream-come-true-maker.

Thank you to the wildly talented cover artist, Katie Turner, and to designers Julia Bianchi and Trisha Previte for bringing this story to life through the power of art.

A huge thank-you to copyeditors Kat Kopit, Ana Deboo, and Veronica Ambrose. Your work is so essential to getting the book where it needs to be!

Thank you to everyone I interviewed or even simply chatted with for this book, on topics ranging from middle school experiences to librarian life to parenting to politics to the magic of K-pop: Jessica Harring, Jacob Appel, Kelly Granito, Rowan Abdelaziz, Lauren Antolino, the Tabnicks, Harms, and Compare families (Natalie Compare, you are a true Once. You taught me so much!), Mike, and Kelly. I must give a special shout-out to Mike and Kelly in particular to acknowledge that your help was indispensable as well as being *incredibly* generous and openhearted. You have my sincerest gratitude.

Never-ending appreciation to my beautiful NYC family: Lauren, Tom, Michael, Lizzie, Jacob, Oliver, and Claudia, as well as my rock in Tacoma, the legendary Michigan sports fan and devoted wolf enthusiast Ian James Young Mikusko. Claudia, my sweet niece, you are the perfect young person to talk to about any topic on earth, because you are authentic, thoughtful, original, and resilient. You perceive the world with such a delightful mix of heart and no-nonsense humor. I love you to death.

A word of thanks to the late, great editor Bob Gottlieb, who welcomed me as mishpocha, was kind enough to take me seriously, and whose advice on writing will stick with me as long as I have pen and paper.

Thank you to Kelly Yang for your kindness and support.

Audrey Dymond, one of Canada's most delightful young people, thank you for your fantastic opinions. Keep 'em coming!

Eternal thanks to my mom and dad—without your love I would not have had the courage to step out into the wider world and explore its many faces and stories. And to Margie and David, my other parents, for the incredible help with the little ones and the gift of knowing we are all always loved. I could not write any book without you four!

To the Cranford Library and all of my writing students there—you inspired me more than I can say. I wish I could name you all, but that would be quite the list. Every single one of you made me a better writer and helped me think about all manners of topics in new lights and with new sensitivities.

Jonathan, Simone, and Ingrid, thank you for giving Mommy writing time and for being the reason for every word.

Lastly, thank you to those long-ago friends who pushed me forward—sometimes too far—and to those who pulled me back. I hope you know who you are. I learned from all of you, and learning is a gift—even when it's hard.